MAGIC
HUNTER

BOOK 1 OF
THE VAMPIRE'S MAGE SERIES

BY C. N. CRAWFORD

MAGIC HUNTER

BOOK 1 OF THE VAMPIRE'S MAGE SERIES

Copyright © 2016 C. N. Crawford

ISBN-13: 978-1533183453
ISBN-10: 1533183457

Edited by Tammi Labrecque
Cover art by Rebecca Frank
Interior design by C.N. Crawford

www.cncrawford.com

Contact the Authors:
cncrawfordauthor@gmail.com

Twitter: @CN_Crawford
Facebook: cncrawfordauthor

First Edition

Printed in the U.S.A

Also by

C. N. CRAWFORD

The Vampire's Mage Series
Book 1: *Magic Hunter*
Book 1.1: *Shadow Mage*
Book 2: *Witch Hunter*
(Summer 2016)

Demons of Fire and Night
Book 1: *Infernal Magic*
(Summer 2016)

The Memento Mori Trilogy
Book 1: *The Witching Elm*
Book 2: *A Witch's Feast*
Book 2.1: *The Abysmal Sea*
Book 3: *Witches of the Deep*
(June 2016)

To the Council.
You know who you are.

1

$\mathcal{A}$ hard rain drenched Rosalind's black clothes, plastering them to her body like a second skin. Despite the downpour, she pressed on over the pavement, skulking past the library. Her thoughts roiled through her mind like the dark storm clouds above.

She really wasn't up for killing someone tonight.

Not someone, she reminded herself. *Something.*

Either way, she'd much rather be spending the night at one of the dorm parties—warm and dry, drinking cheap beer, flirting over red plastic cups. That was what most people did on a Friday night, right? Beer pong. DJs. Hook-ups with hot guys.

Sadly, none of that was an option tonight. *Someone* had to keep the demons from slaughtering Thorndike's student body.

The new iron walls built around the campus had failed to keep the monsters at bay, and two students had been slaughtered in the past month. And to make matters worse for her, personally, if Rosalind screwed up tonight's mission she could kiss her life's dream goodbye. No more demon-hunting for her.

She pulled a hawthorn stake from her belt, whispering the Brotherhood's motto: *"Lux in tenebris lucet."* Light shines in the darkness.

Though right now she could barely see through the pouring rain.

She couldn't let the nasty weather stand in her way, though; she really didn't want to lose this job. For one thing, as a member of the Brotherhood, she belonged to an ancient and noble tradition of Hunters: the protectors of humankind. Not to mention that she got really nice boots out of the deal, and the Brotherhood kept her well-supplied with money and lethal gadgets.

While checking over her shoulder, she almost tripped over a collection of votive candles. A few skittered across the pavement. She scanned the shadows to see if she'd attracted any attention, but nothing moved.

As she pressed on, she mentally cursed the students who left all that crap lying around campus—as if candles or pictures of angels could scare away demons. Superstitions were for the desperate, a way of giving the illusion of control—not that Rosalind was in a position to criticize. No one in the world could pry her lucky ring from her finger.

Stake in hand, she continued on, striding past Thorndike's new mascot: a vampire effigy, made from black felt, impaled on a wooden stake. Some art students had thrown it together after a few local attacks, and the fabric sagged in the rain.

She hurried down a winding path, and thunder rumbled—almost as if nature wanted to ratchet up her nerves—like she wasn't stressed out enough.

Tonight's assignment wasn't just a low-level goblin or a boggart, like the usual jobs she'd had in the past few years. She was supposed to eliminate a redcap, a powerful demon of the mountain goddess.

Rosalind wasn't thrilled about the prospect. Redcaps couldn't live without human blood, and this one had slaughtered two cashiers in the Somerville Market Basket just yesterday, gnawing through their guts while shoppers stared in horror over packaged cupcakes and Twix bars.

Even aside from the supermarket murders, she had a good reason to be nervous. She'd already screwed up *two* assignments—both vampires—and now her whole future was on the line. One more failure, and she'd be kicked out of the Brotherhood—set adrift in the world of ordinary people who relied on angel pictures for protection. And she was fairly certain a redcap wasn't any easier to kill than a vamp.

She paused to survey the lawn, trying to get a sense of magic curling through the air. She let her body attune to the atmosphere's vibrations. This part of hunting was her strength. Many people could feel magic's frequencies, but Rosalind's skills went further. She could actually *see* magic—and smell it, too.

An aura tickled her skin, raising goose bumps. As it moved around her in smooth, blue waves, she shivered. The magic carried the briny smell of the ocean. *Not a redcap's aura. Fascinating—but not my target.*

She slipped into one of the alleys by the old theater, scanning the shadows. Her Guardian still hadn't told her where to find the demon, but she had a pretty good idea. If she were a redcap, she'd be heading for one of the frat parties on Wendell Ave. If a demon wanted to feast on nubile flesh, the drunk college students at those parties would be an easy bet.

At the mouth of the alley, Rosalind tightened her fingers around the stake, knuckles whitening.

She should focus on the positive. If she succeeded in tonight's task, she'd get her chalice—the pendant given to novices after their first big kill. But, after a string of failures, she couldn't shake the cloud of dread hanging over her, and she was just starting to catch a glimpse of a burnt-orange aura curling through the air...

Her phone buzzed, and she nearly jumped out of her boots. She yanked it out of her pocket. It was Josiah, her Guardian from the Brotherhood, texting her an update.

> Redcap is heading for the Delta Theta Alpha house. Intercept him there.

With the fetid smell—like a dank cave—wafting into her nostrils, she didn't even need the text.

She hurried across the lawn. From the top of the hill, she scanned the row of frat houses until she homed in on the aura's source. *There he is.* A shiver crawled up her spine. Wispy copper tendrils rolled off him—the redcap's magic.

His red hat shone brightly under a yellow streetlight, glistening with gore. Crimson drops of blood dripped onto his zebra-print suit. Redcaps didn't normally wear clothes, and the sight was jarring to Rosalind—like she'd spotted a fox walking on its hind legs, dressed in a wedding gown. Perhaps the demon planned to blend in at a *pimps and hoes* party, and hoped no one would notice the human blood dripping from his hat.

Stalking along the sidewalk, she gripped her stake. With the two vamps, she'd hesitated. They'd looked so *human.* But this time, she needed to hit her mark. If she didn't, dozens of students would die. In fact, if the next few minutes didn't go the way she planned, the redcap would be dipping his hat into *her* blood.

He isn't human, she reminded herself. *He isn't even a person. He's a thing.*

One of these days, she'd just like to stay in, playing beer pong.

Gritting her teeth, she broke into a sprint. She pumped her

arms harder, her breath growing ragged. If he managed to get inside the party, the slaughter would be horrific.

Her boots pounded the pavement, and the demon whirled, teeth bared. *Good.* The less human he looked, the easier this would be.

Twisting her torso, she hurled the stake at his chest with all the force she could muster, but his hand flew out and snatched it from the air.

His grin was a thing of terror.

Uh-oh. That's not how it went in training. She screeched to a halt, scrambling to grab the handheld flamethrower from her belt. The weapon wasn't much larger than a can of Coke, but it produced a three-foot flame that burned at 1,000 degrees Celsius.

Before she had the chance to blast him, the creature's hands were on her, gripping her wrists to stop her from accessing the arsenal on her belt. He was younger than most redcaps—his face elegant, his grasp iron-clad. Beauty and strength were just two of the weapons that demons had in their arsenal.

And what did Rosalind have? A bit of wood and some gadgets.

He inhaled deeply, licking his pale lips. "I like it when my dinner puts up a bit of a fight." His voice slithered over her skin.

Ugh. Even for a demon, this one was creepy as hell. Maybe it wouldn't be so hard to stab him.

She brought her knee up hard into his groin, and his pale eyes bulged. He might be a monster, but he still had nerve endings where it mattered. He loosened his grip on one of her wrists, just enough for her to wrench it free. She twisted her hips, bringing the full force of her palm into his Adam's apple. *Crunch.*

As he hunched over, gasping in pain, she grabbed another stake from her belt.

He was lunging for her neck, teeth bared, when she plunged the stake into his heart.

Or, at least, she'd been aiming for his heart. What she got must have been a lung, because he gripped his chest, stumbling back but stubbornly refusing to die. *Shit*. Josiah would be pissed.

As the redcap ripped the stake from his ribs, she pulled the flamethrower from her belt. The demon's eyes widened, and for the first time, she saw genuine fear.

Disturbingly human-like fear.

This caused an extra moment of hesitation on Rosalind's part, and the redcap had the upper hand again.

As he leapt for her, she pressed the button on the flamethrower, but it was too late. The demon knocked her to the ground. Almost instantly, his sharp teeth pierced her neck. White-hot pain exploded through her throat.

At this moment, on the edge of death, she could think of only one thing: *I am the worst demon Hunter in the world.* Pain blazed through her body.

The knife. She had a knife in her belt. *Come on, Rosalind. You got this.*

Just as she pulled it out, a pair of strong hands clamped around the redcap's head, twisting it sharply to the side with a sickening *crack*.

Her stomach flipped, and she shoved the demon off her. She stared, open-mouthed, as a black-clad Hunter sliced off the redcap's head with a sword in one shockingly swift motion. With a morbid fascination, she stared as the stranger plunged his fingers into the demon's chest. For one horrible moment, the air filled with the sound of crunching bone and tearing flesh. As the redcap's headless body twitched on the ground, the Hunter ripped out his beating heart.

Her first thought was: *Shit. I was supposed to kill the demon.*

Her second was: *How the hell could a human rip a heart out like that?*

When she glanced up at the Hunter, her body froze.

Not a Hunter. Not even close.

Despite his beauty, the man before her was twice as horrifying as the demon he'd killed. He was human, but not like her. A tattooed crescent moon, dark and sharp as a dragon's claw, marked his neck, and a raven perched on his shoulder. He held the demon's heart in his hand, crimson blood dripping down his arm.

A cold and silvery nocturnal power crackled in the air around them, old as night itself. Before her stood a shadow mage, and the aura unfurling from his body was ancient and terrifying.

He stared at her, his eyes cold and pale as glaciers, and dark shadows whispered around him. A pit opened in the hollow of her stomach. *He knows what I did, and he's here for vengeance.*

With a flick of his wrist, the mage tossed the demon's heart to the ground. Rosalind gripped her bleeding throat with one hand, grasping for a vial of iron dust with the other. Fear tore her mind apart.

Even as she reached for the dust, the mage was already whispering in a demonic tongue. His spell transfixed her in place, freezing her muscles. She couldn't move, and her mind screamed with pure panic.

As the mage spoke, his aura strengthened, permeating her bones.

Her blood roared in her ears, and she tried desperately to command her muscles to obey her. *This is it. He's going to compel me to bash my own brains out on the pavement.* And the one stupid, useless thought pounding in her skull was: *I haven't even achieved my chalice pendant.*

A powerful magic crackled over her skin as the raven fluttered around her. Rosalind flinched, waiting for the *coup de grace.*

But, instead of a death blow, she felt the sharp pain in her neck subside, and her arms relaxed, free to move. A shuddering breath slid from her, and she pulled her hand from her throat. He'd *healed* her. Why the hell would a shadow mage heal a Hunter? Mages and Hunters were ancient enemies, and if he'd known what she'd done...

She locked the thought away. She had no idea if mage skills included telepathy.

As his magic caressed her skin, it occurred to her she'd never felt this aura before. It wasn't the briny scent from earlier. It was rich and earthy—and strangely sensual, as if it was licking her skin.

As she rose, she gripped the vial of aerosolized dust, holding his gaze. He stood at least a head taller than her, and something about his predatory stillness told her to *run.* Still, she schooled her features into calm. Showing fear to a mage would only provoke his bloodlust.

She swallowed hard, trying to gather her thoughts as she stared at him, stunned as much by his beauty as by his feral gaze. Slate-gray eyes, tousled brown hair, sharp cheekbones— he looked more angelic than demonic. How could a mage be so gorgeous? Magic was supposed to corrupt human bodies.

His gaze slid to her weapon. "Purgator dust." His voice chilled her skin. "You mean to burn the magic off me, after I just saved your life?"

She gritted her teeth. She knew one thing: he hadn't saved her life because he was a nice guy. But either way, she wasn't supposed to kill him. As humans, mages were to be taken back to the Brotherhood's Chambers alive. Of course, that assumed she actually stood a chance against him. In reality, he could probably pulverize her with a spell in a fraction of a second.

She tried to steady her voice, refusing to show submission. "It's my job to catch monsters."

She eyed his physique—pure, lean muscle, his forearms tattooed with a forest of magical symbols. Everything about his appearance screamed at her to get away—yet there was something oddly *familiar* about him. She'd seen those pale eyes before. And what was with his accent? Not American. Not English. Something older, that tickled the darkest recesses of her memory.

The raven—his familiar—perched on his shoulder, its dark gaze fixed on her.

"You think I'm a monster." The mage's tone conveyed only the faintest hint of interest. "Why am I not surprised?" With the bestial glint in his eye, he'd clearly lost his humanity long ago.

"Well, yeah." She didn't want to tempt his wrath, but there was no point lying to a mage. It would only make him angrier.

What was she supposed to do now? She'd just let a mage kill her target and cast a spell on her. And she had *no* chance of beating him in a fight.

She lowered her voice to steady it. "Do you kill Hunters like me?"

His gaze rooted her in place. "Hunters, yes. But not like you."

Her heart clenched, and she held the dust up to his face. He could have stopped her by now—broken her fingers, if he'd wanted to—but he hadn't. But he must know that, if she sprayed the dust, his torment would be excruciating.

"What are you talking about?" She'd gained mastery of her voice, at least, and it sounded far more confident than she felt. His comment had unnerved her, and she couldn't stop staring at him. The shocking contrast of his jaw-dropping beauty with the primal ferocity in his eyes seemed positively otherworldly. "You hardly seem human anymore." She hadn't meant to say that part out loud.

"And yet I just saved your life."

"I didn't need your help. I had it under control."

"That's not how it looked. He was gnawing at your jugular."

Don't show weakness, Rosalind. "I was lulling him into a false sense of security. I was preparing to attack." Her stupid hand trembled, and she hated that he could see her fear. He probably loved every second of her terror, relished the scent of her panic.

His eyes slid over her, landing on her ring—her good luck charm, and one she never took off.

"An iron ring," he said. "That's how you stay sane."

"What are you talking about?"

He slipped closer, his movements fluid, and adrenaline flooded her veins. *Run.*

But she couldn't run. Turning her back on him would mean instant death. She kept her feet rooted to the ground, her heart racing.

Rivulets of rain poured down his skin. "I want to see what happens when you take it off."

It was more of a command than a request, but she knew better than to follow his orders. She had no clue why he found her ring interesting, but his intense scrutiny made her uneasy. Like he was peeling away her armor, or catching her coming out of the shower.

"I don't take it off. Ever. It's my good luck charm. Some people have votive candles. I have my ring to keep the monsters away."

"Doesn't work, though. After all, I'm here." He leaned closer, and despite the rain she could feel the warmth of his skin. She inhaled his powerful magic: air seared by lightning, a hint of sage and earth. She felt a strange wave of something like desire rolling off him, though she had no idea how she could sense that.

He whispered into her ear, "You need to run, Rosalind. They're coming for you."

A shudder crawled up her spine as understanding began to dawn in her mind. He hadn't found her by accident—he'd come for her. But *why?*

She gripped the iron dust tighter, knuckles whitening. "Who's coming for me?"

"The Brotherhood. They want to watch the world burn, and you with it."

Ice closed around her heart. *No. He's lying.* "Why would the Brotherhood come for one of their own?"

"You're not one of theirs. I know what you are. And the Brotherhood will soon find it out."

He turned, slipping silently into one of the alleys.

With a shaking hand, she lowered the dust.

2

$\mathscr{R}$osalind stepped out of the steamy shower, drying her dark hair with a towel. Josiah had been frantically texting her about meeting in the library for a post-mortem, but she wanted to stop by her residence hall first. The encounter with the mage had left her nerves ravaged.

Plus, it was kind of hard to rush to a work meeting when you knew you were about to get fired.

She slipped into a pair of jeans and a low-cut white shirt. The right outfit wasn't enough to get her out of this mess, but it couldn't hurt. She'd chosen her clothes strategically: the white represented purity—Josiah seemed turned on by that, and the low-cut top was just revealing enough to distract him with her cleavage. Only her weapon belt, complete with a loaded gun, ruined the sleek lines of her outfit. But there was no way she was leaving home without it.

She slid her knee-high boots on over her jeans. The iron-lined toes would come in handy if she saw the mage again.

As she leaned closer to the mirror, she pinched her cheeks, bringing out a blush, before glancing at the faint, white scars on her neck. The redcap's attack had been a *very* close call. She should be happy to be alive at all. Still, she couldn't shake the crushing disappointment of her failed kill.

Maybe she could persuade Josiah to bend the rules a little, to keep her on as a Hunter. She'd been *born* for this. Granted, she panicked when confronted with actual demons, but she'd get better if they gave her a chance.

She gathered up her hunting clothes and pushed through the bathroom door. The mage's terrifying warning—whatever he'd meant by it—whispered through her skull. As she walked through the hall, she blinked back tears, trying not to imagine the worst case scenario: exile from the Brotherhood.

She pushed open the door of her cramped dorm room.

Her roommate, Tammi, lay on her bed, playing music through her iPhone. As soon as she saw Rosalind, she yanked out her headphones.

"Rosalind!" Beaming, Tammi flipped her long, blonde hair behind her shoulders. As she took in Rosalind's grim expression, the smile quickly faded from her face. "What's going on? You look like you're about to cry. Is this about Josiah?"

"Sort of." She dropped her clothes on her bed. "I actually have to go meet him in Harvard Square to talk about some stuff."

Tammi crinkled her brow. "What *stuff*? Is this one of those conversations where you have to sit there and listen to him rehash all the reasons he dumped you? Because I would skip that if I were you."

"No. It's work-related, but probably just as painful."

"Oh, right. Your mysterious job that no one is allowed to know about."

Rosalind sighed. "Not for long. I'm pretty sure I'm about to get fired." She shouldn't be talking about this, but she was still so charged up from the encounter with the mage. It was hard to even think straight.

Tammi cocked her head. "Okay, *what* exactly do you do

at night? Because I've been vacillating between *stripper* and *assassin* for a while."

Rosalind's phone beeped, and she yanked it out of her pocket. "Hang on a second. What the hell? It's Mason." Rosalind and her father didn't exactly have a close relationship. In fact, she only ever thought of him by his first name—when she thought of him at all. And he *never* texted her.

When she unlocked her phone to read the text, panic curdled her stomach. It simply read:

> I tried to save you from yourself, but I
> can't protect you any longer.

Her breath caught in her throat. Did her father really know about her failure already? "This isn't good," she whispered. The last thing she wanted to do was talk to Mason, but she needed to find out what was going on.

"*What* isn't good?" Tammi asked. "You seem all dramatic."

Rosalind paced the floor as she dialed his number. His voice mail picked up. *Jerk.* It was just like him to send a cryptic, panic-inducing text and then shut off his phone. A cold sweat broke out on her forehead, and she threw her phone in frustration.

"Rosalind!" Tammi said. "You're freaking me out. What is going on?"

"Mason is an asshole." Rosalind picked up her phone from the pile of discarded clothes on the floor. Luckily, it hadn't broken, and she jammed it into her pocket.

Tammi unscrewed the top of a nail polish bottle and began painting her toenails. "You already knew that. But I'm guessing whatever you're upset about has to do with your father?"

"I don't even know." Rosalind took a deep breath, suddenly desperate to confide in her friend. "Can you keep a secret?"

Tammi stared at her. "Of course I can. Plus, I've told you my secrets."

Rosalind was the only one on campus who knew Tammi's original name: Marcus Robbins. Twenty years before, Tammi had been born into a boy's body. And while that part wasn't a secret, Tammi didn't want anyone knowing about her birth name. And she especially didn't want anyone seeing the photos of her awkward mullet phase.

Rosalind sat at the edge of her bed, just below her poster of a bearded Darwin. "I'm just trying to figure out where to start."

"Oh, just come out with it. Whatever it is, it can't be as bad as the time I had to tell my fundamentalist parents I was transitioning."

She raises a good point. Rosalind dug her fingernails into the duvet. "Okay. The thing is, I'm part of the Brotherhood. I'm a demon hunter. I was supposed to kill a redcap tonight, and I messed up." It came out in a rush. She already felt a weight off her chest.

"*What?*" Tammi knocked over her nail polish, and a pool of crimson stained her duvet.

"Josiah is my ex-boyfriend, but he's also my Guardian in the Brotherhood," Rosalind said. "He dumped me because the Brotherhood forbids novice and Guardian relationships. And I'm supposed to be reporting to him in about fifteen minutes, so he can fire me for screwing up."

"He can wait. This is fucking huge. I did *not* have you pegged as a Hunter. I wasn't even sure if Hunters were real. Can you even fight?" Tammi stood, her face flushed. "Start from the beginning. How long have you been a part of the Brotherhood?"

This really was a long story. "I became a Hunter at eighteen, but I've been in the Brotherhood since I was five. That's when

Mason adopted me. The one good thing he ever did for me was introducing me to the Brotherhood. The order gave me stability and a sense of belonging—everything Mason failed to give me. I always thought a future with the Brotherhood was my destiny. I thought I'd be promoted to Guardian someday, leading a group of novices in the ancient tradition of the hunt. And then, tonight, I messed everything up. Again. They can't risk having incompetent people fighting demons. It's too dangerous."

"What happened?" Tammi asked breathlessly.

An image of the mage's cold, icy stare flashed in Rosalind's brain, and she shuddered. "I've already racked up two failed kills. Three, and you're out. Tonight, I was supposed to kill a redcap, but I let the situation get out of control."

"You let him get away?"

"Not exactly. He bit me."

"Holy shit, Ros. Why aren't you dead?"

"Because a really hot mage showed up, ripped out the demon's heart, and then healed me. And then I let the mage get away."

Tammi stared at her, open-mouthed. "Jesus, Rosalind." She pulled her hair off her face. "Look on the bright side. At least you made it out alive. And it can't be that terrible to get saved by a hot guy."

Rosalind flinched. "I don't think the Brotherhood will be so impressed with those things."

Tammi frowned. "Don't you think we should be making peace with the demons, or at least the mages? I'm just a little wary of the Brotherhood, since they don't do trials and all..."

Rosalind didn't need to hear this lecture right now. When demons were trying to feast on your guts, you didn't always have the luxury of putting them on trial. "Did the mages give us a chance to make peace when they murdered a hundred kids in Boston? Did that redcap ask for peace when he ate the two cashiers in Market Basket? The vamps have killed two people on campus in the past month. Tonight, this guy was going to slaughter ten times that."

"I guess so..." Tammi said doubtfully.

Rosalind could feel the blood rushing to her head. "The Brotherhood have been protecting humans from dark magic since the dawn of civilization. Without Hunters, demons would enslave us all. And the demons aren't going to wait around for us to put everyone on trial while they rape and eat their way through Boston's citizens. Demons don't respect weakness. We have to fight back."

Tammi sat on the edge of her bed, her brow furrowed. "Fine. But why you? Why can't you have a normal job? You're a computer science major. You have useful skills."

Rosalind shook her head. "Because the world needs people like me. Anyway, programming doesn't exactly light my world on fire. I'm not meant for a nine-to-five job. But since I'm about to get fired tonight, coding is probably back in the cards for me."

Tammi raised her brow. "Killing is the only thing that would make you happy? That's messed up."

"I still haven't killed anything. That's why I'm in trouble. And it's not that I *want* to kill anything. I just like being part of something important. And I like the sense of adventure. If I could choose any job in the world, I'd join Darwin's Beagle voyage. But until someone invents time travel and Victorian gender equality, I'll have to stick with the Brotherhood."

Rosalind's phone beeped again, and she scrambled to yank it out. It was Josiah again, demanding to know where she was. "Shit. I really need to go."

"If you get fired, come find me. There's a streak night planned.

We'll get hammered and watch all the naked guys running around campus. You'll forget all about the redcap."

"I'll text you!" Rosalind grabbed her umbrella and rushed out the door, leaving her coat behind. There was no point wearing a low-cut top if you were going to put a coat over it.

And she'd need all the resources she could muster to face Josiah.

3

With an umbrella in hand, Rosalind hurried through one of Harvard Yard's brick gates. She kept her eyes locked on the Brotherhood's towering command center: the Victorian brick building known as the Chambers.

It had once been a performance and lecture hall. Since the mage attacks in Boston, the Brotherhood had taken it over, refurbishing the interior at an astounding speed. It had been refitted with a combination of cutting-edge technology and old world grandeur, and it now acted as the Brotherhood's Massachusetts headquarters.

As she walked up the stone steps to a set of glass doors, she tried to pull her thoughts together. She'd need to project competence if she wanted to convince Josiah she was valuable to the Brotherhood.

She paused next to the small scanner by the door, lining up her iris with the blue circle in the retina scanner. When she heard the beep, she swiped her ID card, and the glass door clicked open. The Brotherhood were a little paranoid with their security measures, but you had to be vigilant when fighting blood-drinking demons.

Through the glass doors, she nodded at Martha, the rosy-cheeked security guard behind the desk, and hurried on to the central corridor. After scanning her retina a second time, she pulled open an oak door, its surface carved with Latin phrases.

The sight of the Great Hall always took her breath away. It was the most stunning part of the building—a cavernous, cathedral-like space modeled after a Roman amphitheater, with semicircular rows of benches surrounding a round stage. She often envisioned herself lecturing beneath its enormous stone dome about the history of witchcraft, instilling students with a sense of reverence for the Sanguine Brotherhood's history.

During the day, sunlight streamed through an oculus onto the lecture stage, illuminating the Guardians with pure white light. But now only pale moonlight lit the interior.

Her footsteps echoed, and she scanned the stone benches for her Guardian. For most, he'd be hard to pick out at all, but she was an expert at spotting tiny movements in the dark, and the slow rise and fall of his enormous chest drew her eye. As she caught sight of him, her heart quickened.

"Rosalind." His voice boomed through the hall. "I've been waiting for twenty-seven minutes. You're late."

"Sorry. I wanted to figure out what the hell I was going to say to you."

He splayed his fingers. "How about the truth?"

He was definitely pissed.

She climbed the stairs, taking in his huge form, nearly as imposing as the Great Hall. The guy could deadlift five hundred pounds. She was still working on three hundred. *Let's just say I never want to get on Josiah's bad side.*

As she approached, he fixed her with one of his stony stares. "What happened? I've been worried sick."

"I'm fine." She sat next to him on the bench, its cold surface chilling her though her clothes. "But there was a complication."

He leaned in, his dark eyes intense. "Tell me."

"The redcap is dead, but I saw a shadow mage. He interfered. Technically, he's the one who killed the redcap. And he healed my neck wounds."

"Your neck *what?* Seven hells, Rosalind." He flicked on a small flashlight and inspected her skin. His face hardened. "You let a demon bite you. And then you let a shadow mage cast a healing spell. I'm going to have to purify you of any magical residue. Why did you allow that to happen? I've seen you fight. You hesitated, didn't you?"

He knows me too well. "The redcap looked human. I saw fear in his eyes."

"Need I remind you what demons have done to human kind? What they did to your birth parents?"

"You don't need to remind me. I think about it every day." It was something she and Josiah had in common. Vampires had slaughtered both their parents. But in Josiah's case, he could remember the event vividly. His trauma could make him a little intense on the subject.

"If given half the chance, that redcap would've chained you up in a dungeon. Demons don't have souls. They're pure predators. As a Hunter, if you hesitate, you die. You're lucky to be alive right now."

She hid her face with her hands. Her low-cut top wasn't working at all. "I know all this."

He pulled out his phone, flipping through his photos before shoving a gruesome picture in her face: a young man lying on the pavement, most of his neck missing. "This is what your redcap did yesterday, a few days after he killed the cashiers. The victim's name was Perry. A writer—recently engaged and planning his wedding. His fiancée lost her mind when we delivered the news."

Rosalind closed her eyes, suppressing the bile rising in her throat. "I know. He looked scared at one point. It threw me off."

Josiah's dark eyes flashed. "Do I need to show you the pictures of the cheerleading team the demons ripped apart two months ago? Since the supernatural world has gone public, they don't care about discretion anymore. They're murdering indiscriminately."

"You've mentioned it once or twice." *Shit.* She needed to keep her attitude in check if she wanted to keep her job.

"It's not just about vindicating human deaths. I want you to be safe. The Brotherhood isn't going to lose you on my watch. You're our strongest novice, and it's my job to guide you. Your physical training is fine. You need mental training."

Our strongest novice. He still thought that? "If you give me another chance, I won't hesitate next time."

"I want to hear about the shadow mage. Why was he there?"

Why *was* he there? "He was terrifying. Insanely powerful." Just thinking about his cold voice chilled her blood. "It was almost like he'd come to give me a message. He said he *knew what I was.* He said the Brotherhood will know soon, too." She shivered, thinking of the powerful thrill of his aura. "What do you think he meant?"

"I have no idea."

"He mentioned my ring. Something about how it keeps me sane."

"He obviously wanted to throw you off guard. And he did. Don't tell anyone about it until we know more. That's the sort of thing that leads to rumors." Josiah ran a hand over his buzz cut. "Tell me what he looked like."

"Beautiful, really. Smooth skin. Pale eyes. Brown hair. Tattoos—I saw a crescent moon."

"Magic deforms human bodies. He's obviously glamoured himself."

"Ah."

"Why didn't you spray him with dust? It would have seared the magic off him."

She shook her head. This was the truth she really didn't want to admit, but she owed Josiah an explanation. "With the demon, I saw fear in his eyes. And he seemed human. But with the shadow mage... *I* was afraid. I thought if he sensed I might hurt him, he'd murder me with his mind. His aura was immensely powerful. And when he first showed up, I was certain he was there for vengeance."

"Vengeance for what?"

A wave of guilt washed over her. "I mean, because of what *we* did in the interrogation room. His eyes looked so much like the inc—"

"You did nothing wrong in that interrogation room," Josiah cut her off. "The Brotherhood need us to act quickly. The mages have infested half of New England now, and something terrible is coming. Worse than the Boston Slaughter. If we show them weakness, they win. It's that simple."

A sigh slid from her. "Something is definitely coming. And I want to be on the side of the Brotherhood when it comes. It wasn't just the shadow mage on our campus tonight. There was a sea mage, too."

"Did you see him?"

She shook her head. "No. He must have been further away, but his magic smelled of the ocean."

He swore under his breath. "I shouldn't have allowed you go out alone tonight."

The comment hit her like a slap in the face. "Of course you should have. I'm a Hunter. Going out alone is part of the job, and you know I can fight."

"Your combat skills are incredible, but mentally you're not battle ready. You can't let your emotions get the better of you." He shook his head. "You need to master your fear, or the demons will see you as prey."

She flinched. "We've been over this. It's why you singled me out for that special session downstairs." She took a deep breath. She had no clue why she'd made it out alive at all, and now, she just needed Josiah to get to the point. "So what's the deal. Am I fired?"

"The Chamber will review the case, but it's not as if you're the first novice to screw up. The Brotherhood won't want to lose you. You'll be giving them intel about two mages on the Thorndike Campus. No one else can sense them from so far away, or with such precision."

"I've had an excellent teacher." She exhaled slowly. He wasn't an unreasonable Guardian, and he always seemed to have her back. On top of that, Josiah was one of the best Hunters the Brotherhood had ever trained. Randolph Loring had promoted him to Guardian at only twenty-three years old.

Her relationship with him should have been awkward after the break up, but she'd quickly stopped thinking of him in a romantic way—even if his chiseled physique excited all the other female novices.

"It's not just your hunting skills that make you valuable," he said, eyes flicking to her neckline. "With your Computer Science degree, the Brotherhood will want you to work on their security systems." He pulled out a small, iron pendant, inset with rubies. "I still have your chalice."

"Next time."

His eyes met hers, and he handed it over. "Take it. You've earned it, anyway."

She forced a smile. It was sweet of him to try make her feel better, though she didn't deserve this. "Thank you, Josiah."

He pulled out an iron flask, etched with Latin phrases, and handed it to her—ambrosia, the sacred drink of the Hunters. "This will help clear you of the stain of magic."

She took a sip of the sweet liquid, and instantly her aching muscles relaxed. The stuff was addictive.

"Better?" He lowered his eyes. "You know I only had to end it with you because the Brotherhood wouldn't allow us to be together."

She handed him the flask again. "I know, Josiah."

"I'll still protect you."

Her father's message flashed in her mind. *I can't protect you.* "That reminds me." She pulled her phone out of her pocket, bringing up Mason's text. "Any idea what Mason is talking about?"

His brow furrowed, Josiah stared at the phone. "How should I know? Why don't you ask him?"

"He's not answering. He shut off his phone."

Josiah arched an eyebrow. "Great parenting."

"He's not really a... parent," she muttered.

"I have no idea what he's talking about, but like I said, I'm here to protect you. Get some rest. I'll let you know when you need to come before the Chamber."

The blood drained from her head as a horrible thought struck her. "Will I need to go in front of Randolph Loring and everything?" He was the flame-haired leader of the Brotherhood. His family's power stretched back centuries. The man was at least ten times as intimidating as Josiah.

"Relax. Randolph has better things to do than listen to a novice."

Rosalind rose, but Josiah touched her hand. "Don't think about the mage. Whatever he said to you, he was just trying to screw with your mind. And stay out of trouble tonight. If a mage has marked you for some reason, you need to stay hidden. You know how much they'd love to take you as a slave for their own disgusting purposes. He'll want to rape and feed on you. Or turn you into a monster like him."

She winced, thinking of how easily the shadow mage could lure someone into a trap. His beauty and sensual aura were all the weapons he needed. "I'll be safe. Thanks, Josiah." She curled her fingers around the chalice pendant.

"*Lux in tenebris lucet.*"

She smiled. "Light shines in the darkness."

As she left the Great Hall, she tried Mason again, but the call went straight to voicemail. At the sound of his clipped voice on the recording, her muscles tensed. It was hard not to remember him calling her an "abomination." Hard not to think of him tying her to a chair to beat her legs every time he lost his temper. She had no idea why he'd wanted to adopt her at all.

As she walked through Harvard Yard, she shoved the images from her mind and tried to imagine her life *before* Mason. Before the vamps ripped her life away by slaughtering her parents. She could remember only glimmers. Buttery sunlight. Someone patching up her knee. Toes sinking into the sand on a beach. Her parents giving her periwinkle and yellow wildflowers on her birthday. Her own face, smiling.

She could have sworn someone else lingered at the edges of the memories: a boy.

With a jolt, she remembered his eyes, pale and gray—not unlike the shadow mage's.

Chilled to the bone, she hugged herself tight.

Of course, it wasn't like gray was such an unusual color.

Yep. That mage definitely messed with my head.

4

$\mathcal{B}$y the time she returned to Thorndike's campus, the rain had slowed to a light drizzle. Rosalind stalked across the quad, trying to sneak through the shadows undetected. She couldn't shake the feeling that someone was watching her. At least she had her weapon belt if the mage planned to stalk her.

Once inside her dorm building, she released a breath. Demons and mages could enter here, but their magic wouldn't work within the walls.

After the monsters had come out of the magical closet five years ago, Thorndike's buildings had been refitted with aura detectors that sprayed iron dust. At least the building would keep her safe from the lethal spells of a psychotic mage.

She strode down the hall to her room and unlocked the door. After pulling off her coat, she flicked on the light.

She gasped. Two men in black suits stood in her room—one thin, with impossibly long legs, and the other roughly the size and heft of an industrial fridge. *What the fuck?*

Instantly, her hand flew to her vial of dust.

Fridge smiled. "Well-trained, I see. But that won't work on us."

"We're from the Brotherhood," said the long-shanked one. "We don't use magic."

Her mind turned from confusion to horror. She really *was* in trouble. "I just saw my Guardian. I thought everything was going to be okay. What are you doing in my room? And where's my roommate?"

Longshanks tilted his narrow head, studying her. "Randolph Loring sent us."

Randolph Loring knew who she was? She wasn't sure if she should be flattered or terrified. "Is this about the mages? How did you hear about that so fast?"

Fridge licked his pale lips, edging closer. "I'm sure we will enjoy hearing about the other mages. But no. This is about *you*, Rosalind."

"I want to see Josiah," she managed. "I just gave him intel about two mages on campus. You should be hunting them."

"Josiah can't help you now," said Longshanks.

Fear crawled up the back of her neck. "Josiah is my Guardian. I need him here for this conversation."

Fridge smiled, his long teeth like a row of tombstones. "No. You don't."

She took a step back, her mind burning with panic. She shouldn't be afraid of her own people, and yet... "Why are you here for me? I haven't done anything wrong. There's a shadow mage *and* a sea-mage stalking the campus, and you're here harassing me."

Longshanks edged closer, and Rosalind took another step back—right into another body. A quick glance behind her told her the third person was a woman—a very large, muscular woman. Her heart clenched. There were three of them, trapping her in the dorm room.

"We know you're a mage," the woman whispered in her ear. "And I know you're not stupid enough to resist us."

A wave of horror slammed into Rosalind. *A mage.* Now *that* wasn't possible, even if she didn't know who her birth parents were. Unlike the other monsters, mages were made, not born. To become a mage, you needed to actually commit to learning magic. It could take years to learn Angelic, the magical language. It wasn't like it happened by accident. "You've made a mistake. I've never learned a spell in my life."

"The Brotherhood doesn't make mistakes," Fridge said. "Cuff her."

The woman gripped Rosalind's arms, and Rosalind's adrenaline surged. Once the Brotherhood had someone in their sights, they didn't tend to change their minds easily. She didn't know what they did with convicted mages, but she was pretty sure no one arrested by the Brotherhood made it into the daylight again.

Tammi was right about one thing: the Brotherhood didn't do trials.

A survival instinct—pure panic—blazed through the ancient part of her brain. *Run, Rosalind.*

Before the woman could finishing cuffing her, Rosalind reached back, grabbing the woman by her neck. She locked her arm around the woman's neck and, using her body weight as leverage, flipped the woman over her shoulder and onto the floor. Free, Rosalind rushed for the door to the hall, slamming it behind her.

By the time Fridge busted through, she'd pulled her gun from her belt, already loaded with silver bullets. She pointed it at the Hunter's head. The bullets were meant for werewolves, of course—not other Hunters—but they'd still kill a human.

Was she pulling the dumbest stunt of her life right now? Probably—but it was too late to turn back. She just needed to get down the stairwell, and out the door, then find a quiet place to get in touch with Josiah. He'd help her sort this out. He had promised to protect her.

Fridge paused at the edge of the doorframe, blocking in the others. He raised his hands, his face reddening with rage. "The mage has a gun."

"If I were an actual mage, I wouldn't *need* a gun. But like I said. I'm not a mage." It wasn't like she was going to *use* it on him, but he didn't need to know that. Slowly, she backed away from him, edging closer to the stairwell with her gun trained on the Hunters.

When she reached the stairs, she bellowed at the top of her lungs, "Streeaaaaaak niiiiiiiiiight!"

Within moments, hallway doors slammed open. Rosalind didn't wait around to watch her classmates strip off. She was already gunning down the steps. The horde of naked college students would cause just enough chaos to let her slip outside undetected.

With a racing pulse, she burst through the front doors, careening for one of the dark alleys between the campus's brick Victorian buildings. She knew exactly how to hide on the Thorndike campus, and slipped past some recycling bins into an unlit passage. From there, she could sneak through to the football field and jump into a cab.

She'd have just enough time to call Josiah—assuming he could help her at all. Maybe she'd just watched her entire life blow up before her eyes.

From the alley, she sprinted past the darkened, tree-lined tennis courts, heading for the football field. Fear blazed, giving her extra speed, until a rhythmic noise stopped her in her tracks.

Rotors beat overhead, and a circular light danced over the

tennis courts. *Search helicopters.* Were they for *her?* When the light swerved over the football field, she saw men, swarming the grass in dark clothes. The light swerved again, and she caught a glimpse of flame-red hair, and the glint of an iron chalice pendant. A chill gripped her spine.

Randolph Loring. He'd come for her, leading the hunt.

Seven hells. What the fuck was going on? The Brotherhood had brought down their whole damn army, searching for her. Her body buzzed with panic. *This is all wrong.* She belonged *with* the Brotherhood—not fighting them. It was her destiny to become a Guardian.

Yet here was Randolph Loring, hunting her.

Tendrils of a cold, ancient magic tickled her body, and she whirled, nearly jumping out of her skin. Someone was coming right for her on a sleek, black motorcycle.

The shadow mage.

Her mouth went dry as he pulled to a stop beside her. "Get on the bike or you'll die."

She wasn't sure if that was a threat or a rescue attempt, but his commanding voice was awfully convincing either way. "I don't understand what's happening."

As if he was going to tell her the truth.

"I already told you what's happening. They know about you. I told you to run, and you didn't listen."

She shook her head. "But—"

"You don't have time. You can come with me, or let the mage-Hunters murder you. Your choice."

She wanted to throw up. She couldn't believe she was even contemplating the advice of a shadow mage, yet Randolph Loring was hunting her. There would be no trial, no chance to explain herself.

Gunshots rang out, and an unholy pain splintered her shoulder. She screamed, instinctively dropping to a crouch, hands clutching the bleeding wound. The pain ripped her chest apart, taking her breath away.

I need to get the hell out of here before they slaughter me. Trying to block out the pain, she jumped on the bike and wrapped her arms around the mage's waist. With her face tucked in close to his leather jacket, she stifled a scream as he took off.

The helicopter swerved above, and another hail of bullets ripped through the night air. She flinched. She was going to die, slaughtered by her own people before she got the chance to defend herself.

The mage sped through a roundabout. A powerful wave of magic vibrated over her skin as he chanted a spell.

The gunshots fell silent, and the helicopter wavered in the night sky before careening off course. Was the mage actually controlling the goddamn *wind?*

Horror punched a hole in her gut. She'd just been shot by the Brotherhood and taken up with a powerful monster—one capable of murdering a whole legion of Hunters. Tears pricked her eyes, and she clamped them shut, trying to gain control. She couldn't let herself fall apart.

As they raced through Cambridge, the wind rushed over her skin, making her shiver. Or maybe she was shivering from the certainty that the rest of her life would be spent as a fugitive. She'd end up as the mage's sex slave, or a vamp's blood-bag, until someone decided to reap her soul for the god of night.

The searing pain in her shoulder stole her breath. *Think of something calming.* That was what she always did when the world seemed in danger of shutting her down. *The beaches in England, the hawthorns, blue and yellow wildflowers.*

It wasn't working.

Nauseated, she heard the sorcerer chant another spell—and gaped as both their bodies glimmered out of view. *Gods, the invisibility is a mind-fuck.*

That's it, then. She'd just hurled herself into the dark side, and now she couldn't help but second-guess her choice. Had Randolph Loring really come for her? What if this was some sort of test—one that she'd failed, wretchedly? Or what if it had been a horrible series of accidents, and she'd just thrown herself at a seductive shadow mage?

She should have gone willingly with the Brotherhood when they'd first arrived, but she'd panicked. They didn't evaluate the guilt of their prisoners, because they operated with one hundred percent certainty. To be honest, she'd never questioned them before either. The Brotherhood was always right, and the world needed them to act decisively or the demons would win.

At least, they'd always been right until now.

Now, even Josiah wouldn't be able to help her. Kind of hard to claim you were innocent of magic when you ran off clinging to a shadow mage's chest.

Her dark hair whipped wildly around her head, and the wind stung her skin through her blood-soaked shirt. The mage had offered to help her, but there would be a price. With mages, nothing was ever what it seemed.

She forced herself to block out the agony. They raced down Mass Ave, heading for Harvard Square—the location of the Brotherhood's Chambers. *Why the hell would he take her to the Brotherhood?* But as they wove through Harvard Square's congested intersection it was clear the mage had other plans. He was probably ushering her to his demon harem right now.

She felt sick. Her life was over, and she didn't even know why. Sure, she'd screwed up tonight, but she was innocent.

If anyone had answers to this catastrophe, it was the shadow mage. She wanted to ask him everything he knew, even though he turned her stomach in knots of fear.

"Why do they think I'm a mage?" she shouted as they tore down Brattle Street.

He ignored her.

They zoomed past a row of old Victorian mansions before veering sharply left—heading right for wrought-iron cemetery gate. It swung open just as they approached.

At the sight of the gently sloping paths and marble graves, she shuddered with cold recognition. He'd taken her to Mount Auburn Cemetery. The place wasn't so much a graveyard as a full-blown Victorian necropolis—a walled city of the dead, complete with street names and towering mausoleums.

And this was the point where she'd learn how she was going to die.

5

She ran through the options of what might happen in the next hour. Hanging? Impalement? Crushed to death by rocks? Like an idiot, she'd come here willingly—though her shoulder hurt so badly that death almost seemed like a mercy at this point.

Just as their bodies shimmered back to visibility, the mage pulled up outside a looming gothic chapel, its towering walls built from dark granite. He parked his bike in the shadows and turned off the engine.

She loosened her grip on his waist, grimacing at the pain when she shifted position. "What are we doing here?"

"This is your safe haven. Abduxiel Mansion." He stepped off the bike. "I'm going to heal your shoulder, and then you're going inside."

Rosalind gritted her teeth, crippled by pain. It felt like the bullet must have shattered her collarbone.

He moved closer. Gently, he tugged down the collar of her white shirt, exposing her wounded shoulder.

Pain ripped through her entire arm. If the agony from the gunshot weren't drowning out all other thoughts, she'd probably be running in terror from the mage right now.

As he traced his fingers over her flesh, he whispered a spell. His aura seeped into her body, drawing the pain from her shattered bones and caressing her skin. She glanced down to see her wound healing, and let out a long breath. Gods, it felt so much better. As if that weren't enough, the blood disappeared from her shirt.

She took a steadying breath as the mage covered her shoulder with her shirt again. Something about his proximity deeply unnerved her. Maybe it was the fact that he served the night god—just like the vamps who'd murdered her parents.

"What about the bullet?" she asked.

"Gone."

She still had no idea why he was helping her. "You even cleaned the blood out of my shirt."

"It would attract vampires."

She shuddered. "Thank you. I guess." He'd just saved her life, yet he was her natural enemy. Frantic thoughts whirled though her mind. "I don't understand what's happening. Why are we here? Why is Randolph Loring hunting me?"

At that moment, the chapel doors creaked open, and a man in a black robe motioned for her to enter. A dark hood cast his face in shadow.

"You're safe here," the mage said. "Orcus will look after you."

"You want me to stay in this mansion?"

"The Brotherhood won't be able to find you here."

The sight of the cleric tightened her chest. He looked like a grim reaper. In fact, he probably *was* a grim reaper. "Do I have a choice in any of this? Am I a prisoner?"

The mage's raven circled overhead, then landed on his shoulder. "You came here willingly, but I have instructions to make sure you're safe, which means staying in the mansion. Orcus will make sure no one hurts you."

Desperation warped her mind, and she struggled to string a coherent thought together. "I can't stay here. There's obviously been some sort of mistake. I'm not a mage. I'm a Hunter. When things have calmed down, I'll explain everything to the Brotherhood. I've never even *seen* a spell book." She suddenly felt a desperate need to convince him.

Dark lashes framed his pale eyes, and his unwavering gaze almost hypnotized her. "The Brotherhood execute people without trials, and they want to burn you," he said matter-of-factly. "You won't be able to reason with them. On some level, you understand that, or you'd never have come with me."

The night wind kissed her skin. "They execute demons. Not people. And they don't *burn* people anymore. That was just a medieval thing."

"The medieval ways are returning."

"I'm not a mage." Her mind raced with panic. What if this whole thing had been an illusion concocted by the demons to tempt her away from her true path? "I've never learned any magic."

Moonlight bathed his cheekbones and pale eyes in silver. "It doesn't matter what you are. It matters what they think you are."

"And I'm supposed to stay with the grim reaper." She had no idea who to trust at this point, but the shadow mage ranked pretty low on the list, and she couldn't see herself going out for Appletinis with the faceless reaper anytime soon. "I'm supposed to just take your word for all of this."

"You're supposed to use your own senses and capacity for rational thought. You saw the Brotherhood coming for you, and they shot you." He glanced away. "I don't have time for this."

"How can I trust my own senses when you have the power to warp them?"

His cold gaze slid over her, and as he stepped closer, her heart skipped a beat. "What purpose would that serve? If I wanted you dead, you'd be in the earth right now. If I wanted you to kill people, you'd be pulling out one of those knives and thrusting it into a heart."

Dread tightened its grip around her chest as she looked up at him. "Tell me why you helped me."

"Ambrose wants you alive."

"And who the hell is Ambrose?"

"You don't need to know that right now."

She bit the inside of her cheek to stop herself from screaming at him. She needed answers, and he was giving her nothing. She steadied her voice. "Okay, let's start with this: You know my name. You apparently know things about me. And who, exactly, are you?"

"Caine Mountfort. We've met before." He cocked his head, examining her. "Apparently, I didn't leave such a lasting impression."

Recognition flickered in the recesses of her mind—the boy with the gray eyes... "Did I know you in England? Before Mason adopted me?"

"England?" He arched an eyebrow. "Is that what the Brotherhood told you?"

She was ready to scream with frustration. "Yes, because that's where I'm from. I lived in England until a few of your vampire buddies murdered my parents."

He took a long, slow breath as if marshaling his patience. Something seemed to have unnerved him. "Look, I don't have the time or the inclination to delve into this with you. You must go with Orcus."

His habit of enticing her with hints while refusing to give a straight answer made her want to punch something. Her world had just been shattered, and the mage had answers he didn't care to share. And there wasn't a damn thing she could do about—not when he had mind-blowing magic on his side.

A hot tear spilled down her cheek. "Can't you just answer my questions? What do you know about me? And why are the Brotherhood hunting me down? You and I both know I can't be a mage if I've never chanted a single spell."

He reached down, lifting her hand. At the touch of his strong hands, she felt a brief thrill from his magical aura, and it surged through her body like a jolt of electricity. What *was* that?

"Keep this ring on and stay away from the Brotherhood. You'll be fine." His gray eyes met hers. "Don't trust anyone. Not Orcus. Not me. Not your best friends. No one. That's all you need to know." He turned to leave.

Don't trust a bloodthirsty mage or the grim reaper standing behind me? Gee, you don't say. His evasiveness infuriated her. "Are you coming back here?"

"No."

"Where are you going?"

"You don't need to know that. Stay with Orcus." It was hard to ignore the ring of command in his voice.

Just like a goddamn mage to leave her question unanswered.

As she stood there like an idiot, he slipped into the cemetery's shadows. *My one chance at the truth—gone.*

"Come with me." Orcus's gravelly voice made her jump, and she nearly staked him. There was no way in hell she wanted to go into Abduxiel Mansion with Crypt Guy.

Scary as Caine was, at least he was human, and a hood didn't obscure his face.

His particularly stunning face.

The way she saw it, there were two options right now. Either the Brotherhood had made a mistake, or Caine had created this whole thing as an illusion. A cool breeze slipped over her skin, and she shivered.

What if Caine had glamoured demons to come for her? What if Longshanks and Fridge had been reapers spelled to appear human—

No. Magic didn't work in the confines of Thorndike's buildings. Plus, Caine had a point. If he wanted to control her, he could hypnotize her to do whatever he wanted.

Still, her heart clung to the possibility that this was all some sort of mistake. She pulled out her cell phone, and a message flashed from Josiah.

Where are you?

While Orcus cleared his throat, she frantically typed a message back to her Guardian.

Why are the Brotherhood after me?
They say I'm a witch. I saw Randolph
Loring. Did he come for me??

"Miss." Orcus touched her arm, his fingers cold and bony. "You must come inside."

She jerked her arm away from his touch, staring intently at her screen until a message popped up from Josiah.

Someone accused you of witchcraft.
I don't know who. You must stay
hidden until I can fix this. Don't use
your phone again. I will find you. *Lux in
tenebris lucet.*

The Brotherhood would track her phone. Panic clenched her heart. Even Josiah wanted her to run. Perfect, loyal Josiah, completely faithful to the Brotherhood, thought she should flee from the Hunters. He knew that once the Brotherhood had their sights set on a target, they didn't give second chances—no explanations, no trials, no pardons.

At least her Guardian stood by her.

She swiped open another message—this one from Tammi, who'd been texting her from a campus party.

> Ros where r u...
> I'm getting drunkeus.
> I lost one of my shoes...

Good. At least the Purifiers hadn't involved her. Rosalind hammered out another message.

> Tammi—things have gotten weird with the Brotherhood. Josiah and I will sort it out. I'm OK, but I'll be offline for a while. Speak soon. XO

She shut off her phone, steeling herself for a night with Crypt Guy.

She turned, but she couldn't force herself to follow Orcus. In fact, there was no freaking way she was sealing herself up in a gothic mansion while Caine slipped off with her secrets. He'd implied her English roots were a lie, and then refused to explain. He'd known that the Brotherhood would come for her, but wouldn't say why.

He was the only person who had the answers she needed, and she would wrench them out of him if her life depended on it.

Which it does, come to think of it.

Her entire world had just shattered, and she wasn't giving up on the remaining fragments without a fight.

She turned to the cleric. "I'm not coming in. I have more questions for Caine."

"You will come with me, Miss," he hissed, grabbing her arm.

A swift elbow to the jaw sent him sprawling in the chapel doorway, and she launched into a sprint over the grass, thundering up a grassy hill.

She wove through weeping stone angels and crooked obelisks, the gravestones jutting from the ground at odd angles like broken bones.

She tore past a row of stone crypts, and down a gently sloping hill. But she was running blindly, and had lost all trace of Caine. He'd slipped somewhere deep into the cemetery's shadows. She ground to a halt near a gently rippling pond, trying to attune her senses to the delicious tingling of Caine's magic.

A chilly wind rustled the leaves, and the moonlight shone on a tombstone's etching. *The Lord of Terror.* Even for someone used to hunting demons, she was getting the creeps.

The breeze brought with it the scent of thunderstorms and wet grass, and the hair rising on the back of her arms told her that a powerful aura lurked nearby.

She followed a winding path that led to the water, catching the smell of burnt air—Caine's magic. She just needed to home in on it.

She crept closer to the pond, drawn by his powerful aura. Anyone could sense magic, if they knew how to tune in to the right vibrations, but Rosalind could actually *see* it too. As far as she knew, no other Hunter had that ability. It was the reason she was born for the Brotherhood.

Goose bumps prickled on her skin as she drew closer to a row of mausoleums overlooking the water. Caine's sensual magic lingered around one of the crypts, nestled among the oak and beeches, pulling her closer.

As she rubbed her arms in the chilly spring air, she approached the arched crypt. Its door hung slightly open, and the crypt walls glowed, faintly silver. This was the one. Caine lurked inside; gods knew why. Probably the entrance to a personal dungeon.

The magic rippled off the stony walls in waves, skimming over her skin. It called to her, sucking her in like the gravitational pull of a black hole.

As she pushed open the metal door, it let out a loud creaking noise that echoed off a high, peaked ceiling. Empty. *What the hell?* He'd definitely come in here. She could still smell his magic and see the lingering glow.

Faint moonlight reached the interior of the crypt, highlighting marble walls and glinting off a deep pool of dark water in the center of the crypt. *What is a giant puddle doing in a mausoleum?*

A powerful aura rolled off it, smelling of ozone—Caine's magic. White-hot excitement surged in her veins. As with everything to do with mages, this mausoleum wasn't exactly as it seemed.

It was a portal.

Of course a mage wouldn't bother with a motorcycle when a portal could get him where he wanted instantly.

Her heart clenched. If she wanted to follow him through, she'd need to act now. Portals didn't last forever.

There was a chance this one would take her right to Caine, and she could confront him to get the answers she wanted. There was also the possibility that he'd fly into a lethal rage. Plunging through the portal meant crossing an obvious boundary. And if she angered him, she'd suffer a slow and painful death at his hands.

Then again, he'd obviously spared her life for a reason. It was just like Josiah said. She needed to master her fear to get what she wanted. And what she wanted right now, more than anything, was answers.

The shadow mage held the key not only to her present life disasters, but to her past. He was the only remaining thread to her golden childhood memories, before the demons had ruined everything.

She gritted her teeth. The idea of jumping into a cold pool of water at the bottom of a crypt ranked only marginally higher than spending a night with Crypt Guy. She twisted the lucky ring around her finger, wondering what Tammi would tell her to do. She was pretty sure what Tammi would tell her *not* to do, starting with "don't follow a psychotic mage through a pool of water in the bottom of a crypt." Tammi was practical like that.

But if Rosalind took the practical route, she'd never find out the truth about herself. She'd never find out if Caine knew something more about her past, or why everyone thought she was a witch.

After sucking in a breath, she took a step forward, and leapt into the icy water.

6

$\mathscr{S}$he plunged deep into the frigid water, the cold piercing her skin. Immediately, she regretted her choice. The pool was far deeper than she'd expected.

Frantically, she kicked her legs to return to the surface, but the shock of the chill disoriented her. For a moment, she couldn't tell which way was up or down, and she flailed in the murky water, her pulse racing.

At last, her head pierced the surface; she tried to suck in air, but the frigid water had frozen her muscles.

Breathe, Rosalind.

As she blinked, waiting for the world to come in focus, she gasped. She was floating in a stone fountain, and her body shook from the cold. Above her, water flowed from the mouth of a stone woman in a torn dress. Rosalind clambered to the fountain's edge, hoisting herself out of the water onto a cobblestone street. The air smelled of jasmine and sandalwood.

Where the hell *was* she?

The force of the magical aura sickened her, seeping into her skull like a poisonous miasma. She doubled over, retching. Good thing she'd skipped dinner.

Freezing, she rubbed her arms, trying to catch her breath. Her white shirt now clung to her skin, her blue bra showing through the sodden fabric. *Great.*

She stood on a narrow lane, constructed entirely of stone. Pale moonflowers and gardenias hung from vines growing on the buildings that surrounded her, as though nature were trying to reclaim its domain.

But something drew her gaze upward: a steep-peaked castle stood on a high rocky hill, bathed in silvery moonlight. The towering gothic palace loomed over the land. *What the hell...?*

She couldn't breathe. She hadn't taken a portal to Caine's house, or even his dungeon. She'd transported herself to another world. Everyone had heard the legends, but she'd never believed them to be true.

Maremount, Mount Acidale, Lilinor... What if these mythical places were real? And what if she'd just leapt into one of the demon realms? If that were the case, she needed to get the hell out of here. Fast. She could fight one or two demons—in theory. But she wasn't ready to fight a whole demon realm.

Her imagination roamed free, and her mind spun with all the horrifying things she could remember about demons. Some killed fast, and others savored their victims' agony, plucking apart the sinews and muscle like artists of gore.

At this point, only two things were certain: she was a complete idiot for plunging through the portal, and she should have stayed with the grim reaper.

She hugged herself, overcome by a sudden urge to plunge back into the cemetery. But when she glanced back into the fountain, all the water had disappeared.

Her world tilted; it felt like all the blood drained from her head. What the hell had she just done? Sure, she was probably safe from the Brotherhood here, but she wasn't safe from anything else. In fact, she'd just thrown herself right into the monster's lair. She *really* needed to find Caine now, assuming he still wanted to keep her alive.

She swallowed hard and took a tentative step, her teeth chattering. If she were lucky, she'd thrown herself into the mage's realm. *Which one is that? Maremount, maybe.* At least, that's what Josiah had once told her.

As she stepped over the damp cobblestones, cold fear washed over her skin. There was no sign of Caine in the city's dark shadows, and she felt none of his dark magic caressing her skin. She reached for the flamethrower at her belt.

She needed to master her fear and plan strategically, practically. It was what Josiah would tell her to do—at least, after he'd finished going apoplectic at her current situation. Gods, she wished he were here.

Think, Rosalind. Since Caine was a shadow mage, he was aligned with the night god. So were the vamps. Hadn't Josiah said something about a vampire kingdom? Lilinor, perhaps? If that's where she'd come, she would soon meet her parents' fate.

Mentally, she tallied the weapons in her belt. If she had to face vamps, her gun would be useless. Silver bullets were fantastic against some monsters, but silver was the night god's element. Contrary to popular belief, vampires and incubi actually *liked* silver. It made them stronger.

No, if this was Lilinor, she'd need her flamethrower, the one remaining hawthorn stake, and maybe the iron dust. That alone could cause intense pain to any magical creature.

She just needed to stop the damn shaking in her hands if she wanted to use a weapon.

She tiptoed over the old cobblestones. As she followed the narrow alley into a town square, she suppressed the urge to scream for Caine at the top of her lungs. He was her best chance at survival, but she couldn't draw attention.

She sniffed the air. Her ears pricked as something rustled nearby, and she pulled the stake from her belt, followed by the flamethrower.

Thud.

She spun, just as two pale vamps leapt to the street. A giant, ginger-haired man stood next to a raven-haired woman.

No hesitating this time, Rosalind.

"Well, look here," the man said. "A human, offering herself up to us."

"I can see her veins through that shirt, pumping blood," the woman said.

Rosalind pressed the button, unleashing the flames, and the vampires scuttled back, clothes blazing.

Someone grabbed her hair from behind, and Rosalind slammed her elbow into the monster's ribs before reaching for the stake. She spun, ramming the wood into another female vamp's heart. As the creature turned to ash, Rosalind snatched her stake from the dust heap.

"She murdered Domenica!" someone shrieked.

Rosalind whirled at the sound of footfalls, and jammed the wood into another vamp's chest.

They were on her like a plague of locusts, and before she could even get to her feet again, one of them grabbed her from behind, pinning her arms in a vice-like grip. He ripped the stake from her hands, then spun her around and slammed her up against the wall. Her back cracked against the stone. As he pinned her arms above her head, the vamp's sharp nails pierced her wrists. Revulsion spread through her. *This is how Mom and Dad died.*

The vamp's hair was long and black, flowing over his shoulders, and his eyes blazed blood red. "She's looking for someone strong. She wants me to keep her as my pet. She came here because she wanted it."

Rosalind burned with anger. The vamp's vise-like grip dug into her arms, and he pressed his body against hers. Vampires were lusty creatures, but the look in this one's eye screamed something more like "sex offender."

As he sniffed her neck, her legs flailed. Her kicks to his shins did nothing. His cold tongue shot out of his mouth, and he licked her neck, moaning.

Freaking vile. Rage exploded in her mind and she rammed her knee right up into his groin. She heard a pained grunt, and his hands loosened just long enough for her to free herself. She whipped the iron dust from her belt, spraying it on the small crowd of vampires.

Their screams pierced the quiet, and her stomach turned as the scent of burning flesh filled the air. Four vamps, blazing like torches—all except the raven-haired vamp, who turned on her again as his buddies turned to ash.

Her mouth went dry. The screams would only lure more vamps. How the hell was she supposed to master her fear in this situation? It's not like *any* human could hack her way out of a demon realm.

"What the hell is going on?" A deep voice interrupted from the shadows.

The vampire's head whipped around, and he gaped as Caine stepped into the moonlight.

Caine's voice was cold and steady. "Were you trying to kill this girl?"

"She belongs to me, sir." The vamp licked his lips. "She murdered five of Ambrose's soldiers. I'm going to play with her a while, and drink her slowly. I'd like to keep her as a pet."

Caine's raven circled his head. Ice tinged his voice. "Step away from her, Horace. Ambrose wants her alive."

Horace's lip curled. "But, sir. She came into our world. That means she *wants* to be my pet. She wouldn't have sought us out if she didn't want us."

"I already told you not to touch her." Caine flicked his fingertips at the vamp.

Horace's body lurched, his neck arching backward at an awkward angle. The silent square filled with the sounds of snapping and crunching bones, then Horace's agonized screams. When Caine lowered his hand again, the screams faded to a whimper.

Horace crumpled to the ground.

Rosalind gaped. *Seven hells. Remind me never to get on his bad side—if I'm not already.*

Caine crossed to her, his eyes flashing. In fact, he looked like he might rip her head off. "What exactly do you think you're doing here? Please don't tell me you've got everything under control again."

She straightened. "I'm looking for answers. My life just fell apart within the span of an hour, and I want to know why. You apparently know a thing or two about it." Her voice rose in volume. He scared the wits out of her, but she had nothing left to lose. And what good was living when your life was over? "I want to know who you are, and who I am, and why everyone thinks I'm a witch. And you're going to tell me." For once, she kept the tremble out of her voice.

Caine's predatory gaze slid over her transparent shirt, and she remembered what Josiah had told her: to someone like Caine, other humans existed only to satisfy their depraved desires.

"You can't stay here," he said. "We're going to see Ambrose. We'll talk on the way."

We'll talk. So he was going to tell her something. "And who is Ambrose?"

"The Lord of this realm. And considering you just slaughtered five vampires in his kingdom, he's just about the only person who can save your life at this point."

7

$\mathcal{S}$ide by side, they crept through the city's winding streets. Caine's raven perched on his shoulder.

Rosalind suspected one thing: the angry set of Caine's jaw suggested he regretted saving her life, or that he might hypnotize her to choke herself to death at any moment.

"Are we in the vampire realm?" she asked.

"Lilinor. I suppose you cleverly deduced that by the presence of all the vampires," he said, his voice glacial. "How did you find me?"

The vampire's mythical realm wasn't so mythical, apparently. "I followed your magic."

"How?" he demanded.

"It smells like rainstorms, and it leaves behind a silvery shimmer."

He slid a disbelieving gaze at her. "You can *see* magic?"

"Yes. It's what makes me a good Hunter." She might have been overdoing the bragging, but something about his cocky attitude really irked her, and she wanted him to know she had her own talents.

"You didn't look skilled when I first met you."

Jerk. "My skills are not the problem. I just felt bad for the redcap for a fraction of a second. It's called empathy. Something that most people have, unless magic has sapped your humanity."

"That hesitation suggests a certain lack of skill. A lack of mastery over your own emotions."

Awesome. So even in the demon realm, I'm getting lectured. "Do we have to have this conversation?"

"You're the one who came after me for answers," he said.

"I want answers about why the Brotherhood think I'm a mage, not your analysis of my lack of skill." She shivered, rubbing her arms. Even if his arrogance grated, she should probably be a little nicer to Caine—she was completely dependent on him for her survival right now, and had to keep him happy. "Thank you for helping me."

Only the bird responded, with a puff of feathers.

"How do I leave Lilinor?" Rosalind asked. "What happens when someone gets to the boundaries?"

"Do you always chatter like this?"

She hugged herself, trying to stay warm in her waterlogged clothes. "I'm just curious. This is the first time I've visited an alternate universe. I never knew they were real before."

He cut her a sharp look. "There are no edges. When you get to the boundaries, you end up in another part of Lilinor. Only magic will get you from one world to another. That's why you need me."

She'd always wondered how the alternate universes worked, and the raw fascination almost suppressed her fear. This sort information was *gold* to the Brotherhood—another bit of ammunition if she wanted to redeem herself. "Do you think space-time is warped at the boundaries by an intensely dense magical aura? Maybe shadow magic and light magic are magnetically attracted at a universe's edges. The aura is staggeringly dense there. That might explain why I felt so sick when I came through."

"Gods below. Are you still talking?" His bird twitched her wings and flew off. "You've even managed to bore Lilu."

Rosalind narrowed her eyes. "I had to fight a flock of vampires to get this far, and I endured a neck-licking from Horace. I realize it was immensely stupid of me to come, but can I at least get an answer or two? Starting with an exit plan?"

"There's no way out of Lilinor unless I create another portal. We must speak to the Vampire Lord first."

"You need his permission? Interesting. I thought you were powerful." Hunting for psychological weaknesses—not a lesson the Brotherhood taught, but one she'd learned from the mean girls who made fun of her clothes in middle school.

"I *am* powerful. I command Ambrose's entire army against the legion of light demons." His voice betrayed only the faintest hint of irritation.

"You've commanded an entire army, but you have to ask permission to make a door."

"A portal. It's not a door. And, more than that, the shadow demons have a hierarchy." Caine's attitude suggested he didn't bend easily to authority. He must struggle with his own rebellious impulses.

"I have more questions."

Caine pressed his fingers to his eyes as if trying to manage a migraine. "I deeply regret pulling the vampires off you."

As she followed him up the winding cobblestone road, she gazed up at him. "I need to know why everyone thinks I'm a mage."

"Fine." His pale gaze met hers for a brief instant. "But you're so ignorant, I don't even know where to start."

"Start from the beginning."

"For one thing, the Brotherhood are notoriously inept."

"No, we're not," she protested. Though obviously, they'd screwed up in her case.

"The Salem Witch Trials. The Scottish Witch Hunt... all the European witch crazes. The Brotherhood's rampant slaughter led to panic. That's why the magical lands were created in the first place."

That wasn't how she'd learned it, but she got the idea. He was talking about magical lands like Maremount—New England's own hidden land of mages.

"The real demons needn't have bothered, because your Hunter predecessors spent most of their time murdering the innocent. The Brotherhood—or the Purgators, as they used to be known—have been screwing up for thousands of years."

Of course, he saw things from the demon point of view. "When I said start at the beginning, I didn't really mean thousands of years ago."

"Almost none of the Brotherhood's victims were actual mages," he continued on. "The Hunters went after the poor, the weak, the desperate. The cranky and ill-tempered. Those who worshipped the wrong gods. Anyone they didn't like. Anyone who didn't fit in. If any real mages were among their victims, it was pure accident."

An extremely biased account. "So, assuming you're telling me the truth—" which, by the way, she really wasn't assuming "—what you're saying is that they've screwed up again with my case."

They passed a candlelit tavern, and she caught a glimpse of vampires packed inside, drinking from silver goblets.

"That's actually not what I'm saying. For once, they got it right."

A cold sense of dread snaked up her spine. Everything he said was pretty much the opposite of what she knew to be the truth.

Or what she'd *thought* was the truth.

And yet, somehow something about the way he spoke suggested *honesty*.

"I don't understand. How can I be a mage if I've never learned a single spell? No one is born a mage."

He led them up a narrow, winding lane. Steep-peaked stone houses towered over them at crooked angles. "That's true. Neither you or I came into this world as a mage. Neither did we learn magic in the conventional way. We both have your parents to thank for that."

A cold sweat broke out on her brow. He knew who her parents were. "What did my birth parents do? How do we know each other? Were you there when they died?" He wasn't her *brother*, was he? She remembered his gray eyes...

He paused, his gaze locking on hers. "We're not from England, for one thing."

"And where are we from?" Her voice was barely a whisper.

"From Maremount."

The ground wavered beneath her feet. She came from a land of *mages*?

She took a shuddering breath. "But I've been with the Brotherhood since I was five. I was too young to be a mage. They can't possibly blame me for a spell I cast when I was a little child."

When he stepped closer, she had to fight the instinct to step away. *Don't show fear, Rosalind.*

He touched her hand, and his energy fluttered over her skin—that strange, inexplicable thrill. As he lifted her fingers, he examined her ring. "Iron dampens the magic. If you take this off, you'll lose your mind. That's because you're possessed with an extra spirit. You have two souls. One is your own, and the other belongs to a mage, long-since dead. Your parents imbued us both with a mages' souls. The spirits they gave us were supposed to grant us powerful magic, and your parents believed they could control the mages within us. It didn't work out. And without a lot of training, your mind will splinter. You won't be able to handle both souls."

She slipped her hand from his grasp, horror vibrating through her skull. For about the tenth time tonight, the world almost seemed to stop, and an overwhelming sense of vertigo flooded her mind.

Two souls? Her mind rebelled against everything he was saying. She was stuck in an unending nightmare.

She was a Hunter, but one corrupted by a dark magic. And her own parents had done it to her. If she took off the ring, she'd devolve into a predatory beast, like Caine.

She wanted to believe he was lying—just another mage trick—but in the darkest recesses of her mind she had the strangest sense that he was telling the truth.

"So that's what Mason meant about me being corrupted."

"You're not corrupted. You could have tremendous power if you accepted it."

"I don't understand." She could hardly breathe as her world crashed down on her. "Did vampires kill my parents?"

"No. Your parents sent you out of Maremount. They gave you to someone from the Brotherhood to keep your power in check. They probably paid someone to keep the magic hidden. To make sure you kept that ring on."

"Mason," she said, her pulse racing. "And all this time, my parents let me think they were dead. And they're alive in Maremount." Her voice broke.

"Please don't start crying."

She tried to force the tears back. "Why did they send me away?"

"They saw what happened to me."

Something in his tone told her not to ask what he meant—not now, at least.

No wonder Mason had never shown any interest in her. He wasn't really a father at all—more like a warden. Her stomach hollowed out. This was all too much to take in. "My parents ruined me."

Her drenched clothes hung like ice against her skin, and she shivered, trying to keep her teeth from chattering.

He looked her over. "We need to get to Ambrose before you freeze to death. Let's go." He turned, stalking up the hill.

Caine's revelation crushed her. She'd always imagined her parents as loving and kind, maybe other Hunters. Not demonic cultists who'd been paying someone to look after her, and who'd let her think they were dead. *Seven hells*. That wasn't how it was supposed to be. Her fingernails pierced her palms, but this time, she wasn't going to let herself cry.

She glanced at him. "Why is it that you're able to live with two souls? Why haven't you lost your mind?"

"Keep your voice down. You're going to attract a legion of human traffickers who will force you into one of the brothels."

Obviously, she needed to get this witch's soul the hell out of her body. And *then* she'd explain it all to the Brotherhood—how none of it was really her fault. If she exorcised the spirit, she could get her life back. After all, she was still human. "How do I get the mage out of me?"

"I think you need to focus on the problem at hand. You must have had ambrosia recently, because you smell like a Hunter.

It marks you out as a demon's natural enemy. Any one of this world's inhabitants would love to keep you as a pet. And if you get even the slightest cut on your skin, the whole city will descend to feast on a Hunter."

She frowned. He was being dramatic. "That seems a bit extreme. And *you're* human. Why don't they kill you?"

"Never mind that."

The narrow street opened into a long esplanade dominated by the towering stone castle. Moonlight glinted off its sharp spires, and a silver portcullis barred the gate. Gargoyles leered from buttresses high above.

She had no desire to go through that gate, but apparently she needed to speak to the Vampire Lord. This was what her life had become.

Caine paused, touching her wrist. His fingers warmed her skin, sending a thrill through her arm.

"When we go in there, someone might attack." He reached for his back pocket, pulling out a hawthorn stake. "From what I saw earlier, I understand you know how to defend yourself."

"Believe me. I've killed plenty of vampires." And by "plenty," she meant the few she'd just killed.

Caine led her to the portcullis, and chanted a spell to lift the silver gate. When it cranked and groaned to the top of the entrance, he led her into a long hall. Ivory rib vaults towered high above them like bones and, within steep-peaked arches, the walls were painted a deep crimson. Since her parents were apparently mages, they'd be right at home in a place like this, Rosalind sure as hell wasn't. The look of the place sent a shudder up her spine.

As they walked through the hall, she caught glimpses of tapestries. Some were threaded with portraits of Nyxobas, the cloaked god of night. Others depicted horned demons with red eyes.

At the end of the hall, ornate wooden doors barred their path. Caine whispered another spell, and the doors creaked open into a great hall, its walls formed by what appeared to be human bones inset with sapphires, pearls, and moonstones. An array of silver weapons lined one of the bone-walls, and the air smelled of gardenias.

Vampires stood along the sides of the room, their shoulders rigid with military discipline. Horace stood among them. Of course, vampires easily outpaced humans.

Candles burned in chandeliers that hung from arches thirty feet above, casting a wavering light over the room. Horace's cold, dark eyes darted to Rosalind, and he flared his nostrils.

But Rosalind's gaze was most drawn to the stunning blond vampire in the silver throne: Ambrose, his face cold and beautiful as a renaissance statue. He didn't look more than twenty-five, but as a Lord he was probably centuries old.

As she followed Caine into the hall, her muscles tensed. Her little hawthorn stake suddenly seemed inadequate in a room full of vampire nobility.

Her eyes flicked to the rows of vamps. She could actually *see* their desperate attempts at restraint. Horace trembled visibly, working his jaw. Apparently, her ambrosia-filled blood smelled amazing—or maybe her second soul smelled amazing. Either way, she was a rabbit in the center of a pack of wolves right now.

As she straightened, she took a deep breath. She wasn't going to show fear. Human terror only stoked a demon's bloodlust.

But before she could take another step, Horace's rough nails clamped into her shoulders. For the second time that night, a demon's fangs punctured her throat, and pain lanced her neck.

8

$\mathcal{S}$he snatched the stake from her belt and slammed it into his back. She felt a sharp tear in her neck as Horace ripped out his fangs, but he wasn't turning to ash. She must have missed the damn heart again.

Caine rushed forward, a silver sword in his hand, and swung for Horace, severing his head. Blood sprayed, and the body convulsed, twitching on the floor as though electrified. Fast as lightning, Caine reached down, ripping Horace's heart from his chest.

She stared as Horace's headless corpse blackened, turning to ash.

Sweet earthly gods. That was disturbing.

From his silver throne, Ambrose arched an eyebrow, his green eyes trained on Caine. "Did you just kill one of my favorite lieutenants? For a *human*?" His nostrils flared, and he sniffed the air. "One of Blodrial's followers, by the smell of her blood?"

Rosalind touched her neck, and her hand came away crimson.

"Rosalind," Caine said.

Uh-oh. Hadn't Caine said something about getting cut?

The vampires' bloodthirsty stares bored into her. A pregnant silence filled the room, broken by the low growling of ravenous vamps. They shifted, trembling at the effort of restraint. The pack of wolves was just about ready to feast on this rabbit.

Ambrose stood. "Control yourselves—"

From all around the room, the vampires lunged. Rosalind gripped the stake, crouching as a female vamp leapt for her. She thrust the stake upward, right into the vamp's heart. This time, she didn't miss, but another had already grabbed her from behind. She slammed her elbows into his ribs. She caught a glimpse of Caine cutting through a line of vamps in a whirlwind of silver and black, sword through bone. His jaw-dropping speed seemed almost otherworldly.

She whipped out the flamethrower, and as a hulking vamp leapt for her she depressed the button, unleashing a torrent of flames. Fire engulfed him, and his agonized shrieks turned her stomach. He flailed, screaming, until Caine sliced off his head in one smooth arc.

She glanced at Ambrose, but he was no longer in his throne. Her mouth went dry. He was right next to her, his fangs bared. Holy shit. She'd neither seen him nor heard him approach.

His green eyes locked on hers, and though her mind screamed *run,* her body wouldn't obey. The Vampire Lord was a perfect predator, freezing her in place with his penetrating gaze. She stood in stunned silence as he licked his lips.

"Ambrose," Caine spoke sharply. "Step back. That's Rosalind."

Ambrose growled, closing his eyes. His blond hair was unruffled—as if he hadn't just witnessed a massacre in his own home. He reached out, swiping a cold finger through the blood dripping down her neck. He licked it, moaning almost imperceptibly. "Heal her before I rip her little body to shreds. She tastes exquisite." He spoke with a clipped English accent. As he backed away, she saw that his eyes were a deep red.

Caine rushed to her, his body soaked with vampire blood. He looked like something from a nightmare. She had no idea how a human had managed to cut down a roomful of vampire nobility. Aside from Ambrose, only one vampire remained, a willowy female with dark skin.

Caine lifted his fingers to Rosalind's neck, sending a hot thrill through her skin—an almost addictive sensation. He closed his eyes, chanting in the Angelic language, and the sharp pain in her neck subsided. As her wound healed, the Vampire Lord's shoulders visibly relaxed, but his eyes remained fixed on Caine with a lethal glint.

"Why did you bring her here?"

"I didn't," Caine said. "She was supposed to stay in Abduxiel Mansion. Instead, she followed me through the portal."

Ambrose steepled his fingers. With his perfect lips and sharp cheekbones, he could have been a model. Just like Caine. It was almost as though vampire aristocracy was determined by sheer beauty alone; maybe that was why Caine commanded such respect around here.

Ambrose's eyes burned with ferocity. "You *let* her follow you here. A Hunter, who might tell the Brotherhood how to find us. And you see what's happened. Eight of my best advisors, slaughtered. Not to mention that Rosalind nearly died. Has your mind become muddled because of your familial connection?"

Familial connection?

Caine's mouth twitched with apparent irritation. "My mind is perfectly sound, Ambrose. I had no idea she'd be so stupid as to rush through a portal into a demon realm."

Now that is just insulting. "Okay, hang on a second," Rosalind said. "First of all, I'm not stupid. Apart from everything I've done tonight. But I was acting desperate because I needed answers.

This is the first I've ever heard of this mage thing, and it seems that both the Brotherhood and the demons know more than I do about my two souls. And why do you all care if I live or die? No one has explained that to me yet."

The female vampire crossed to Ambrose, handing him a cloth. The Vampire Lord wiped the blood off his hands, green eyes locked on Rosalind. "Why did you come, girl? What exactly was your plan?"

"I wouldn't say I had a plan, as it were." She added that last bit to sound more formal. It wasn't like she'd ever spoken to a Lord before, even if he was a demon.

"Not a plan." His eyes roamed over her wet clothes, lingering on her transparent white shirt. "Just a desire."

She flushed. She could imagine what he was thinking. "Exactly."

"I can understand that." He licked his lips. "And what was your desire?"

"I needed to learn why the Brotherhood think I'm a witch. I needed to know where I came from. I need to know how to get my life back."

Ambrose cocked his head. "Your life back? Why would you want that?"

"I was happy."

He frowned. "No, you weren't. And now you know why you're important. You have the potential for great power, just like Caine. In fact, you've just seen him demonstrate a bit of that power, when he cut down half my Council."

Caine shrugged. "Horace was an ass, and he needed to be put down. I did you a favor. And now, I must return her to her own world. I'm going to need to open another portal."

"I hope that when you train Rosalind, you'll instill obedience in her even if the concept doesn't suit you." Ambrose's green eyes drank in Rosalind. "Her blood tastes of hawthorn bark. Funny, that."

How do I respond to a comment as creepy as that? It was an odd coincidence. "They're my favorite trees." It was the best wood for staking vamps, though now was not a good time remind him of that. Anyway, it was more than that. Her best dreams took place in hawthorn groves, the earth carpeted by white petals. "The blossoms are pretty, and they bring good luck."

He stepped closer, staring into her eyes again. "Tell me, Rosalind. Do you dream of the forest?"

Another creepy comment, but—how does he know that? Can vamps read minds? "Yes. Often."

He edged closer, touching her neck, and she shuddered. Apparently, vampires weren't big on personal space. The candlelight flickered over his porcelain skin, and she caught a hint of his scent—burning cloves. "You will stay here tonight. I'll make sure you're safe. Tomorrow, Caine and Aurora will take you back to your world." He nodded at the willowy female. "I'm assigning them to protect you from the Brotherhood. Your behavior is unpredictable, and they will need to watch you closely."

"What?" Caine asked through gritted teeth. "I'm the General of your army. I just won a victory for you against the hellhounds in Uffern. And you want to put me in charge of minding a pedestrian girl?"

Asshole. It wasn't like she wanted to spend time with him either, but his tone was more than a little insulting.

Ambrose studied him. "If you don't like your new role, Caine, you shouldn't have brought her here."

Aurora didn't speak, but the rage contorting her face told Rosalind that she didn't like this plan any more than Caine did.

Rosalind narrowed her eyes at the Vampire Lord. "What do you get out of this?"

"Clever girl." Ambrose studied her. "Let's just say I'm protecting a personal interest. A mage with your powers could be useful to me some day. I trust Caine will be able to break your faith in the Brotherhood."

Apparently, Ambrose wouldn't be on board with her plan to exorcise the second spirit. *Best not to mention it now.*

Caine's gaze was pure ice. "She's impulsive, completely unprepared to practice magic, and deeply committed to the Brotherhood. It will be a long time before she becomes a functioning mage."

"You know she's not just any girl." Lifting Rosalind's hand, Ambrose examined her ring. "What happens when you take it off?" he asked her—but before she had the chance to respond, he slipped it from her finger.

She gasped, and her body exploded with an earthy, vernal aura. An ancient creature stared out from her eyes. A *thing,* taking over her body, one vein and muscle at a time. An overpowering scent of rotting leaves filled the air, and she stared into Ambrose's emerald green eyes, his skin pale in the flickering candlelight. Such a strange, perfect beauty, life and death in one vessel.

She wanted to crush him. The thing inside Rosalind made her reach for his face, but the Lord slipped out of her grasp.

Rage ignited her body, and her legs trembled. Someone screamed in her skull—a wild, unquiet mind inside her own, and it said only one word. *Ambrose. Ambrose.* It was the only word in her mind now, and the thing inside her drowned out her own thoughts.

The mage inside her wanted to touch his cool, pale skin, but he kept slipping away from her. His retreat only stoked her desire. The spirit wanted to rip his clothes from his body. Ambrose would burn with her, would feel her lust and her wrath stoking the flames of the funeral pyre. The mage forced her hand to Ambrose's neck, and some part of her screamed at herself to stop.

But that was the weak part.

Ambrose. She would shatter his bones, drink his blood, grip his pulsing heart in her fingers, she would glory in ripping out his entrails—

Someone else stood before her now, his hand on her waist, face gleaming like moonlight on water. His shocking beauty struck her dumb. The spirit didn't know his name, but lust and rage screamed in her skull, splintering her thoughts. Her body burned white-hot like a dying star, blazing from the inside out. Her skin blistered and cracked from the heat. She wrapped her arms around the stranger's body, quenching her blazing agony—

In an instant, the voices went still, and relief washed over her.

Rosalind. She was Rosalind, the Hunter, in control of her own body once again. Her arms tightened around Caine, and her body trembled, wracked by the remnants of pain. The spirit had gone. She glanced at her hand. Caine had slipped the ring back on her finger.

She wrenched away from him, clamping her hand over her mouth. She didn't want to puke in front of them.

Never again. She never wanted her mind to splinter like that again. She'd been in hell.

She dug her fingernails into her palms, clamping her eyes shut. She needed to get this insane spirit out of her body. The demonic force would completely shatter her.

Caine's arm encircled her waist, holding her up. "She isn't ready for that yet."

Rosalind straightened. She *really* hated looking weak, especially in front of the demons. "I'll never be ready for that. This thing inside me is a monster."

"What was it that the spirit wanted?" Ambrose's words slid over her like cold rain.

"I don't know," she snapped. She hated him right now for ripping the ring off her with no warning, and she had a strange feeling the mage inside hated him, too.

Her body wouldn't stop shaking.

This was why people shouldn't mess around with the dark arts. Her birth parents were obviously raving lunatics.

The vampire inched closer, running his thumb over her cheek, and she shuddered. His beauty was cold and empty.

She couldn't wait to get out of there. She wanted Josiah and Tammi more than ever.

"Never mind, little sparrow," Ambrose said. "Delicate little thing. You will stay in Aurora's room for the night. She can sleep elsewhere. She will be perfectly hospitable. Tomorrow, the three of you will leave." He shot a glance at Caine. "I trust you'll take good care of her. Don't let her out of your sight, or she'll betray us to the Brotherhood. She still believes in them. Begin teaching her as soon as you can. Once she's trained, she'll be quite useful to me."

9

rained. According to Ambrose, she was a delicate little thing who required training and obedience. Rosalind wasn't stupid enough to argue with the Vampire Lord in his own kingdom, but there was no way in hell anyone was going to *train* her.

She followed Aurora down a dimly-lit hall. Stone vaults arched high above like a gray skeleton, intricately carved with moonflowers and stars. Candles flickered in jeweled sconces along the walls, casting dancing shadows over the marble floor. Gods, she really wanted to go back to her little dorm room. This place was creepy as hell, and she needed to run through this whole disaster of a night with Tammi.

Her mind reeled. Tonight, her world had been blown apart.

Whatever it took, she was going to rip this witch's soul from her body. She'd felt the thing's mind, its sickness—a demented spirit, one full of dark, twisted impulses. She wasn't going to give up her own body without a fight.

Aurora's heels clacked over the stone floor, and Rosalind glanced at her. The vampire wore a tiny red dress that hugged her body, and long silver earrings. She was gorgeous. While she didn't look like she wanted to tear into Rosalind's neck, appearances could be deceptive.

"All the other vampires tried to kill me, but you didn't."

"How perceptive of you." Aurora had a British accent, just like Ambrose.

"Why didn't you?"

"I have better self-control, and you were with Caine. I'm quite fond of him." Her eyes met Rosalind's. "I hope you don't try to slay him with your witch-hunting bollocks. You won't be able to kill him, but if you get a stake in him, I'll have to drain your blood."

Fantastic. Aurora already hates me.

"Of course not. He's human. I only kill monsters." She sucked in a breath. *Best not to mention the monster-killing thing again.* "No offense."

"None taken." Aurora halted before an oak door, pushing it open into an expansive bedroom. Moonlight shone through tall, stained-glass windows into an untidy room littered with papers, mounds of clothing, old cassette tapes, and eyeless dolls. A desk stood below the window, its surface covered with flasks of blood and bottles of amber liquid.

Aurora plucked a white dress off the floor, tossing it to Rosalind. "You can change out of your wet clothes. A white dress should be pure enough for you."

Aurora *definitely* hated her.

As the vampire lit candles around the room, Rosalind changed into the tight white gown. The thin fabric was practically sheer and not great for fighting, but at least she was no longer freezing. She draped her sodden clothes over a chair to dry.

Rosalind swallowed hard, glancing around the room. Oil-painted portraits hung all over the walls, but the subjects' eyes were scratched out. Interspersed among the paintings, someone had scrawled notes in the frantic, irregular scrawl of a serial killer. She caught a glimpse of a few words, *BlOoD* and *RaGe* among them. Instead of a bed, a coffin lined with red silk lay in the center of the room.

The room looked like a playground for the criminally insane. *Holy shit. This is who I've thrown in with.*

Aurora turned to stare at her. "What do you think of my room?"

Rosalind took a deep, steadying breath, her foot crunching on a cassette tape. "The paintings are... interesting."

For the first time, she saw Aurora's face brighten into a smile. "Do you like them?"

"Are the crossed-out eyes a vampire thing?"

"What? No. I made those when I was human. I was an art student at Goldsmiths before I died."

That was a slight relief. "Ah. And the handwritten notes, too?"

"I've been dead nearly thirty years, but I like to think of my art as avant-garde, you know?" Aurora looked her up and down. "Just be careful what you touch in my room, Hunter."

"I'm not exactly eager to rifle around."

Aurora narrowed her eyes. "Like, if you touch my Tears for Fears cassette tapes, I will rip your head off and light you on fire."

Rosalind's stomach lurched.

Aurora stared at her. "It's just an expression."

"I won't touch them." Rosalind nodded at the casket, her skin growing cold. "I didn't know vampires actually slept in coffins."

"Most don't. I just thought it was kind of cool, so I made a coffin. Only they're not so good for shagging." Aurora cocked her head. "I've never seen Ambrose take such an interest in a human before."

"I didn't enjoy his interest. He seemed a little off-key." *Insane, really.* Then again, everyone here was obviously slightly mental.

"He's six hundred years old, so he's a little old school; that makes him different. Like, when he was a kid, there was nothing to play with but a wooden circle and a hoop. Public executions were entertainment in those days. But he's sexy as hell, and he's always been good to me. And if anyone messes with him, I would feast on their heart."

Rosalind tried to force a smile. "Another vampire expression?"

Aurora blinked. "No. That was literal. Anyway, he said I'm supposed to be hospitable and shit. So what do humans drink?"

"Water is fine."

"We don't have that here." Aurora rifled around on the desk, bottles clinking. "I know!" She unscrewed a cap from a bottle labelled *whiskey*, pouring it into a silver goblet, then decanted a measure of blood for herself, topped with whiskey.

She handed Rosalind the bloodless goblet and gazed at her, raising her own. "To the dark side."

Rosalind lifted her drink. "To the... whatever." She didn't want to be rude, but she wasn't about to toast to the *dark side*. She took a sip, and the whiskey burned her throat.

"You know," Aurora said. "Vampires aren't as bad as everyone thinks. People think that we're horrible monsters, but we're not really. We're just like regular people."

Right—apart from all the slaughtering, and walls made of human skulls. Rosalind scanned the room, and her eyes landed on something that churned her stomach: fingers poking out from below a pile of clothes on the floor. "Is that a human hand?"

Aurora turned and snatched a severed hand from the floor. "Oh, yeah." She looked up at Rosalind, her face a picture of innocence. "But he was a very bad person."

Oh gods. Do I really have to spend the night in here?

"Are you hungry?" Aurora asked. She dropped the hand on the

desk and rummaged through the papers, pulling out a half-eaten Snickers bar. "We don't really eat food, per se, but I took this off the severed-hand guy. He didn't look like he had any diseases or anything, so it's probably fine."

Rosalind's mind spun like a cyclone. She didn't belong here, yet she'd willingly plunged into a city of the dead. Maybe the demented witch's spirit had compelled her to do it. Either that, or she was a first-rate idiot like Caine had said.

Whatever the case, Rosalind was desperate for human company right now—even the evil kind. "Where is Caine?"

Aurora narrowed her dark eyes. "You're not going to try to hurt him, are you? It won't go well for you if you do. He's a bit full of himself, but he also happens to be the most lethal mage I've ever seen. As you could probably tell from tonight's slaughter."

"I won't try to hurt him. I just wanted to see another human face. Preferably one that's attached to a living body."

"Two doors down, past the portrait of Lord Byron."

Rosalind shivered. In a world of demons, she was forced to rely on someone as terrifying as Caine for an ally.

10

Rosalind walked down the hallway, pausing just after the portrait of Lord Byron dressed in some sort of orange turban. She knocked on the oak door, trying to figure out what she wanted to say to Caine.

She'd have to enlist his help to get the mage out of her body, but she couldn't ask him about the exorcism here. Even the gargoyles were probably spying for the Vampire Lord.

Was Caine really any better than the vampires, just because he was human?

As his footfalls crossed the floor, she half wanted to turn around and run back to the serial killer suite.

Caine pulled open the door, his hair disheveled and wet, like he'd just stepped out of a bath. Droplets of water beaded on his bare chest, and her eyes lingered on his muscled body. Tattoos covered his flawless skin: constellations, a raven, a moon cycle, and Angelic script.

Washed clean of blood, he now wore only his black jeans. She tried not to stare.

For the first time, she saw a flicker of a smile. "Rosalind. It seems the only thing that can rob you of your formidable powers of inquisition is the sight of me without a shirt on."

Cocky bastard. Why had she come here? She couldn't remember anymore. She just needed to keep her eyes on his face. "You're not my stepbrother, are you?"

Gods. Why had she just said that?

"Why? Is your delicate mind troubled by impure thoughts?" He leaned against the door frame, his gaze slowly trailing over her white gown, like he was memorizing every curve of her body. He smelled amazing—a fresh scent, like the earth after a rainstorm. "Don't worry. The vampires wouldn't begrudge a little brotherly love if that's what you're looking for. Unlike the Chambers, we don't judge here."

"Oh, please. First of all, that's disgusting. And second of all, you're not my type." She clamped her hands on her hips. "Can you just answer the question? Ambrose said something about a familial connection. I don't like the idea of being related to a man who's been completely corrupted by magic."

"I knew your parents, but we're not related. In fact, they would have been horrified by the thought. I was merely part of their experiment. When it didn't go as planned, our relationship was over."

"I see. If we're not related, why did they imbue you with an extra soul, too?"

"They wanted to make sure the spell worked before they tried anything on their own flesh and blood."

It was hard to decide the worst thing Rosalind had learned tonight: her exile from the Brotherhood, the mage in her body, or the fact that her birth parents were a couple of assholes. She couldn't take any more shitty news without completely losing her mind—assuming she still had a mind to lose.

She couldn't reconcile Caine's description of her parents with her happy memories of her early childhood, even if they were vague. "I don't understand. I thought my parents were loving. I remember when they gave me flowers and patched up my knee. And I think I remember you. There was a boy with eyes like yours."

"I'm sure you were happy. But things aren't always as perfect as you remember them."

She hugged herself. "We get out of here soon, right?"

"Yes. Before the sun rises. Aurora can't travel in the light. Go to sleep, Rosalind." There was that commanding tone again. "You only have three hours of rest before we move."

But she knew she wouldn't be sleeping at all. Not in the serial killer room, and certainly not with the news that a crazed spirit had infected her body.

11

$\mathcal{R}$osalind jolted upright, gasping for breath. After their rapid departure through another portal in Lilinor, they'd arrived in Caine's Salem apartment, twenty miles north of Boston.

When you hung around with creatures of the night, sunrise signaled bedtime. Now, the sunset streamed through the windows, washing the living room and kitchen in pumpkin light.

Despite its warmth, she shuddered, wrapping Caine's blanket tighter around her shoulders. She'd been dreaming of Mason. Her nightmares were no different from her memories. In her dream, he'd tied her to a chair, beating the bottoms of her feet with his leather belt, all the while ranting about corruption.

As if staying in a mage's apartment weren't bad enough, reminders of Mason had brought her out in a cold sweat.

It was so obvious to her now: Mason had known about the possession all along. It was why he'd always been so repulsed by her. When she'd first arrived, he'd started off reasonably nice— warm mugs of cocoa to warm her in the cold mansion, letting her watch TV as long as she wanted. But then he'd catch her drifting off, losing herself in thought, and something about her dreaminess made him angry. She understood now—it was the mage inside of her. He wanted to beat the magic out of her.

She straightened, pushing the blanket off her to survey the room. For a tattoo-covered mage who lived among corpses, Caine kept a surprisingly tidy apartment. Oak bookshelves, packed with alphabetically arranged poetry and spell books, lined one wall. Midnight-blue sofas stood on the bare wooden floors, and the tall windows overlooked one of the old colonial cemeteries, where the setting sun cast long shadows over the grass.

Four silver-framed mirrors hung on the rough stone walls. Of course he had four mirrors in one room. The guy obviously loved himself.

Rosalind glanced down at herself. The white dress Aurora had given her was crumpled from sleep, and her long hair was tangled into knots. She looked like a disaster, and she tried to smooth out her tangles

Footsteps sounded behind her; she turned to see Caine, his hair gently rumpled from sleep. He wore an undershirt that showed off his athletic form.

She had a bad feeling that the only way to get this mage out of her body would be through powerful magic—the kind that Caine had—except the Vampire Lord wanted her to remain possessed. Ambrose had some sort of big plans for her. What was the likelihood of Caine defying him?

She'd have to tap into his anti-authoritarian nature.

"I hope you slept well," he said. "Might as well get comfortable for a while since you're apparently staying here."

"I slept fine." There was no way she'd be staying, but she'd wait a moment before bringing that up. "I take it you're not thrilled about having me here."

He leaned against a granite countertop. "As it happens, I have better things to do than to train a novice Hunter in the dark arts. Especially a noble-born girl who will go into hysterics every time things get a little difficult."

Arrogant prick. Everything about him irked her. "That's fine by me, because I'm not actually going to train with you. I'll be out of here as soon as I get... everything sorted out."

"And what do you expect to sort out? Do you have a plan now? Or still just a desire?"

Her stomach rumbled. How was she supposed to come up with a plan with a stomach this hollow? "I have a strong desire for some food."

"I don't keep the house well-stocked. I'm not exactly the cooking type. When Aurora gets up, we'll go out somewhere."

"Is she your girlfriend?" Rosalind asked.

He arched an eyebrow, crossing to the living room. "No. Interesting that you asked though. I seem to recall you saying I'm not your type. I'm not sure that I believe you anymore. You've now inquired about our family affiliation and my relationship status."

She failed to suppress an eye roll. *The ego on this guy is unparalleled.* "You're probably glamoured, just like my Guardian said. Under your demigod facade, I'm sure you look like a beast."

His flashed a half-smile. "Is that so?"

She flushed. Why did he make her so nervous? She usually made men nervous, not the other way around. "It's basic witch lore. Magic pollutes the body and turns humans into monsters."

"Demigod, was it? Tell me, what is the most impressive part of this beautifying spell I've woven? Do you think I did a better job on my face or my body with this—demigod spell? I'd really love to hear more."

Her stomach fluttered. *Shit.* Josiah hadn't been wrong about the disfigurement, had he?

She gritted her teeth. "Please tell me it's a spell. Because based on the number of mirrors around this place, I'm a little worried about what would happen if your ego grows any bigger than it already is."

"Can you blame me for loving something that's so—demigod-like?" He cocked his head contemplatively. "That phrasing is unwieldy. Let's shorten to *godlike*."

"If self-love had mass, yours would create a singularity that would warp space-time and destroy the universe."

"Has anyone ever said you're charming when you talk about science?"

"No."

"Unsurprising." He folded his fingers behind his head, in all likelihood trying to give off the best view of his muscled arms. "If you don't believe me about the glamour, why don't you spray that purgator dust on me? If it's a spell, you'll see the real me. The demonic, twisted Caine that lurks below the surface, warped by magic."

"Since you have an aura, the dust will burn you."

"I can handle a little pain."

"Anything for your vanity, right?"

She snatched her purgator dust from the coffee table, pausing for a moment at the self-satisfied smirk on his face. This was going to hurt—a lot. What if the agony flipped a switch in his brain? He could slaughter her in an instant.

Still, maybe now was a good time to practice that whole fear-mastery thing. She had to get used to hurting the bad guys.

She strengthened her resolve and pushed the button. Shiny red dust poured from the canister, coating his skin. A flicker of pain registered on his face, though in reality he must be withstanding indescribable pain. All this to prove to her that he was pretty.

And, gods damn it, he was right. The guy was stunning, and it wasn't because of magic. She sucked in a breath. "Fine. We've established that you're not deformed."

He brushed the dust off his face. "I think we agreed on the term 'godlike'."

Rosalind wanted to hide her face. This was mortifying.

As the last of the sun dipped below the horizon, Aurora strode into the room, clad in a tight silver dress. "What the bloody hell do you think you're doing to Caine, Hunter?"

"It's fine," Caine said. "I asked her to do it."

Aurora crossed her arms. "I don't even want to know."

Caine rose, visibly trying to manage the pain. He soaked a kitchen cloth in water and began cleaning himself off. "Would you like to help me clean off my body, Rosalind, since you're such a fan of my godlike physique?"

Gods, kill me now.

"I've walked into something really weird, haven't I?" Aurora said. "Please don't tell me you fed his ego."

With the dust washed off him, Caine smiled. "Our Hunter has spent a little too much time among the impure, and now she fancies a bit of shadow mage. Her mind must be corrupted like ours. Funny. I wouldn't have guessed a follower of the True God, not to mention one from lofty Maremount nobility, would be so easily warped. I suppose, in the face of godlike beauty, a little lust is only to be expected even in the purest of creatures. I wonder how far we can take that."

She shielded her eyes with her hand. *What an ass.*

She needed to get out of there before she gave in to temptation. The longer she stayed around Caine, the harder it would be to piece her life back together, to resume her life among the Brotherhood.

If such a thing was even possible at this point.

12

"Speaking of becoming corrupted," Rosalind said. "I'm not letting you train me. I want to get this mage's soul out of me. The Brotherhood can't blame me for something that was done to me when I was a child. Once I have this thing exorcised, I can get out of your life."

"Uh-uh," Aurora said. "Ambrose said Caine's going to train you. So that's what's happening."

"You can't force me to learn something," Rosalind said.

"Actually, he can," Aurora snapped. "He has mind control abilities."

"I'm not going to hypnotize her," Caine said. "She'll go along with it willingly. What other options does she have?"

"Actually, I'm not going along with it," Rosalind said.

Caine stared at her. "Don't be ridiculous. You're completely irrational."

"I'm *irrational*? I just learned that I'm possessed by a lunatic spirit. I think it's perfectly rational to want it exorcised."

Aurora's face was stony. "You think the Brotherhood would take you back, after you spent time with us, using Caine's magic?"

"I'm still human. Humans have rights." Maybe the vampire had a point, but Rosalind couldn't even consider that option. She had no life outside of the Brotherhood—no future. "None of this has been my fault. I was only a kid when this happened. I have to make them see that. I don't want to be here, and you don't want me here. If you help me with the possession, we're done with each other for good."

As the room darkened, Caine chanted a spell to light the candles in the iron sconces around the room, then folded his hands behind his head. "You must understand that your actual guilt isn't the point. The Brotherhood convict whoever they want. Sometimes it's demons and witches, and sometimes not. Look outside the window. You can see where they pressed Giles Corey to death with a load of rocks during the Salem Witch Trials. The old man had never looked at a spell book in his life. Did that stop them? No. They had their sights set on him, so he was dead."

"He actually deserved it," added Aurora. "Not for being a mage. He was just an arsehole. Apart from that, Caine has a point."

"That wasn't the Brotherhood." Rosalind wanted to clamp her hands over her ears. It couldn't be true. The Brotherhood had to be certain of guilt, or it meant they'd been interrogating innocent people—even *killing* captives, according to Caine. The blood rose to her cheeks. "The Brotherhood know what they're doing. I've committed my life to them. I belong with them."

Caine arched an eyebrow. "The Brotherhood won't dig too deeply into extenuating circumstances. Any hint of magic is enough for them to stoke the flames of your funeral pyre."

"You're wrong," Rosalind said. She needed to remember what Josiah said. Mages would do whatever they could to mess with your head.

"They're barbaric," Aurora countered.

Rosalind's temper flared. The demons would love people to think that good and evil were merely subjective concepts with a whole lot of gray area. "*We're* barbaric? And what about you? I found a severed hand in your room last night. You drink human blood."

"So? Hunters drink inhuman blood," Aurora shot back.

"What are you talking about?" Rosalind asked.

"The ambrosia you drink," Caine said. "It's made with the blood of furies, kept as slaves against their will. You do worship a god of blood, you know. Honestly Rosalind. It's almost like you don't know anything useful."

"Why do you think vampires are so keen on Hunter blood?" Aurora asked. "Lucky for you, it fades fast, or I'd be taking a little nip from your wrist."

"And speaking of barbaric," Caine said. "Let's not forget that the Brotherhood have reinstated burning as a punishment for witchcraft."

No. They're lying. The Brotherhood didn't touch humans, and she'd never heard anyone talk about burnings or blood drinking.

Her mind was racing now. The mage had already muddled her thoughts, trying to lure her to the dark side.

She had to remember the pictures Josiah had showed her, the ravaged and burned bodies of the mages' victims. "Forget about the blood. Your people—vampires, mages, demons—they slaughter humans like prey, just for sport. You both know it. Look at what happened in Boston. Mages rampaged through a high school. They shot students with arrows. Burned them to death. For what?"

Caine nodded. "There are some sadistic mages out there. I won't deny that."

Somehow, this admission felt like a victory to Rosalind.

"Too bad the Brotherhood never manages to actually catch them," he added, "since they're always too busy murdering doddery old widows."

Rosalind had to stop herself from throwing the canister of dust at his head. Of course he was just screwing with her mind, but everything he said seemed to strike a chord. It was getting harder to believe the Brotherhood only went after the bad guys, when they were so busy chasing *her* down.

It was as though her whole future as a Guardian had just gone up in flames, even if she knew Josiah was looking out for her. "Whether or not the Brotherhood will take me back, I can't live with this mage inside my head. It's like having an invader in my own body."

"Some people would be thrilled to have that power, you know," Aurora said.

Rosalind didn't even want to think about the crushing, raging agony that had pierced her mind when Ambrose ripped off the ring. "What if the ring doesn't stay on me forever? What if someone pulls it off again, like Ambrose did? I was in hell." She shot a glance at Caine. "You understand, right?"

"Oh, I understand." He traced his finger over his lower lip. "But you need to get over it."

Arrogant prick. "And what exactly happened to you? What went so terribly wrong that my parents cast you off into the streets? You obviously lost your mind. Did you kill someone?"

Caine's body went still, and his eyes darkened to deep, black pools, as deep and vast as the cosmos. Shadows swirled around him.

At the sight of his pitch-black eyes, panic hit her like a fist. Caine wasn't just a mage. He was a *demon*, and she'd just pushed him into attack mode. Dread clenched her heart, and for a moment, she thought she saw the ghost of dark wings unfolding behind him. His predatory, midnight glare whispered into the darkest parts of her mind, *run*.

A moment later, his eyes cleared, and he rolled his neck.

She clasped her hands together to hide the shaking. She couldn't let him see her fear, even if she'd just come within whispering distance of death.

"I can't take any more of this," Caine said. "If I have to listen to her talk every night, I'd just as soon face the wrath of Ambrose. I want her out of here. Now."

Rosalind clenched her trembling fingers. Maybe she'd gone too far.

Aurora's eyes bulged. "You can't be serious. You're going to defy Ambrose?"

Caine's eyes flashed like storm clouds. "If I have to listen to her carrying on every night and asking me stupid questions, I'm going to murder her myself."

"So you're handing her over to the Brotherhood?" Aurora asked.

Caine shot Rosalind a cold look. "I will get you the information you need for your exorcism, and then you need to leave. I don't want to see your face again. Do we have a deal?"

Still rattled, she lowered her voice to steady it. "I swear on my honor as Hunter."

Aurora snorted. "Hunter honor. That's obviously bollocks."

"I'll take what I can get," Caine said. "And then we'll send her back to the people who want to kill her if that's what she really wants."

"You're acting crazy," Aurora said. "What if she tells the Brotherhood all about us?"

He stared out the window at the cemetery. "I'll erase us from her memory."

Rosalind didn't like the sound of a supernatural lobotomy. "I don't want you to erase my brain."

He leveled his icy gaze on her. "That's the deal. If you want the exorcism, take it or leave it. I can't risk you running back to the Brotherhood to tell them where we are. Even you must be able to understand that."

He had a point. "Fine." She didn't trust him, and didn't know what he might find in there. Maybe she could slip away just after the exorcism.

"You're both insane," Aurora said. "I'm going to make sure Ambrose understands this was done against my advisement."

Rosalind let out a long breath, still trying to hide the raw fear she'd felt at the sight of Caine's black eyes. "Is there some spell you need to find, to get this mage out of me?"

"This is beyond even me," Caine said. "We'll need to find the sybil."

Rosalind stood. "Great. Where do we find this sybil?"

"I don't know," Caine said. "But Jorge will. He's a vampire who runs Salem's blood bar."

"The blood bar is the only part of the plan that I can get behind," Aurora said. "Because I'm a little cranky before I have my evening drink."

Caine eyed Rosalind's outfit. "But you can't go in there wearing that virginal white dress. They'll eat you alive."

"Literally," Aurora said.

"What am I supposed to wear?"

Aurora looked her over. "I'll take care of the outfit."

Great. Not only were they muddling her mind, but she was going to start dressing like them, too. "Is that really necessary?"

Caine narrowed his eyes. "Unless you have a death wish, which I'm starting to think you do."

13

*R*osalind, sitting on the back of Caine's bike, wrapped her arms tight around him. They roared down a narrow Salem street, past crooked colonial houses, on their way to meet Aurora at the bar. Lilu trailed behind them.

A marine wind rushed over Rosalind's bare arms, and moonlight dazzled off puddles as they rushed past.

It was beautiful by the water, but she didn't belong in Salem with her arms wrapped around a mage's body. Her plan had been simple: become a Guardian and fight evil. Until now, her worst-case scenario involved leaving the Brotherhood to become some kind of software engineer. Maybe a computational biologist, to keep things a little interesting.

No part of her plans had involved donning a black leather dress, covering herself in fake alchemical tattoos, and straddling a sorcerer's motorcycle. But things didn't always go to plan.

Caine had cast a spell to cover her in magical markings that snaked around her arms and back, disguising her as a mage. It so happened there was a lot of exposed skin to cover, thanks to Aurora's outfit choices. Apparently, demons didn't like leaving anything to the imagination. As she sat on the back of Caine's bike, the short dress was hitched all the way up her thighs. At her insistence, she'd kept her own boots on.

As they pulled up to a rickety old pier, Rosalind spotted Aurora standing in the amber light of a streetlamp not far from the harbor. The low-cut back of her dress exposed a brutal network of scars.

Gods, what happened to her? It looked as though she'd accidentally exposed her skin to the sunlight and never healed.

As Rosalind stepped off the bike, she shuddered. Whatever had caused those scars must have been agonizing.

Aurora turned, eyeing Rosalind's outfit. "I told you that dress would suit you."

Maybe it *did* suit her. Rosalind hadn't failed to notice Caine's jaw drop when she'd stepped out of the room in the tiny black dress. Still, she felt exposed, and tugged the neckline up.

"But you've got to stop fidgeting," Aurora added. "You're acting like a pedestrian."

Rosalind frowned. "A pedestrian?"

"Ordinary people," Aurora said. "Those without magic. Boring. Stuck on the ground. Like you with that stupid iron ring. I told you. Stop fidgeting."

"This isn't how I normally dress. And there's no room in this dress for my weapon belt." Not to mention a bra.

"Only pedestrians need weapons," Caine said.

She *liked* her weapons. But even without them, a Hunter had other tools. Josiah had taught her to scan her environment for anything that was usable as a weapon. Ingenuity was the one area where Hunters had the upper hand. Iron dust could defeat magic, and Hunters knew how to fight the old-fashioned way: fists, broken bottles, big blocks of wood—whatever they could find.

In the cool sea air, goose bumps raised on her skin. Nothing stood on the wharf apart from a ramshackle, two-story house labelled *Sail Loft*. Weather-beaten and boarded with old wood, it must have been deserted for centuries.

She hugged herself. "That's where we're going?"

"Glamoured," Caine said. "Unlike me."

Rosalind paused, touching his arm. "I'm supposed to act like a mage, and they'll believe it?"

Caine nodded. "As much as you can. They'll know you're human by your scent, but they won't touch a mage. If they think you're pedestrian, things will become unpleasant fast. And if they discover you're a Hunter, you can expect an excruciating death."

"Fantastic," she said.

"That's why you should take the ring off," Aurora said. "What if a high demon comes in? Some of them could smell your Hunter blood even if you haven't drunk ambrosia in a day. A bit of real magic would protect you."

Instinctively, Rosalind tightened her hand into a fist. The whole point of this was that she'd never again have to suffer the wild, burning rage of the witch's soul, that uncontrolled animal mind that threatened to swallow her whole. "That is *not* a good idea."

"It's true. She's not ready for that yet," Caine said. "We'll just hope no high demons are there tonight."

Aurora arched an eyebrow. "You just want to hope? That's your plan? We should've left her at home."

"We can't leave her anywhere until I erase some of her memories," Caine shot back. "She could still run to the Brotherhood with everything she knows, in the hopes of making a deal."

Rosalind scowled. She really hated that whole memory-erasing idea. "I'm not taking off the ring again until I can get this spirit out."

Caine looked her over, his gaze lingering on her skin. "It's fine. With the tattoos, she can pass as a mage. As long as she can manage to refrain from lecturing everyone about morality for the next twenty minutes."

"We'll just go in and ask about the sybil, right?" Rosalind asked.

"No," Caine said. "You don't want to launch right into the sybil thing. It's never good to let vampires know you're desperate. It gives them power over you. We'll blend in, get some food, act like normal shadow mages, and then casually ask Jorge about the sybil."

"Little problem," Aurora said. "She doesn't smell like a mage."

Caine arched an eyebrow. "Mages don't have a smell."

"Yours is like fresh earth," Aurora said. "A bit of peat and some sage. I think that part belongs to you. But the magic has its own scent. Anyone who's conducted Angelic spells in the past several days smells like a lightning storm and singed air."

Rosalind furrowed her brow. "Are you telling me I need to smell like ozone?"

Aurora shrugged. "If you don't want the vampires to kill you, you need to smell like Caine. Or you need to take off the ring and do one little magical spell. Or we can leave you outside and chain you to the pier."

Rosalind's eyes widened. "I'm not just being stubborn. I'm afraid of losing my freaking mind. This witch's soul is like an inferno. It's completely warped, and I don't even want to know what it would do if I let her out. It wouldn't be pretty. I think in that case *I'd* be the one ripping out throats."

"Fine. So rub up against Caine." Aurora flicked a hand at the mage before staring at Rosalind again. "Don't look at me like that! You don't know how many pedestrian girls would pay good money for that."

"She's not lying," Caine said, with a small shrug.

Aurora sighed. "Bollocks. I fed the ego."

Rosalind took a tentative step and a deep breath. The thought of getting close to Caine sent her pulse racing, though she wasn't sure if that was because he was a demon from the shadow hell, or because he looked like a Greek god. "Rub up against Caine? You have got to be kidding me."

Caine flashed a half-smile. "Given your well-established appreciation of my beauty—"

"The scent is strongest on the neck," Aurora cut in. "And don't pretend to be disgusted, Rosalind. I can hear both your pulses racing."

Rosalind glanced away, cheeks burning, though she wasn't even sure why she cared what they thought. She was a Hunter, for crying out loud, and this was all part of a mission for the Brotherhood—albeit, a severely screwed up mission. Caine was just part of the job, a means to an end.

In the silence, the only sound was water lapping against the pier. "Right. It's just a body. Just two bodies, coming together..." Had she really just said that out loud? *Rosalind, you absolute moron. Please stop talking.*

Aurora rolled her eyes. "Are you going to do this weird babbling all night? If I get any hungrier, your pedestrian smell will no longer be a problem."

Chilled by the ocean breeze, Rosalind rubbed her tattoo-covered arms. "Right."

"Because I would have eaten you," added Aurora for emphasis. "Not an expression."

"Yeah. I got that." Rosalind stepped closer to Caine, her heart thumping. Just part of her mission. Her shockingly, wildly fucked-up mission, completely unsanctioned by the Brotherhood, who wanted to arrest her. Or possibly kill her. This was the mission of a demon-infected Hunter gone rogue.

What would Josiah make of all this?

Aurora threw her arms up in the air. "Ugh. I'll give you two some privacy. I'm going in for a drink before I murder you both." She stalked away over the pier.

Rosalind stepped closer to Caine. Moonlight bathed his skin in milky light. With his tousled hair and sharp cheekbones, he really was stunning—obnoxiously so, in fact. As a mage, he was supposed to look like a withered hag... but if he was a demon, maybe that explained his otherworldly beauty.

He held out his hand, and she took it, edging closer to his body. Wordlessly, he lifted her wrist to his warm neck, pressing it against his smooth skin. In the night air, she could feel the heat coming off his muscled body, the blood pulsing fast in his veins. As she stood close to him, a strange thrill whispered over her skin, and she had to restrain herself from closing the last few inches between them.

He's not human, she reminded herself. *He's a predator.*

She cleared her throat. "I saw your eyes change earlier. When you were angry."

"Yes."

"It happens to demons. You're not human." It seemed an oddly personal conversation—yet she was standing here, pressing her wrist against his throat. Might as well get to know him.

"I'm half demon."

"What kind?"

"Incubus."

At that word, horror churned in her gut, and she snatched her arm away from him.

A look of confusion flickered across his features. "I'm not going to hurt you."

She swallowed hard, trying to shut out the guilty thoughts echoing in her mind. "Josiah told me that all incubi were brutal rapists."

He took a long, slow breath. "Josiah is wrong," he said softly.

She stared at him, trying to control the thoughts swirling in her mind. *But Josiah can't be wrong—because if he is, then I've committed a far worse sin than I thought.* "Are you sure?" she asked, her voice barely a whisper.

A mixture of emotions flitted through his gray eyes, hurt and anger among them. "Of course I'm sure. I feed off sexual energy. That's true. But I've never forced anyone against their will." The cocky smirk returned to his lips. "You've seen how I look. Why would I need to?"

Remorse tightened her throat. If Caine were telling the truth... She couldn't let herself think about what she'd done—not now. She was close enough to losing her mind as it was. "But some incubi must be evil," she said.

"Demons don't have the same concept of evil that you have, but if you're asking if some demons are rapists and murderers, the answer is yes. Just like humans."

She forced the guilty memories deep into her mental vault. If she pored over them now, she'd never make it out of this situation with her wits intact. "Are there many like you?"

He shook his head. "Not many, no. And even fewer succubi. Even mages hate the females."

"Why?"

"When succubi feed from humans, it's not quite as pleasurable as when incubi do it."

"Oh." She swallowed hard, moving closer again to press her hand against his neck. "I'm sorry I freaked out. I thought incubi were... evil." She drank in his clean, earthy scent, her eyes lingering on the flawless skin near his collarbone before drifting up to his full lips. They looked soft, and she couldn't help but stare. If he ever wanted to feed from her, she wasn't sure she'd be able to turn him down—assuming he was telling the truth about only choosing willing partners.

"You've been brainwashed. It's not your fault." He lowered her wrist. "There. It's not always so bad when you get close to the monsters."

Not bad at all—horrifyingly, disturbingly *not bad*. Obviously, the mage's spirit inside was leading her into dark, animalistic places, drawing her to other corrupted souls.

Okay, fine. The truth was that Caine was just hot as hell.

As she stepped away from him, she steadied her breath. *Keep your composure, Rosalind*. Somehow, the fact that he wasn't a real monster—that she actually *liked* him— was more horrifying than anything else she could have learned about him. It raised questions she didn't want to answer.

She followed him over the old wooden pier toward the bar, and the breeze lifted her hair. As much as she hated herself for it, his warmth had been delicious, and she could almost imagine what he'd look like without his—

Stop it. She clenched her jaw. She was on a Hunter mission, and couldn't get distracted by his beauty. And more than that, she now had a duty to report back to the Brotherhood what she knew about incubi. Of course, people like Josiah would say that Caine was a liar, but his voice had the ring of truth in it—not to mention the fact that he hadn't once tried to force himself on her, even though he could easily overpower her.

They reached the shoddy old door to the bar, and Caine yanked it open, revealing a room fit for vampire royalty. White stone swooped high above them, and candles blazed from ornate chandeliers. Vampires stood around, drinking blood from champagne flutes.

Or at least, they *had* been drinking moments before. Right now, they were all staring at Rosalind. In fact, it kind of seemed like the whole *wrist on neck* maneuver hadn't worked.

A tall, thin man stood behind an oak bar, his hand paused mid-pour. His fangs glinted in the candlelight. "Caine. Did you bring a Hunter into my bar?"

Shit. Was it the smell of her blood? She scanned the room for weapons. A marble fireplace with burning logs and silver pokers. Chandeliers, and champagne flutes all over the place. *I can work with this.*

"Jorge." Caine smiled. "Would I bring a Hunter into your bar?"

"She smells like a mage, but she's wearing an iron ring. And by the frisky glint in her eye, it doesn't look like she's been hypnotized."

Oh. So they did notice the ring.

Caine stared him down. "Of course she's a mage. But a bastard fire cleric put a curse on her, and now she has to wear the ring to suppress the spell or her whole body will go up in flames. And I'm quite fond of her body."

"I'm sure you are. I know your type." The bartender winked, returning to his blood Martini. "Fine. Keep the ring on. As long as you can vouch for her."

Apart from the fangs, the guy *really* didn't seem like a vampire. Vampires weren't supposed to wink.

Caine grabbed Rosalind's hand and led her to the bar. She shot him a quick glance. His features were relaxed. Impressive lying—a crucial skill in any mage's repertoire. *Is there a chance he'd been lying about incubi?*

Apparently, she was supposed to pretend to be his girlfriend. She could live with that if it meant she was going to get her life back. *All part of the mission.*

Caine led her to the silver bar stools, where Aurora was already knocking back a glass of blood.

Blood-drinkers and demons. This was her new crowd. She took a seat next to Caine, who leaned on the bar.

Drying a Martini glass, Jorge nodded at him. "What can I get for you? The usual?"

"The usual. And the same for my girlfriend."

Jorge nodded. "Two bourbons, and two dinners of food."

She turned to Caine, her stomach rumbling. She didn't have high hopes for the menu. "Two *dinners of food*?"

He leaned in to her. "He hasn't eaten food in several centuries. Don't expect anything amazing."

"What are you implying?" Aurora asked. "Vampires can't cook?"

He stared at her. "You tried to make me ramen noodles in a tea kettle."

Aurora shook her head. "What's the problem? That's what I ate when I was a human."

"I guess that's what happens when you die in college," Caine said.

Jorge filled two tumblers with bourbon, sliding them over the bar.

Rosalind cocked her head, glancing at Caine. "You don't drink blood?"

His eyebrows shot up. "Why would I drink *blood*?"

"I thought mages drank human blood. From skulls. But if you're an incubus..." She let the thought die out on her tongue. There was no way she was going to bring up that he gained power through sex.

"Right. Mages drink blood. Just like we all have to glamour ourselves to hide our deformities." He leaned in to whisper in her ear. "No. I'm pretty sure we've established that's bollocks. I'm gorgeous, and you're the blood-drinking human."

Shit. She'd forgotten about the ambrosia. Maybe it *was* possible. After all, Blodrial was known as the sacred god of blood. The Guardians were a little obsessive about the drink. It wasn't human blood, but—on the other hand—maybe trying to rationalize blood drinking was not a good sign.

Jorge dropped off two white plates, piled with food. At least, technically it was food: a pile of Swedish fish, two uncooked tortillas, a stack of American cheese slices, and a frozen pancake, artfully presented on a doily.

It was the most screwed-up meal she'd ever seen, but her mouth watered anyway. Hunger gnawed in her stomach.

With her fork, she lifted a tortilla, grimacing. Within the tortillas, candy hearts were stuck in a smear of jam. Red slogans emblazoned their surfaces: *Love Me, Hot Lips,* and *XOXO.* This had to be the weirdest quesadilla in the history of "dinners of food."

Caine handed her a blue heart: *Adore me.* "This one's for you. A reasonable suggestion."

"It doesn't seem fair to take that from you. I don't think I could ever adore you as much as you do."

"Give me your pancake."

"What?"

"There are only two edible things on that plate. The candy fish and the pancake. At least let me warm it for you." He reached over, spearing the pancake on his fork. After he chanted a quick spell, it thawed and toasted to a golden brown. He dropped it on her plate again. "Don't say I never did anything for you."

She nearly cracked a smile for the first time since the Brotherhood had come for her. The truth was, Caine *had* been helping her.

She just had no idea why.

She took a bite of the pancake. Sweet and fluffy. Within about twenty seconds, she'd chomped through the entire thing, before stuffing a handful of Swedish fish into her mouth. She moved on to the American cheese slices, and when she was unwrapping the final piece she looked up to find Caine eyeing her with concern.

"I don't think I've ever seen anyone eat that fast," he said. "I'm a little alarmed."

Aurora stared over her drink. "Unsettling, really. It reminds me a little of that time I saw Horace eat a truck driver outside a McDonald's."

"I haven't eaten in a full day." She was still grumpy, in fact. She whispered, "What do you think the chances are that a high demon will come in?"

He shrugged. "Fifty-fifty. Might be fun, really. But if it happens, you should get out of here. Let me handle it."

The arrogance on this guy. "What are you going to do, toast some waffles for him? Burn his bagel until he's cross?"

"You're still cranky." Caine handed her his pancake. "Have mine."

He glanced down the bar, catching Jorge's eye.

Smiling, the bartender sidled up to them. "How were the dinners?"

"Amazing, as always," Caine said. "We'll just need two more bourbons. Neat."

"No problem." Jorge pulled a glass bottle from the shelves, unscrewing the cap to fill two more glass tumblers. "I'm just happy to see you with a girl who isn't trying to murder you for once."

"Give it time," Aurora said.

Rosalind frowned. "Wait. Why is Caine always with girls who want to murder him?"

Jorge scratched his chin. "The vampire girls get obsessed with him after he screws—"

"We don't need to get into that," Caine snapped. "Has no one ever told you that bartenders are supposed to be discreet?"

Jorge furrowed his brow. "I've never heard that."

Caine scowled. "I don't know why I continue to be surprised whenever vampires fail to be empathic."

Jorge leered at Rosalind, waggling an eyebrow. "I'm perfectly empathic."

Given the way he was looking at her, she was pretty sure he thought "empathic" meant *horny*.

Caine knocked back his drink. "Speaking of my new girl—as you mentioned, she's not trying to kill me. Obviously, I'm quite fond of her for that reason. And there's that little curse. It's not a big deal, of course. But it would be nice to take that ring off her so she could use her magic again."

Jorge flashed a wolfish smile. "You want to get some of those kinky spells going?"

She nearly spat out the pancake. *What does that even mean?*

Caine nodded. "Exactly. So if we could figure out how to lift the spell..."

Grinning, Jorge leaned on the bar. "You need Sambethe. The sybil."

Caine swirled his drink. "And where would I find the sybil?"

Jorge let his eyes roam over Rosalind's body. Whatever "kinky magic" meant, he seemed to like the idea a little too much. "The sybil is allied with Borgerith."

"Ah," Caine said. "The goddess of the mountains. So she won't speak to us."

Jorge leaned in further, looking around the bar. "You can find her in Elysium. It's an underground club where demons get together, no matter what the alliances. Fire demons mix with night, rock mixes with sea. It's chaos. But you can't tell people. The gods wouldn't exactly approve."

Rosalind took a sip of the bourbon. "And where would we find—"

Something halted her sentence. A wave of shadowy magic rippled through the bar, crawling over her skin like spider legs. She glanced around. The magic was a deep red, the color of dried blood, and it smelled of moldering hemlock—a smell of death.

"Caine," she whispered. "We should go."

"Why? I haven't even finished my drink."

"Because something powerful is headed right here. Something deadly."

Caine studied her, but before she could get an answer out of him, the bartender's eyes flicked to the door, and his face went even paler. "Bileth," he whispered.

Rosalind turned to the entrance. In the doorframe stood a hulk of a night demon, his skin pale as moonlight and cheekbones sharp as razors. He must have been three hundred pounds of pure muscle, and horns grew from his skull. His eyes were empty, ivory pools.

A shiver ran up her spine. She'd seen him before—his portrait hung in Lilinor Castle. Every fiber of her being screamed at her to run. She'd read about high demons before, but she'd never seen one. And hadn't Caine said something about smelling her blood...

Caine slipped an arm around her shoulders, pulling her close to him. He whispered, "I'll handle this. Get out of here."

She was terrified, but she wasn't going to run from a demon. She was a Hunter.

The high demon cocked his head, sniffing, then licked his lips. His gaze slid over Rosalind's body, and Caine whispered, "Run. You too, Aurora."

Aurora was out the door in a split second. But Rosalind stood rooted to the spot. She was a Hunter, damn it, and this was her chance to prove herself. She wasn't going to leave Caine to fight alone.

On top of that, it wasn't like she could run that fast. Bileth would stop her in a second.

In the next moment, the high demon was before them. Caine squared off with him, muscles tensed.

The demon opened his mouth, revealing jagged teeth. "Is this Hunter with you?"

Oh, shit. Hadn't take long for him to suss her out. His fetid magic coated her body, roiling though her blood like a poison. But Caine's magic was there, too, cool and silvery. With their auras blazing, the two demons seemed to be gearing up for a serious battle.

"Her? A Hunter?" Caine asked, obviously stalling. He glanced at Rosalind, his eyes burning into her. "She's a mage, and she was just leaving. Though now that you mention it, she may have accidentally ingested—"

Bileth gripped the mage's throat with both hands, and long, ivory nails pierced Caine's neck. Crimson tendrils spiraled from the demon's fingertips, wrapping Caine in a web that pinned his arms against his body, binding his legs, sealing his mouth shut to stop his magic.

14

The silver glow around Caine began to weaken, and fear screamed through Rosalind's mind.

Bileth's power only grew stronger, and his red magic exploded from him like a dying star. He was about to murder Caine.

She grabbed Aurora's champagne flute, smashing it over Bileth's head. She plunged the fractured stem into his back.

His pale eyes swiveled to her as she grasped for another glass. This time, he grabbed her wrist, crushing it in a death grip. Holy hells, he was breaking her bones.

In another split second, he pinned both her wrists, black talons piercing her skin. He pulled her closer, so close she could smell the blood on his breath.

He smiled, and the sight of his long, white teeth made her shudder.

"I like touching your things, incubus," he growled.

Revulsion welled in her gut as his inky red magic swirled around her head. It coiled into her mind, whispering through her own thoughts, until her body was no longer quite her own. She gaped at him, her heart beating fast as a hummingbird's.

The demon released her hands, but she no longer controlled them. *Touch him,* a voice whispered in her mind.

She watched in horror as the demon's magic forced her to reach out for his chest, hands sliding over his skin. Revulsion rose in her throat as Bileth propelled her closer, forcing her arms around his neck until she was practically grinding against him.

As he growled, his magic forced her to lurch away from him. *Grab the broken glass.* Her hand flew out for a broken shard on the bar, and her blood roared in her ears. She gripped it hard, slicing open her flesh. Blood dripped onto the floor. The vamps gasped, scenting fresh blood.

Bileth forced her hand to her throat. She strained against his magic, her arm shaking. The shard pierced her neck, and pain ripped through her skin. She whimpered, concentrating on the magic that invaded her mind like a noxious ink. She needed to master her fear, to shove this magic out before he forced her to slit her own throat. She shivered, trying to push his poison from her body.

Nearby, Caine's tingly aura grew stronger, filling the room. It caressed her injured hand and healed the gaping wound. With a tremendous force of will, she cut a glance his way, watching as he ripped himself free from Bileth's magic. His body blazed with his pearly aura. In a split second, his knife pressed against Bileth's throat. At that moment, Bileth's magic completely snapped from her mind.

Caine's eyes—dark as an abyss, glinting with an ancient violence—sent a shiver up her spine.

His voice came out low and steady. "You know I hate to argue with you, Bileth. But she's a mage."

Bileth's body vibrated with barely contained rage. "Then where is her aura?"

"I'm not allowing her to use magic now. She was getting out of control."

"And yet I smell the god of blood. You're attacking *me* to save a Hunter?"

Rage bloomed in her chest. The way Bileth had controlled her body filled her with intense loathing, and she wanted to hurt him.

Right now, the demon's attention was on Caine. She needed to help the incubus anyway. If anything happened to him, she'd be responsible for his death.

With a racing pulse, she leapt onto the oak bar, then jumped for one of the chandeliers. She kicked her legs, swinging in a wide arc. As the air charged with Caine's nocturnal magic, she propelled herself to the next chandelier, clutching at the silver. Below, the vamps hissed.

"Rosalind," Caine shouted. "I told you to run."

Blazing candles tumbled to the ground, and hot wax spilled on her skin as she swung from one chandelier to the next, toward the fireplace. *What the hell was my game plan?*

With an enraged snarl, Bileth ripped himself free from Caine's grasp. "Hunter!"

The scent of rotting hemlock drew closer, Bileth's blood-red magic curling around her skin. Panic punched a hole in her chest. He wasn't fighting Caine anymore. He was coming for her.

She jumped to the ground, grabbing the silver poker. Hot anger burned through her, and she whirled. She threw it in a high arc as he lunged for her, and it pierced the center of his chest.

The demon froze, gripping the metal. He opened his mouth, and the chorus of shrieks that emerged from his throat turned her blood to ice. There wasn't enough time to consider how proud Josiah would be, because her attack had stoked the vampires' fury.

As she leapt over a table, Jorge jumped for her. She ducked, bringing her fist up into his groin. With a twist of her body, she kicked him into the fireplace. As she did, another vamp grabbed her by the hair, yanking her head back with a sharp snap. But the attack was short lived. Something had stopped the vampires.

She glanced at Caine who murmured, his body luminescent.

Bound by Caine's magic, the vampires lurched, bodies contorting in pain. The horrifying crunch of vampire bone echoed through the room. She released a breath. As long as he was chanting, he had the vampires under control.

She cut a glance to Bileth, and terror crawled up her spine. His dark, wide eyes were fixed on her, and he ripped the poker from his ribs. She needed to get out of here *now*.

Leaping onto the tables, she crashed through champagne flutes of blood in a frantic rush to the door. "Caine! Let's go."

His eyes met hers, and he broke his spell over the vamps.

Rosalind flew, bursting through the door, and Caine followed in a black blur.

Once outside, he flicked his wrist, and the door slammed shut. Enraged shouts reverberated through the walls as demons pounded on the door. Her heart leapt into her throat. Bileth was still in there, and it couldn't be long until he tore through the rickety walls.

Caine glared at her. "Do you realize that you just impaled one of the most powerful demons in the world? There was a reason I didn't slit his throat."

The blood drained from her head. This "master your fear" thing wasn't working out so well. Maybe she still needed to work on distinguishing bravery from flat-out stupidity.

This time, she wasn't going to wait for Caine's instruction to run.

She took off in a sprint over the pier, charging for the bike. Somehow, Caine was already there by the time she arrived, waiting for her on his bike.

She jumped on, gripping his waist. He revved his engine, peeling off into Salem's narrow streets. His magical aura rippled over her skin. Dizzy, she watched her body disappear as the street sped by below them.

She tried to control the shaking in her hands so Caine wouldn't notice. The way Bileth had controlled her mind made her sick. *That* was a demon's true nature—the reason that Hunters had been fighting evil for centuries.

She clamped her eyes shut. Here she was, clinging to a demon as though he were any different.

Caine roared through Salem's winding streets and up a dark hill—away from his apartment. Where exactly was he taking her? For all she knew, he could be dragging her to Nyxobas as punishment for assaulting Bileth. He could be sentencing her to the shadow hell.

Fear tightened her chest as they sped past tiny wooden houses on a tree-lined street. She still didn't trust Caine, and the recent display of his power told her just what she'd be up against if she stopped being useful to him.

He pulled off the main road into a parking lot, slamming to a stop near the wooded edge of the pavement.

Rosalind shot a nervous look to the darkened pharmacy nearby. *What the hell?*

He stepped off his bike, and she followed, taking a tentative step away from him. They were completely alone.

He stepped closer, casting a scrutinizing gaze at her neck. When he touched her skin with his fingertips, she flinched.

"Did Bileth bite you?" he asked.

"No. He didn't get that far."

"Good. If he had, you'd die an agonizing death in the next hour." He frowned. "But you realize you just got me barred from my favorite drinking hole when you lit the bartender on fire."

117

"I was revolted by Bileth's magic in my mind. It disgusts me that demons want to control humans' minds. We're just their toys."

"You think that's how I see you?"

The question caught her off guard. "I don't know yet."

"It should be obvious that I don't, or our interactions would be very different. Anyway, Bileth isn't an ordinary demon. He commands eighty-five legions, and he reports directly to Nyxobas. He's as ancient as the god himself, a fallen angel from the celestial wars several millennia ago."

She swallowed hard. "But you held a blade to his throat."

"That would be difficult to fix diplomatically, yes. But I've angered him before, and I could usually make amends by supplying him with expensive vodka and a particularly stunning courtesan or two. Plus, I've never actually stabbed him. I don't think he'll forgive impalement with a fireplace poker so easily. You should have run."

"I did tell you that something was coming. But you wanted to finish your drink. Plus, I wouldn't have made it out fast enough." She couldn't tell him the truth—that she'd needed to save him to atone for what she'd done.

"You had a second chance to run."

Her legs were still trembling, and the memory of Bileth's complete control still haunted her. "I wanted to hurt him. He deserved it. And anyway, I thought you needed my help."

"I don't see how that would be any of your concern. According to you, I'm a monster. And more than that, I told you I'd handle it." His voice had a razor-sharp edge; his eyes were dark storm clouds. "And I would have. Aurora ran when I told her to."

Despite the look of primal wrath in his eyes, irritation spurred her on. "I don't like being bossed around. You need to stop giving me commands. I'm not your soldier. And why couldn't you just tell people that Ambrose wanted me alive? Surely the Vampire Lord has some clout."

Caine took a deep breath, and his eyes returned to their normal gray. "It's not that simple. Ambrose doesn't want Bileth to know what he's planning."

"What's he planning?"

"You don't need to know that. Not as long as you still plan on exorcising the spirit."

Exasperated, she glanced around at the empty lot. "Can you at least tell me what we're doing in a parking lot?"

"Come with me." He stopped himself, taking a deep breath. "Please come with me, Rosalind." Turning abruptly, he marched up the thickly overgrown, rocky hill.

She followed, slipping on the steep, rocky slope as she scrambled to catch up. "Is there some sort of botanical emergency that needs addressing?"

"You should rethink your plan. About purging the mage's soul."

"And this rethinking needs to happen in the woods?"

Maples loomed high above them, blocking out most of the moonlight. They crunched over fallen leaves and twigs.

Caine led them up a steep hill into a grove of maple and poplar trees overlooking the parking lot. "In 1692, this is where the Brotherhood hanged nineteen people who had nothing to do with magic."

Another history lesson. "I'm not saying the Brotherhood are perfect. So they get it wrong sometimes, and they need to modernize. But they're trying to protect humanity, and no one else is fighting the predatory demons like Bileth."

"The Brotherhood aren't perfect, and neither is the magical world. We've got that in common. The difference is that the

Brotherhood is gaining an unprecedented amount of power. People are terrified of magic, and that means the Hunters no longer have any restraints. No more trials. No more mercy. They're starting to execute mages, and people they mistakenly think are mages. They want to watch the world burn. They want to watch *you* burn. And you want to run back to them. Do you have a death wish, Rosalind?"

Executions. Burnings. That stuff wasn't true, was it? "First of all, I'm human. They won't hurt me. Second of all, they don't burn anyone."

"Running back to the Brotherhood would be suicide."

Tears pricked her eyes. What good was her life if she had no home, no family? She didn't even know who she could trust anymore. "I don't see myself having a lot of options." She shook her head. "I don't understand what you want from me."

"You have a gift. You're meant to fight. Just like I am. And call me crazy, but I think you should fight the people who want to burn you to death. Your plan to throw yourself on their mercy is utterly stupid."

She cocked an eyebrow. "That's your mage-recruitment pitch? Calling me stupid?"

"I said your plan is stupid. Not you."

"You haven't explained why we need to be knee-deep in shrubbery for this conversation."

He stepped closer, fingers grazing her hand. His touch sparked her with a warm, electrical charge. *Must be an incubus thing.*

"Take off the ring." He winced as though in pain. "It is your choice to take off the ring, but I would strongly suggest that you do it. You need to see the magic that lurks under the surface—what the Brotherhood is so terrified of. Then tell me if it scares you, too. Because I've seen you fight. You're a warrior. Like me."

At the thought of taking off the ring, raw panic burned through her nerves. "What is it with you people and wanting me to lose my mind?"

"Like you said, you don't have a ton of options. The people you plan on running to for protection want to kill you. Now the demon world wants to kill you, too, and they will hunt you unless you convert. It's your one chance at saving yourself."

She narrowed her eyes. "How do I know I can trust you?"

"I've saved your life more than once now. And I'll be here now, when you take off the ring. If the spirit tries to hurt you, I'll put the ring back on. Just like I did in Lilinor."

The wind rustled the elm leaves, whipping her hair around her head. She couldn't bear the thought of that wild rage and agony. "I'm not doing it."

"Running away from your true nature won't keep you alive. You can't be scared of it."

"It's not my true nature. It's an invasive nature, just like Bileth's aura in my skull. And I don't want the magic to corrupt and deform my body."

Caine furrowed his brow. "I thought we'd established that my godlike beauty dispelled that myth."

"That's just because you're an incubus."

"No, it's because magic *doesn't* deform the human body. When will you understand that the Purgators are wrong about nearly everything?"

"I *felt* this thing corrupting me. I felt the evil when Ambrose yanked off the ring."

"You've been trained to fundamentally reject magic, and that's why it feels evil. You've been hiding from it for most of your life, and that means you're at war with it. You need accept that it's a part of you now."

If he thought she could master this particular fear, he was wrong. The spirit's mind was the seventh circle of hell. Of *course* she was scared. Fear was a normal human emotion, absent only from demons and psychopaths. And while Caine fit at least one of those categories, Rosalind still felt a natural, human terror at the idea of losing her mind.

Even so, it wasn't like she'd admit to being scared. She had her pride.

She lifted her face. "If anyone should be scared of me taking off the ring, it's you, since I'm pretty sure this mage is a psychotic murderer. But if that's what you want, then fine. Just stand back so I don't rip your spine out through your throat."

Nice. I'm starting to talk like a vamp.

Caine smiled. "Don't get cocky. You speared one demon prince, but I'm not overly worried about my chances in a fight against you."

Now she kind of hoped the mage would do a tiny bit of damage. She sucked in a shaky breath, and slipped the ring off her finger.

15

$\mathcal{A}$s soon as she slid the ring off, the second soul inside her opened like a flower, and another presence filled her mind.

"Druloch calls to me," it whispered. "I live within the tree's shadows."

Someone looked out at the world through her eyes, and sent energy though her legs, forcing her to run. Bright, silvery light pierced the oak leaves above her. Elms towered over the forest floor. In the bright moonlight, they cast long shadows—the woods' fingers.

The forest teemed with life. Hawthorn petals carpeted the mossy earth. Around the path, blueberry bushes grew, and wild fox grape vines climbed over trees, their branches full of sparrows and blackbirds. The rich, peaty scent of the woods hung thick in the air. But there was death here, too, and sacrifice. Something drew her into the trees' shadows.

She slammed to a halt, feeling the vibrations of the surrounding woods. A flutter of movement caught her eye from a tangle of roots on the ground—black wings, a squawking bird. In the shadows, a crow ripped out a sparrow's entrails, and the tiny bird screeched in agony. The crow was eating it alive. Lost somewhere in the aura, Rosalind felt sick. She wanted to wring the sparrow's neck to end its misery.

But the thing inside her relished the electrifying cycle of life and death. *In the dark parts of the forest, the strong feed on the weak.*

The spirit wanted to feed.

It forced her to her knees, and made her plunge her fingers into the ground. Vernal power coursed through her veins, and a green aura swirled through her body. This mage wanted her to bury herself in dark moss.

I'm in here, her mind screamed. *My name is Rosalind.*

The mage forced back her head, scanning the woods. Sage-colored algae grew on felled tree trunks. In the distance, an elk tore along a path. The trees' spirits breathed around her, trunks swelling like bellows, the air thick and sweet with their whispered breath.

Power charged her body, and the mage compelled her to rub the dirt over her arms and chest. The rejuvenating power of fertile soil.

Her mind shrieked with the invader's thoughts.

The hawthorns. The sharp claws of lust. The fire. You led me to the fire. You will burn.

Somewhere inside this chaotic mind, Rosalind tried to make herself stand. *Rosalind...* The name grew fainter.

Something was wrong. Rage tightened around her heart like a cinquefoil vine. The moonlight burned too strong, dazzling through the leaves, blinding her. The smell of burning flesh filled the woods. Within moments, agony ripped her apart, her skin burning, blackening, and cracking. Pain splintered her mind until the world tilted.

The mage was burning her body.

Something else needed to die to stop this. Her blood boiled, and around her, oak leaves blazed like candles, lit with the witch's fury.

Oh gods. The agony warped her mind. Someone was here. An agent of the night god. *Break his ribs. Rip his heart from his chest. Drink the blood to cool your flames.*

She leapt up from the ground, her pain blinding, and slammed into the mage, her fist ramming into his skull. After knocking him to the ground, she jumped on his chest, hands slipping around his throat.

But the flames faded, her skin cooled, and a long sigh slid from her. Now the pain was just memory. She could see him now—so beautiful, his eyes a pale gray. The mage wanted him, and now Rosalind wanted him, too. She ran her fingers over his chest. The spirit forced her to lower her mouth to his and lick his lower lip, pressing her body against him, burning with need as she kissed him—

He slammed the ring back on her finger, and the thing withered in her mind, its presence only a faint echo.

She was lying on top of Caine, her hands fisted into his tousled hair and her mouth pressed against his. His soft, warm lips were electrifying, sending a different kind of heat through her—one that she liked. She forced herself to inch back, and stared into his eyes, trying to catch her breath.

Caine's breath warmed her neck. He murmured, "Apparently, your spirit wanted to get her hands on me, but not for fighting."

Her dress was torn, hiked up to the waist. Heat warmed her cheeks, and she said the first thing that popped into her head: "This is why I don't wear dresses."

His eyes blazed with a pale light, and he trailed his fingertips down her back, leaving a trail of tingles. "If you're going to straddle demons in the woods, you might as well show a little leg."

Oh, gods. She'd just pushed him onto the forest floor and assaulted him. And he'd clamped the ring back on her finger. For an incubus, that must have taken an awful lot of self-control—or maybe she wasn't his type.

Caine glanced at the mud and dirt coating her body, and whispered a spell. As he spoke, his aura whispered over her skin. She watched the muck lift into the air.

As much as Caine's aura soothed her, the thought of the mage inside controlling her body made her stomach turn. She unclenched her fingers from Caine's hair, gazing into those glacial eyes. "You shouldn't have made me take it off. I don't want that thing inside me, forcing me to do things against my will. Just like Bileth."

He frowned. "Forcing you to do horrible things like kiss me."

"Exactly." Seven hells. If the other novices knew what she'd been getting up to, they'd celebrate her downfall. The golden Hunter, covered in alchemical tattoos and mud, straddling an incubus in the Salem woods.

His hand slipped around the back of her neck; at his touch, another electrical charge sparked through her skin. "And yet, I don't see you jumping off me very fast."

Shit. He was right. Embarrassment warmed her face. She leapt up, tugging down her hem. Though, really, it was probably a little late to reclaim her dignity now. "I don't know what happened. I couldn't stop the witch."

He propped up on his elbows. "You can't expect to master it right away. You need to be stronger than the spirit."

A ghost of that crazed blaze still burned in her mind. Her fingers trembled as she brushed the leaves off her dress. "That's not the kind of war I know how to fight. She's completely crazy. I'm not taking that ring off again. Not until I get the spirit out."

"She's absolutely not crazy. Jumping on top of me was the first sensible thing I've seen you do, and honestly the first time I've seen you enjoy yourself."

She shivered. Didn't he realize? The agony had been unbearable. "My body was on fire."

He flashed a smile, and she knew he was thinking of the kiss.

"I don't mean with lust. I mean my skin was literally charring, and so were the trees. My body was blistering with flames."

He arched an eyebrow. "When you were on top of me?"

"No, before that. I was angry. Enraged. And everything was aflame. And then when I—when the mage jumped on you, I guess she felt something else. The pain subsided, and it felt calm again."

"See? I'm magic." He rose, pulling a stray leaf from his hair. "Maybe the flames were a vision of your future if you give yourself back to the Brotherhood. I don't know what else it would be. Your spirit isn't a fire mage. Ambrose said you tasted of hawthorns."

Rosalind nodded. "She's a forest mage. That explains all the tree stuff. I should have felt it through her aura, but it's too intense for me to even think straight."

"My spirit worshipped Nyxobas. Yours was aligned with Druloch, the god who lurks in the woods' dark shadows."

"The mage was drawn to the darkness. Something about the cycle of life and death. But the flames were so strong. She must be using fire magic."

"It's not possible. There are three shadow gods—sea, night, and forest. They've been warring with the gods of fire and light for millennia. That means there's no way you're connected to fire magic."

The sea god. A chill whispered over her skin. She'd scented a sea-witch on the Thorndike Campus. Could that mage be connected to all this? Something told her not to mention it to Caine. It was entirely possible that Rosalind was responsible for yet another mage's capture, and she had no way of knowing if that mage had been evil or just another poor idiot caught up in things beyond her control. She wanted to change the subject. "I'm not well versed in the shadow gods and fire gods. I've only been taught about Blodrial, the one true god."

"Blodrial fell from heaven after the celestial wars, just like the others. The only thing that sets him apart is that he doesn't believe humans should speak Angelic."

Of course they shouldn't. She'd just seen evidence of what the Angelic language could do to a human mind. "Right. Because it's evil in human bodies, and it screws people up. Blodrial is right."

"He's against it because the gift of magic to human kind was the original sin that banished our gods from heaven. The gods are all trying to free themselves from their punishment."

She'd never heard this version before. "And what is their punishment?"

"The celestial gods—those who won the war, trapped them in matter. The shadow and fire gods are trying to gain freedom by collecting human souls, competing with each other. But Blodrial thinks he can repent by stamping out magic on earth. Erasing the original sin. None of them can accept their punishment, and we all lost something. Even humans."

"What did we lose?" She was grateful for the temporary reprieve from thinking about the flames.

"Ignorance. Knowledge comes with a price. When humans learned to speak the Angelic language, they also learned about something else—their own mortality. Pedestrians have a story about a snake and a fruit tree that covers that concept."

"Don't eat from the tree of knowledge, or you'll die."

"Exactly."

She rubbed her throbbing temples. This was all too much for her now. She didn't want to think about her own death, not after she'd felt so close to it just moments ago. "Okay. So you have no idea why I felt like I was on fire?"

"No idea. It never happened to me. I had a whole lot of rage and bloodlust, but no flames. Still, as long as you stay near me while you learn to control the aura, I can help. You said it didn't hurt when you were near me."

He still wasn't telling her the whole story. "Why are you and Ambrose so invested in my power?"

"Unlike the Brotherhood, we want you alive. Isn't that enough information for you?"

"No. It isn't. And I don't get it. How are you able to stay sane with two souls?"

"I had to accept the mage, and then bend him to my own will. I had to become stronger than him. Now I use his knowledge and power, but he doesn't control me."

Shuddering, she thought of her blackening skin. "If I don't wear the ring, she'll consume me from the inside out. I won't be me anymore."

"I won't let that happen."

She wanted to see Tammi and Josiah, and walk the halls of Thorndike University. She didn't want to live in a world where people casually tossed human hands onto the floor, and she definitely didn't want to live with a violent lunatic invading her brain, forcing her to do things against her will.

How could my own parents have done this to me? Magic had obviously twisted their minds into insanity. "I don't want to be a mage. I don't want to be like you. I need to at least try to get my old life back."

"The Brotherhood will not give you your life back."

"Josiah will help me. He's my Guardian."

"That's absurd. No one in the Brotherhood is trustworthy."

"*I'm* in the Brotherhood. And anyway, am I supposed to believe you're trustworthy? You still won't tell me what Ambrose wants me for."

Josiah simply *had* to help her. Even if she couldn't rejoin the Brotherhood, she needed to claw some kind of normal life back.

His voice grew cold. "Your Guardian obviously hasn't guarded you very well so far, but it's your own life if you want to throw it away. I hope the burning you endure at the hands of the Brotherhood is somehow less painful than the illusion of burning that so terrifies you. Though it's highly improbable."

He turned, striding down the overgrown slope, and she followed, trying to maintain her balance on the slippery rocks. At the bottom of the hill, Caine paused to look at a small, flowering shrub.

His hand hovered over a cluster of white flowers before he plucked them from the plant. Wordlessly, he handed them to Rosalind, then stalked into the parking lot.

She twirled the delicate stem in her fingers. Hawthorn blossoms.

16

After they returned to the waterfront, Caine parked his bike under an oak. He climbed off, and Rosalind followed him across a patch of grass by Salem Harbor. The briny wind kissed her face, skimming over her tattered dress.

She had no idea what they were doing now. It wasn't like he'd filled her in or anything. But she had a bad feeling he was going to change his mind about his promise to help her exorcise the spirit. He seemed to think she was making a terrible mistake, but he wasn't the one who had to feel the flames when the ring came off.

He paused before a small gray stone in the ground. Chanting, he flicked his wrist. She gasped as a dark, steep-peaked house glimmered into view. She had to catch her breath at the illusion— or maybe it was the other way around. The house's invisibility was the illusion.

Caine opened a red door into a hall, warmly lit by candles. "My other home. The secret one." He motioned for her to enter, and she followed him into an ivory-walled hall. "Right now, you're the only person who knows this exists. Aurora will be only the second person. If you're still going to insist on rejoining the mage Hunters, I'll have to steal this particular memory from you before you leave. Or I'll have to kill you. Your choice."

Rosalind cocked her hip. "I don't really like the idea of you rooting around in my brain."

"What are you afraid I'll see?"

She toyed with her ring. *You'd slaughter me if you knew the terrible thing I did.* She pushed the thought away. "It's more that I don't particularly want brain damage."

"I'm an artist of dark magic. I'd leave all your computer science jibber-jabber intact."

"Mmm. Sounds like you really know what you're talking about." She frowned. "When are we going to see the sybil? Where's this nightclub?"

"We'll go tonight, once Aurora gets here. Hopefully, none of Elysium's patrons have heard about your little incident with Bileth." He motioned for her to follow him into a high-ceilinged living room. "In the meantime, let me introduce you to my parlor."

Parlor. It was a strangely old-fashioned New England word for a delicately beautiful place. Silvery wallpaper covered the walls, decorated with ethereal spider-web patterns. Midnight-blue curtains hung from bay windows overlooking the water, and candles burned in silver candelabra. The entire place was impeccably tidy. He probably had cleaning spells to do the work for him.

She sat on a deep blue sofa, smoothing out her tangled hair. She looked like a mess. At least the tattoos had faded from her skin, but her dress was hanging off her—probably shredded around the time she threw herself at Caine.

He sat next to her, and she glanced at him, trying not to stare at his beautiful features and strong jawline. "I think I might remember you. I remember glimpses from when we were kids. I remember someone like you on the beach. A young boy with gray eyes."

He eyed her cautiously. "I'm older than you. My memories are a bit clearer."

Curiosity bloomed in her mind. "What do you remember? What were my parents like?"

"Powerful."

He wasn't giving details, and she had the unsettling feeling they'd done something terrible to him.

A sigh slid from her. "I remember feeling loved. Even if my parents were witches, I felt safe then. But you weren't safe. They threw you out."

He gazed into the candle flames. "Nothing I didn't deserve," he said, so softly she barely heard him.

A lump rose in her throat. "You were just a kid."

"Is that so?" A muscle feathered in his jaw. "You don't think like a Hunter with all that empathy of yours."

"Maybe the Brotherhood isn't as bad as you think." She thought of Mason, making a mental correction. "Some of them are awful. But most of the Brotherhood made me feel like I had a home again. I felt valued, and important. I had a place among them. They give me a purpose."

"Is it worth your life?"

"They have to take me back. I don't have anything else," she said.

"That's quite a lot of faith you put in them."

"It's not so much faith. It's more like—"

"—A desire," he said. It was the same phrasing Ambrose had used, but on an incubus's lips, the word had an entirely different association. Her mind burned with the memory of his lips on hers, of her body pressed against his, fingers coiled into his hair.

But he'd put a stop to their kiss. It was stupid, but she almost felt the sting of rejection.

"You know when I kissed you earlier?" She flinched at her own question. *Shut up, Rosalind.*

His lips curled in a faint smile. "The image is fresh in my memory."

"I was just wondering, since you're an incubus..." Why in the gods' names was she bringing this up? She'd lost all her impulse control since she started hanging out with demons. "Why did you stop me? I thought incubi fed off—" She cleared her throat. "You know."

He arched an eyebrow. "*You know.* Is that what you call it in the Brotherhood?"

Her chest flushed. She had no idea why she'd gotten sidetracked by this conversation. She should be focusing on the sybil right now, and finding a way to piece her life back together. "You know what I mean."

He ran a finger over his lower lip, studying her. "Why did I stop it? Because you weren't in control. I can tell you it took a tremendous amount of restraint on my part."

Rosalind stared at him, entranced by the flickering candlelight dancing over his skin.

"Hello?" Aurora's voice broke the silence.

Rosalind let out a long breath, letting some of the tension uncoil inside her.

"Caine!" Aurora shouted from the doorway. "Am I invited in?"

"Of course you're invited in," he said.

Beaming, Aurora glided into the living room. "So *this* is the secret lair of the great shadow mage."

Rosalind arched an eyebrow. "Vampires can't enter without an invitation? I thought that was a myth."

"It is," Aurora said. "But I just feel awkward barging into someone's house. I mean, Lilu led me here—but she's a bird so it wasn't, like, a proper invitation with words. And I didn't want to be a third wheel in case you were banging."

"You're welcome here," Caine said. "Bileth won't find this house. He may track us to the waterfront, but we're invisible to him."

Aurora threw herself down on a chaise lounge. "I would have stayed to help with the fight, but I had a feeling you'd be doing that bone crunching thing, and I didn't want to get caught in the crossfire. You need to tell me everything that happened." Her eyes landed on an oak liquor cabinet, and within moments, she was across the room, rooting around the glass bottles. "I'll need a cocktail for this."

"Bileth knows I'm a Hunter," Rosalind said.

"How the hell did you make it out of there alive?" Aurora pulled out three Martini glasses, laying them on a tray. She filled them with whiskey. "You must've blinked your big eyes at him to charm him. Showed off a little of that perky cleavage."

"Not exactly," Caine muttered. "She impaled him with a fire poker."

Aurora whirled, the tray of cocktails in her hands. "She did *what?*"

"I'm a Hunter," Rosalind said. "I hunted him. I didn't know he was some kind of demon royalty. And I was worried about Caine."

Caine quirked a smile. "You were worried about me? I thought you were a Hunter. I'm pretty sure I'm among your intended prey."

Flustered, she plucked a cocktail glass off the tray. "Maybe, but right now you're my one hope at exorcising the spirit."

Aurora shoved a glass in Caine's hands, before downing her own in one go. She collapsed into a chair. "None of that matters now. We're all dead. For real this time. Did you know Bileth is known as 'The Scalpel' for the way he removes people's skin just for fun?"

Rosalind's stomach turned a flip. When Caine had been trying to convince her that demons and Hunters were somehow morally equivalent, he'd conveniently left out the bit about The Scalpel.

Caine traced his finger along the rim of his glass. "It's not a good situation. And, to make matters worse, we can't kill Bileth without provoking a major war."

"If you gave him the Hunter," Aurora said, "he might forget the whole thing."

Rosalind tightened her grip on the Martini glass. "You can't give me up. It wasn't my fault. I thought I was helping Caine."

Aurora arched an eyebrow. "You're really caught up in this fault thing, aren't you? Hasn't anyone ever told you that sometimes bad things happen to good people?"

"We're not going to give her to Bileth," Caine said. "Ambrose would never forgive it—and anyway, the Hunter is growing on me. At least in the rare moments when she's quiet."

Aurora was already refilling her drink. "You're directly defying Ambrose's orders to train her, so I'm a bit confused why you're suddenly worried about his forgiveness."

"I wasn't going to defy him entirely," Caine said. "I have a solution that meets Ambrose's needs as well as hers."

This was the first Rosalind had heard of this concept. "Wait. *What* solution that meets both our needs?"

"Ambrose wants the mage's spirit to survive," Caine said. "The spirit will simply need another body. And I have a willing host who would gladly accept this power."

"Who?" Aurora asked.

He sipped his drink. "Me."

Rosalind straightened. "I don't think that's a good idea. The mage's mind will break you. It was physically painful. Her body was on fire. And can you really handle another soul?"

Aurora glared over her Martini glass. "What do you care what happens to him? Once you run back to the Brotherhood, it will be your job to ram an iron spear though his heart. You get that, right?"

"I won't come for him, even if he doesn't erase my memories." It was the first time the thought had ever occurred to her, but as soon as the words were out of her mouth, she knew them to be true. Even if he was a demon, he'd done nothing but help her so far.

The longer she spent with the demons, the less she wanted to hunt them.

"Oh, really? You won't hunt him now, and he's growing fond of you?" Aurora's eyes raked over Rosalind's dress. "Did something happen between you two? And would that something have anything to do with the state of your clothes, and the fact that you both smell like you've been rolling in dirt?"

"Don't be ridiculous," Rosalind said.

Aurora rolled her eyes. "I was wondering how long it would take. At least maybe now that she's taken the edge off, she can relax a little and listen to some sense."

"It wasn't like that," Rosalind said. "We were trying to take the ring off to see what would happen."

"I get you. I haven't 'taken the ring off' in weeks and it's making me crazy." Aurora sloshed her drink.

Rosalind blushed. "I meant literally. My actual iron ring."

Aurora's face brightened. "Thank the gods. Taking that off is the first good thing I've heard you say since I've met you. You're going to let Caine train you, like Ambrose said?"

Rosalind tightened her fist. "It's not possible. There's something wrong with the spirit. She was on fire, and so was I."

But Rosalind was almost starting to see Aurora's point. With a demon lord hunting her, she needed the protection of someone powerful. Once she exorcised this spirit, there would be no more Caine and no more Ambrose.

Only the Brotherhood, who wanted her dead.

Her chest tightened. What if Caine and Aurora were right? What if the Brotherhood would never accept her innocence?

Aurora glared at her. "You'll be on fire if you run back to the Brotherhood, but I don't see that stopping you."

"Caine already made that point." She sipped her cocktail, which tasted of straight whiskey. "What is this?"

"A Manhattan," Aurora said. "Except I forgot the bitters and that other stuff, so it's just the whiskey."

Caine's eyes darkened, his body tensing to a predatory alertness. In a fraction of a second, he was at the window. "There's a Hunter nearby."

Josiah? Spilling her bourbon, she leapt up and rushed to the glass. She peered into the dim harbor walk, but she could see no one out there.

Caine stared. "He's not that close. He's prowling somewhere around Essex street, a few blocks away."

"What if it's my Guardian?" she breathed. "I haven't been able to contact him. I destroyed my phone when I went through the fountain."

"What if it's your executioner?" Caine asked. "Or what if they're one and the same?"

This was her chance to find out what the Brotherhood were thinking. What if they'd changed their minds, and Josiah had come to deliver the news?

She dug her nails into her palms. "I need to see for myself."

"You must have lost your mind," he said. "You want to show yourself to a mage Hunter?"

"Yes. I need to find out where I stand."

He pressed his palm against the window, studying her. "I'm not letting you go alone. It's too dangerous. Also, I can't risk you passing along information."

"Fine." She had no idea how Josiah would react to learning that she was actually *living* among the witches. There would be no way to hide it if he met Caine, whose entire body hummed with magic.

"I'll have to erase his memory after," Caine added.

"He'll never agree to that."

"I don't need him to agree."

She rubbed the bridge of her nose. "This Hunter could tell me what's going on with my case. Maybe they've forgiven it by now." If nothing else, she needed to know if Josiah was going to sell her out. She'd rather find out now than later.

Caine nodded at the door. "Let's go."

Running a hand through her wild hair, she followed him out his front door, and they stepped out into the cool spring air. The wind rushed over her skin as they stalked down a street lined with weather-beaten wooden homes.

Cringing, she cast a quick glance at her outfit. *Ugh.* She looked like some kind of vagabond stripper. "With all the magical spells at your disposal, I don't suppose you have one that could mend a dress?"

His gray eyes roamed over her body. "Of course I do. But I don't see the point. You look perfect as you are now."

A blush crept up her chest. Of course he'd say something like that. He was an incubus.

They turned the corner onto Essex Street, and she hugged herself.

Maybe the outfit didn't matter. There were only two possibilities for Josiah. Either he had faith in her, or he didn't. If he trusted her integrity, he'd listen to her explanation—even if Randolph Loring and the rest of the Brotherhood wanted her dead.

Just outside a crooked yellow home, a figure prowled through the shadows. While most people wouldn't have seen anything in the dim light, she was used to spotting movements at night. *Josiah.* She'd recognize those broad shoulders anywhere.

He'd come for her. A smile brightened her face, and she broke into a run.

17

$\mathcal{S}$he wrapped her arms around him, but Josiah wasn't looking at her. His eyes were too busy burning a hole in Caine. Josiah's fingers wrapped around his flamethrower. "Did this monster hurt you?"

She touched her Guardian's wrist. "Josiah. Relax. He's been helping me."

"*He's* been helping you? A mage?" He spat out the last word like a curse.

Caine crossed his arms "Not just a mage. I'm an incubus if that makes you feel any better."

Rosalind flinched. *Shut up, Caine.*

"An incubus." Josiah's face reddened. "I told you about them. Has he touched you?"

"No," she said. No need to tell him what happened in the woods. "But I'm so happy you found me. How did you know where I was?"

"No one in the Brotherhood will tell me anything. Apparently, they think I might help you. And they're right, of course. I had to spy on Randolph Loring when he was speaking to one of his associates in the Chambers. They know you're in Salem, but they don't know where. I've been searching the streets all night." A deep growl slipped into his voice. "And here I find you, with an incubus. He needs to be put down."

"You seem cranky," Caine said. "I suppose it can't please you to know that an incubus is protecting your girlfriend when you failed to do so."

Rosalind glared at Caine. "I'm not his girlfriend anymore. He's just worried about me." She glanced at Josiah. A vein pulsed in his forehead. He was about to lose it. "Look. Caine is a demon, and he's got an ego problem. But I knew him when I was a kid. And he's going to help us sort all of this out, so I can get my life back."

Josiah studied her carefully. "You spent your childhood with an incubus? How is that possible?"

She took a shaky breath. This was it. This was the point when she'd learn if her Guardian would stand by her, even with her magic-tainted background. "He explained to me the reason Randolph Loring thinks I'm a witch."

"What is it?" Josiah asked.

"I'm not from England. I was adopted from Maremount. My parents were... corrupted by magic. They did something to me, but I was only a little kid. I didn't have a choice. I don't even remember it. And when they realized what a terrible mistake they'd made, they sent me off to live with the Brotherhood. With Mason."

A streetlight glinted off his dark eyes, and he brushed a strand of hair off her face. "What did your parents do?"

"They summoned a mage's spirit into my body. I'm possessed with it, even now. As long as I keep the iron ring on, it dampens the magic, and I feel normal. The true god protects me. But if I take it off, the mage takes over my body. She can make me do things I don't want to. She can turn me into a mage and force me to cast spells."

Josiah paled. "Are you sure this is all true?"

"Twice now I've had the ring off, just for a few moments. I felt her invade my mind. It's horrible. I was splintering, and my skin was burning."

Josiah glared at Caine again. "And how is a demon going to help you rid yourself of magic? And, more importantly, *why* would he help you?"

"I'm just a caring person," Caine said.

"He's going to help me find a sybil in one of the demons' clubs, and she can tell us how to exorcise it. Caine will absorb the spirit into his own body."

"He's doing it to gain even more power," Josiah said.

She sighed. "Probably. And if he doesn't exorcise the spirit, he's stuck training me under the orders of the Vampire Lord. He seems to find the idea kind of tedious."

Josiah's eyes bulged, and she half-wondered if he was having a heart attack. "The Vampire Lord?" Clearly, she shouldn't even mention Bileth, or her Guardian would hurl up his dinner.

She touched his arm. "Once I'm free, we can explain it all to the Brotherhood, that I'm cleansed again, and they can stop hunting me, right?"

Josiah stared at her intently. "I'll see what I can find out. Maybe there's some sort of precedent in the Brotherhood's history of exorcisms. I can tell you that I'll fight for you."

Relief washed over her. "Thank you, Josiah." She'd nearly forgotten to ask him the questions that had been burning in her mind for the past twenty-four hours. "Josiah. Have you heard anything about the Brotherhood burning people?"

The vein bulged in his forehead again as he clenched his jaw. "Did this demon tell you that? You can't possibly trust him."

He wasn't answering the question. "Does that mean there are no burnings?"

"Of course there are no burnings," he shouted. "Do you think I'd be on board with that? And I'm not leaving you here with an incubus. It's out of the question."

"What are you going to do?" Caine asked. "Take her to Randolph Loring before she's been exorcised? I suppose from where you stand, it's better to risk burning her at the stake than leaving her with an incubus who might get his hands on her. One of these things would irreparably crush your ego, while the other would just be a bit unpleasant. All that ash and blackened bone to clean up."

Caine just *had* to make things worse. *Asshole.*

Josiah's nostrils flared. "You're not even human. You're a depraved beast, and you belong in the shadow hell."

"I'm pretty sure I could steal your woman from there." Caine's voice was glacial.

"Stop it, both of you." The wind rushed over her bare skin, giving her goose bumps. Of course they hated each other. What had she expected? "I'm calling the shots here. I'm the one with the demonic possession, and I'll decide what to do with it. I'm sticking with Caine until we can exorcise the spirit. I don't know what's happening after that, or if the Brotherhood will take me back or hunt me to the ends of the earth. But I do know I can't live with this monster inside of me. I've felt it, Josiah. And if I don't get it out, it will torment me until I die. Caine says he can help me, and I believe him."

Josiah's eyes were desperate. "I forbid you to stay with him."

Rosalind clenched her jaw. "You're not listening. There's nowhere else for me to go right now."

Her Guardian jabbed a finger in her face. "Do not let him touch you. I'm not messing around, Rosalind."

Was this really the most important issue right now? "I won't let Caine near me." She touched Josiah's arm, trying to mollify him. "Please try to find out about my case—if the Brotherhood will take someone back after they've been cleansed. Or at least maybe they'll stop sending goons to arrest me so I can go back to Thorndike."

"Of course I will."

"Are we done here?" Caine asked.

"We're done," she said. "You don't need to erase his memory, do you?"

"Like hell he's—" but Josiah couldn't continue the sentence, because his face had gone slack.

She whirled to find Caine chanting, his hand raised.

"Caine!" Frustration simmered in her chest, and she shoved him. "He needs his memories to help me. And it's not like he learned anything that Randolph doesn't already know. You don't need to erase his mind."

Dead-eyed, Josiah turned, walking jerkily as though warring with himself.

What the hell is Caine playing at? Anger coiled through her, and she yanked out the iron dust, aiming it at Caine. "Stop fucking with him. He's here to help me."

Caine cut her a sharp look, and lowered his hand. "I didn't erase his memory. I just wanted him to leave. He was annoying."

Anger exploded in her skull. What was it with men and needing to dominate others?

But Caine was no ordinary man. Not only did he have this natural impulse for domination, but he had the means to exert complete control over others through his magic. "You just wanted him to know that you were in charge."

"It's better for him if he understands that."

She narrowed her eyes, losing patience. "Do you have some kind of god complex?"

"He must understand that he can't fight me, or he'll end up dead. He's not really on your side, Rosalind. He's only helping you because he's scared of what will happen if you get too close to the demons."

"Of course he's scared. He doesn't want me to get hurt."

"That's not what I meant. He's scared he couldn't satisfy you the way a demon could."

"That's bullshit. Just because you're an incubus you interpret everyone else with your own disgusting flaws. And maybe your mind-blowing arrogance clouds your judgment. You just met him, and you already think you know everything about him, based on a two-minute conversation? And I didn't even get to the part about how you lied about the executions."

"My judgment is clouded?" Ice tinged his voice. "That's a bit rich coming from someone whose defining characteristic is chronic wrongness, mixed with a staggering dose of condescension. You and your insecure boyfriend are so preoccupied by evil that you've entirely overlooked all the Brotherhood's transgressions."

He was a genius at mixing truth with lies, and right about then she was seriously sick of his shit. "I wasn't wrong about a high demon coming into the bar, but you ignored me, because you think you know everything."

"It's hard for me to value the opinion of a staggering hypocrite. You belong to an organization that believes in their own superiority over others, that uses torture as a tactic. You are completely blind to your own faults. But, of course, knowing how you were as a child that's not surprising. A superiority complex is in your nature."

"What the hell is that supposed to mean?" She shook her head. He was trying to distract her. "Never mind. The point is, demons thrive on control over humans. Just look at what Bileth did to me. The Brotherhood have their faults, but we don't hurt people just for enjoyment. We're not sadists. We act strategically. If some people get hurt, that's unfortunate, but we don't take pleasure in it."

"Whatever helps you sleep at night."

Angry heat warmed her cheeks. "We don't take away people's free will and force ourselves on others. That's a demon thing, because you are abominations. Even if you compel yourself to be nice most of the time, the facade will crack eventually. You can't help forcing your will onto others. You're corrupted." A part of her needed it to be true—needed the monsters to be real, for the lines between good and evil to be clear. But the other part of her despised the words coming out of her own mouth. She'd called him an "abomination," and "corrupted," echoing Mason's favorite insults.

He flinched. For a moment, his features looked so human that she almost forgot what he really was, but in the next instant his pale irises darkened into a fierce, animal glare. Silvery light swirled off him, and his true demonic form emerged.

18

His cold magic crackled in the air, the power washing through her in waves. The dreadful ghost of dark wings rose up behind Caine, beating the air with a freezing wind. The temperature dropped by at least ten degrees, and Rosalind shivered. Apparently, she'd hit a nerve.

Her body buzzed with nervous energy, and Caine's dark gaze rooted her to the spot. If it came down to a fight between them, would she have *any* chance of survival, or would it only be a matter of time before he hypnotized her to bash her skull into the street?

An unnatural stillness overtook his body, like a beast of prey waiting to pounce. "If I'd wanted to take away your free will, this night would have gone very differently."

Nearby, heels pounded on the pavement, and Caine's gaze cut away.

Rosalind let out a long breath, and turned to spot a tall, blonde girl struggling to run in high heels.

She frowned, straining her eyes in the dim light. "Tammi?"

The charged air calmed, and Caine's eyes cleared as the air began to thaw. "Please tell me that's not another Hunter. I can't take any more of your kind."

"Rosalind!" Tammi sprinted over. Her blonde hair flew wildly around, and her usually impeccable makeup streaked her face. After nearly crashing into Rosalind, she stopped to rest her hands on her knees. "That's it," she gasped. "My life is over. My parents disowned me years ago, and now I can't go back to Thorndike."

Panic coiled in Rosalind's chest, and she touched her friend's shoulder. "Tammi, what's going on? What are you talking about?"

Tammi straightened, still catching her breath. "I can't believe I found you."

"Are you okay?" Rosalind asked. "*How* did you find me? What's going on?"

"I've been following Josiah from a distance," she said. "He took the train here, and I trailed after him, but I lost him in the park. He walks fast. And by the way, I know way too much about him now. Did you know he reads billionaire romances? Am I babbling? I'm kind of jacked up on the excitement. I'm basically a fugitive now. From the law."

Rosalind's blood turned to ice. "What are you talking about?"

"Did you say billionaire romances?" Suddenly playful again, a smile played about Caine's lips.

Tammi's eyes landed on the incubus. "Oh, hello."

"Tammi, meet Caine. He's a demon, but he's helping me solve my... issue..." She'd gloss over the fact that she'd just called him an *abomination*. Clearly that was a bit much—even if he had hypnotized Josiah. "Anyway, what do you mean you're a fugitive?"

"Okay. We *really* need to talk. You would not believe the shit storm that's been going on since you left. The Brotherhood have been hounding me ever since you disappeared. They yanked me out of my art history final and then pulled me in for a bunch of interviews in the Chambers. During the last interview, I was interrogated by some asshole named General Loring—"

Rosalind's mouth went dry. "Randolph Loring interrogated you? The red-haired guy? What did he want to know?"

"If I've ever seen you conduct magic. If you had friends who used magic. And what were the names of all your friends? And did I notice if there were any deformities on you, signs of corruption by magic? And if I wasn't going to be helpful, they were going to arrest me and try out some of their enhanced interrogation techniques. And I don't imagine he was going to be particularly accommodating about putting me in the women's prison. I got kind of a fanatical vibe."

"Your friend is a great deal more sensible than you are," Caine said.

Anger ignited Rosalind's nerves, and something else, too. Guilt, maybe. This was the other side of that swift justice she'd been so quick to excuse. "But you haven't done anything wrong. How could they arrest you?"

"They called it obstruction of justice." Tammi wiped some of the smudged makeup from her cheek. "They're a freaking cult. I know, because I was raised by crazy fundamentalists. The difference is that my parent's church had a broken neon sign outside of it, and the Brotherhood have taken over half our country."

A wave of grief washed over Rosalind, yet something inside her wanted to cling to the gleaming image she had of the Brotherhood. "It's a war between good and evil. We're fighting to destroy monsters, like the demon who tried to control my mind not that long ago." That was the Brotherhood's explanation when their methods were questioned. In a war between good and evil, they must do whatever it took to win. Only the weak-willed complained.

"Nothing is that simple," Tammi said. "You can't divide people neatly into two different categories. I know that better than anyone."

Something clenched tightly around Rosalind's heart. "But you can divide humans and demons. Think about everything they've done to us. I've seen the pictures of the children they murdered—the school in Boston, the vampire attacks in Maine. That's what evil is."

Tammi cocked her head. "Demons kill humans. Humans kill demons. It's the same thing."

"It's not the same thing. We're fighting back. The demons want to use us and control our minds."

Caine's eyes flashed. "The only reason Hunters don't use that particular skill is that they don't know how. Have you asked Aurora how she got those scars all over her back? They're from one of the Brotherhood interrogation rooms before she escaped. They used iron and hawthorn wood to carve her up. Fortunately, she's oddly proud of the scars. Demons are no more evil than humans. Some of them just happen to be a lot more powerful."

Guilt tightened her chest. "I didn't know Aurora was in there."

Tammi placed her hands on her hips. "I'm confused. You told me Caine was helping you, but you also seem to think demons are evil."

"She did just call me an 'abomination,'" Caine said morosely.

Rosalind sucked in a sharp breath. "Okay. That was... a little harsh, I admit. I just thought you were being controlling, but you're not completely evil."

"I'm sorry, am I interrupting a lover's quarrel?" Tammi scowled. "Because I was talking about the fact that I'm a fugitive. It's kind of a big thing for me right now. All I'm saying is, the Brotherhood want to throw me in jail and torture me until I crack. So if that's not evil, I'm not really clear how we're defining that particular term."

Rosalind's tears threatened to break through the surface. Tammi was right—Rosalind just hadn't wanted to admit it. She still thought Caine was an arrogant jerk, but she didn't want him tortured to death, and she definitely didn't want her closest friend thrown in the Brotherhood's prisons.

Sorrow welled in her chest. What about all the innocent people who'd gotten caught in the Brotherhood's crossfire? Or what about people like *her,* corrupted by magic through no fault of her own, hunted down like she was some kind of murderer? The Brotherhood's reach had spiraled out of control. Even she could see that now.

Yet she'd been a willing part of this system, refusing to let herself think about the casualties and the collateral damage. After all, in a war between good and evil, anything was justified, right?

"I can see how the Brotherhood's methods are... problematic." She glanced at Caine. For once, he was keeping his mouth shut. Maybe he understood that her whole future was collapsing before her. "I suppose my loyalty to the Brotherhood is just another example of my chronic wrongness."

"It's really the primary example," he said.

Grief overwhelmed her, and she fought to keep the tears at bay. She'd been thinking of the Brotherhood as her family for so long. But maybe they were a severely dysfunctional, abusive family—not unlike Mason. And if they were coming after Tammi, it was time to move on. "I won't go back to the Brotherhood. I still want to protect humans and fight the real monsters." Suddenly exhausted, she rubbed a hand over her forehead. "Maybe the monsters aren't as easy to identify as I once thought. Only the really horrible ones, like Bileth, and the mage inside me."

Tammi crinkled her brow. "The what inside you?"

Rosalind glanced at her friend. "I'm possessed. By the ghost of a crazy lady."

Tammi narrowed her eyes. "That's what they told me in the church I used to go to."

"Yeah, but mine is a real possession. I have access to magic, but I can't use it without being possessed by a maniac. And not only that, but if I take my ring off, my skin starts burning, like I'm standing in the center of an inferno."

Tammi's eyes widened. "Holy shit, Ros."

"There was one way around that, if I recall," added Caine.

"I can't throw myself at you every time..." Flustered, she let her sentence trail off.

Tammi twirled a strand of blonde hair around her finger, eyeing Caine. "That doesn't sound so bad to me."

A smile played over Caine's lips. "I told you your friend was sensible."

When she thought of taking off her ring, panic blazed through her nerves. "Forget it. How soon can we go see the sybil?"

"You still want to do that?" Caine asked. "Even though you're starting to understand that the Brotherhood are wrong about everything—including that magic is evil—you're still running away from your own power like a scared child."

The way he spoke to her still irked her. "Yes. I want the exorcism. But if you need to hear it, you're right about the Brotherhood, Caine, and I no longer have a future. I hope that makes you feel better. You obviously like control over things, and now another thing is going your way." Still flickering between anger and a burning disappointment, she felt a sudden need to lash out at him again. "Out of curiosity, does anything ever not go your way, or do you just seduce or hypnotize your way into getting anything you want?"

Anger flashed in his eyes. "That's quite the statement from someone noble-born and raised in a mansion. I'm guessing this is the first terrible thing to ever happen to you and that's why you have no idea how to handle it."

"You're guessing wrong."

Caine studied her with an unreadable expression.

Tammi cleared her throat. "This conversation is fun and everything, but I can't really go back to the Thorndike campus without getting arrested, so...."

Rosalind touched Caine's arm. "Can she stay with us? Please? Just until we get the spirit out. Then we'll figure something else out, and we'll get out of your life."

"Another human to look after?" he asked. "It's not a good idea."

"What else is she supposed to do?"

He traced his fingers over his jaw, considering her plea. "Fine. At least she's more sensible than you are."

Tammi wiped away another tear. "And then what? Where can we go that the Brotherhood won't find us?"

Rosalind turned to her friend. "It's going to be okay. Josiah said he'd help work on my case. I know the Brotherhood are unreasonable, but Josiah isn't. He said he'd help look for a precedent. If they're not after me, they'll stop harassing you."

Tammi crinkled her brow. "You think Josiah can do that?"

"I can't guarantee it, but..." Her sentence trailed off. *It's the only option we have* just didn't sound very reassuring. She glanced at Caine. "How soon can we go to Elysium?"

"We can go as soon as you want." His cold gaze met hers. "But if you want to come with me, you'll have to learn to act submissive for a few minutes. The only pedestrians allowed in Elysium are there as courtesans to offer pleasure to the demons."

She crossed her arms. "You have got to be kidding me."

19

Rosalind wasn't sure which was worse: the fact that she was willingly going into the demons' night club—pretending to be a courtesan—or the ridiculous outfit Caine had created for her, using magic.

After studying her body to take her measurements, he'd transformed her ragged outfit into a tiny white dress. Now, she tottered along the road in six-inch heels, practically tripping over her own feet.

For a demon associated with pleasure, he'd created bizarrely sadistic shoes. Still, as he'd pointed out defensively, the heels contained actual stiletto blades in case things got messy, and the hair sticks pulling her locks into an untidy bun were fashioned from large hawthorn spikes, inset with iron. Perfect for staking vamps if anyone got bloodthirsty. As an extra precaution, she'd collected a vial of iron dust, now tucked in her cleavage. This time, she wasn't going into a demon lair totally defenseless.

Elegant in her slinky leather dress, Tammi had already mastered the art of walking in heels. In fact, her new ensemble had almost brightened her morose mood. As they walked, she smoothed her hair over her shoulders.

Draped with stunning silver jewelry, Aurora took a swig of something from a flask—blood, probably. "You sure it's a good idea to bring the pedestrians into these places? Demons get hungry. Shit. I'm hungry."

"We don't have a choice," Caine said. "Rosalind will have to meet the sybil directly to get the oracle."

"What about Tammi?" Aurora asked. "She could've stayed at your house."

"No way I'm missing a demon sex club," Tammi said. "This is the only good thing to come out of this shit show."

Caine wore dark jeans and a form-fitting T-shirt that showed off his athletic physique and his tattoos. Rosalind couldn't stop her gaze from lingering over his body.

"I'll make sure nothing happens to them," he said.

Rosalind stumbled over a stray brick, then righted herself. "I can fight, too. I've come prepared with several weapons. It's almost like no one is impressed that I speared a high demon."

"You can't even walk normally," Aurora pointed out. "The spearing was obviously pure luck."

"It's these shoes," she shot back through gritted teeth. At this point, she was almost hoping things got rowdy so she could demonstrate her real skills—not that she had any desire to run into Bileth again. In fact, a shiver inched up her spine at the thought of him. "Speaking of my amazing skill at spearing demon princes, Bileth won't be there, will he?"

"No chance," Caine said. "These types of places, where light and shadow demons mix, are completely forbidden by the gods. A high demon like him can't know this place even exists, or everyone inside would be cast into the seven hells."

"If they're risking that, the cocktails at this place must be amazing," Tammi said.

"While they go off to find their sybil, I'm going to get you a thyme-tini," Aurora said. "They are to die for. Not literally."

"If this place is for all kinds of demons, what sort of demon runs it?" Rosalind asked.

"A valkyrie named Mist," Caine said. "Try to avoid her. She can be—difficult."

That was probably an understatement, considering valkyries were ancient demons of war and death. The aristocratic demonesses not only collected souls for the storm god, but they could instill other people with battle-crazed wrath.

Tammi flipped her hair over her shoulder. "How, exactly, does one act like a courtesan?"

Caine walked with his hands in his pockets. "All courtesans have been trained by Arielle, a succubus. She has taught legions of humans over the years, and she's an expert in seduction."

"So, we're supposed to be seductive?" Tammi asked.

"Yes," he replied. "And, if you can, try to give the impression of underlying desperation and maybe some emotional issues."

Tammi touched her lips. "Oh, I've got all that covered."

Goose bumps covered Rosalind's arms, and she hugged herself. "Acting seductive wasn't exactly part of my training."

Caine's eyes trailed over her body. "You'll be fine. Just—try not to speak."

"Thanks."

Aurora took another swig before wiping the back of her hand over her mouth. "And if anyone asks, you two human courtesans belong to us. I'm claiming Tammi, since she's less stupid than Rosalind."

Ouch. "There's that classic vampire charm again," Rosalind said.

They turned into a small, tree-lined square dominated by a stone church built to look like a castle. Their footsteps clacked over the pavement, and the only other sound was the wind rushing through maple leaves. Rosalind hugged herself tightly, trying to control the nervousness buzzing through her body. She was about to step into a nightclub full of monsters, dressed as bait, with only a few tiny weapons.

Steeling her resolve, she followed Caine to a heavy oak door. As he chanted a spell, she felt the sensual touch of his aura, trailing over her skin like butterfly kisses. The sensation was extremely distracting, and she tried to focus her thoughts on her weapons. They'd be the key to saving her life—and Tammi's—if any of these demons tried to devour them.

The door swung open into a packed dance hall, lit by glowing balls of light. Rhythmic music blared, the bass vibrating deep in her body.

Waves of magic unfurled from the creatures inside, skimming her skin with red, periwinkle, emerald, nectarine, and gold. She'd never been around so many magical auras at once, and they rushed through her chest. Shivering with their power, she tried to pick them apart. She had a sense that some belonged to powerful hellhounds and vamps. Others belonged to simple nature spirits: wood nymphs and tree sprites. She couldn't get a read on their intentions, but her overall impression was that the creatures inside this club were here for one thing: pleasure.

The auras were intoxicating, almost overwhelming. She reached out to anchor herself, gripping Caine's arm. At his touch, her mind cleared again, and she could feel only his clean, tingling aura caressing her skin. *Interesting*. She hadn't known you could block out other auras with touch.

Caine turned to her, his eyes trailing over her dress. "You look perfect."

Embarrassingly, her cheeks flushed, and she glanced into the club. Aurora and Tammi were already pushing into the crowd, heading for the bar, but a small group had gathered around Rosalind and Caine. The human women wore a vivid collection of jeweled hot pants, corsets, glittering underwear, and fishnets.

Apparently, her own outfit was rather conservative.

A green-eyed beauty at the front of the group ran a finger down her ruby red bra. She had a perfect hourglass figure, and her eyes were fixed on Caine. "Are you an incubus?"

"How did you know?" he asked with a smile.

The woman flicked her hair over her shoulder. "I've never seen anyone so hot in my life."

A smile played over Caine's lips. "You obviously have good taste. Seeing as you're someone who knows things, do you know where I'd find a woman named Sambethe?"

She smiled, obviously thrilled at the chance to help him. "Yeah. She's the weird gray-haired lady. She's always in one of the booths back there." She pointed to a far corner. "She just sits there, hammering margaritas."

Gold lights pulsed over Caine's smooth skin. "You've been most helpful."

The woman took a step closer, eyes hopeful. "Are you looking for a human mate? I've been dying to meet an incubus. We all have."

He slipped his arm around Rosalind's waist, the bass vibrating through his skin. "I've chosen my courtesan for tonight."

Courtesan. She was a Hunter, damn it. Or at least, she used to be, back when her life had a point. She schooled her face into a wide-eyed expression that she imagined courtesans wore, mouth slightly open. She tried to ignore the flash of self-loathing.

The blonde frowned, casting a critical eye over Rosalind's body. "Her? Why? What's so special about her?"

Rosalind opened her mouth to defend herself before realizing that she'd been about to extol her own virtues as a courtesan. So she did the wide-eyed thing again. *Gods, kill me now.*

A wicked grin flashed over Caine's face. "She's beautiful, obviously. But more importantly, she's mute."

Rosalind's mouth clamped shut. *Jerk.*

Disappointed, the woman strutted away.

A mute, adoring woman—that would suit him. She gave his arm a squeeze that she hoped hurt just a little, but before they could move beyond the door's entrance, another woman approached—this one clearly a demon. Seven feet tall, she wore a metallic gown that shimmered over her body like liquid mercury. Translucent black wings rose from her shoulders, a stark contrast to her platinum hair. Gray eyes bored into Rosalind.

Caine inclined his head. "Mist. Thank you for welcoming us."

"I haven't seen you here in a while," she said, eyes still lingering on Rosalind. "I see you brought a human. I trust you know the rules here. The only humans allowed must be courtesans, trained by Arielle in the art of serving demons."

"Of course," Caine said. "Arielle gave me this one as a gift. She loves to serve my needs."

Rosalind cringed. The urge to roll her eyes was almost overpowering.

Mist scanned the length of Rosalind's body, like she was assessing a prize horse. "She looks surprisingly strong for a courtesan."

Caine slid his arm around her waist. "I chose her for that reason. I don't like my girls to break when I play with them a little roughly."

Rosalind bit down a retort. *This excursion better be worth it.*

"Well. Enjoy yourselves." With a last, lingering glare at Rosalind, Mist slipped into the crowd like her namesake.

Caine held Rosalind's hand, leading her further into the club.

She tried not to stare at the demons and humans grinding against each other, or the nymphs gyrating in cages, wearing sequined pasties.

A few human men stood in archways, offering up their necks to female vamps, or following after them on leashes. All fairly pathetic from the human side of things.

As she and Caine pushed further into the club, Rosalind caught a glimpse of two female water nymphs wrestling in a sparkly liquid, surrounded by a crowd of leering male onlookers. The demons certainly had more exciting parties than the Brotherhood—she'd give them that but she was completely out of place here.

She focused on forcing her features into an approximation of a "doe-eyed" expression, though she'd never really known what that meant.

Caine turned, frowning. "What are you doing with your face?"

"I was trying to look seductive." She kept her hand locked in his, anchoring herself to his aura.

"You look terminally alarmed."

Frustration simmered in her chest. "I told you. Acting seductive wasn't part of my training."

He leaned in close, his breath warming her neck as his aura gently licked her skin. "I can, of course, help you with that—one of the incubus talents."

Warmth radiated off his body, and she glanced at his full lips, slightly open. Her eyes trailed down his arms. His skin looked gloriously soft, but the muscles under them hard as steel. She inched closer, overcome by a sudden urge to pull him in for a kiss. *Get a hold of yourself, Rosalind. He's using his incubus magic.* "I didn't say you could do that."

"Do what?"

"Use your incubus seduction talents."

He whispered into her ear. "I'm not using any magic."

Her pulse raced. He *wasn't* using his magic, or she would have felt his aura strengthen. She swallowed hard, trying to gain mastery of herself. She wasn't going to fall for the charms of an incubus. "I knew that."

"You've got that seductive look now." He brushed a strand of hair out of her face. "Shall we continue on?"

She tried to ignore the heat tingling through her body. She was here for the sybil—not to enjoy herself.

As they approached the booths at the back, a human woman in an emerald-green corset held a tray over her head. A single margarita stood on it.

Caine touched the woman's arm, and she turned, flashing a stunning smile at him. Flame-red hair cascaded over her shoulders. "Hi, gorgeous."

"Hello. I need this drink." He plucked it from the tray.

"Oh." The girl's face crinkled in confusion. "It's for Sambethe."

"I'll bring it to her. And while you're at it, two Manhattans for us. Dry."

Looking him over, she licked her lips. "I'll be right there."

Caine threaded his fingers through Rosalind's, and wove his way to a darkened corner of the club.

In a booth, lit from above by glowing golden orbs, sat a white-haired woman in a stunning, coppery gown. Her frosty hair contrasted starkly with a smooth, creamy complexion. The woman's milky eyes landed on the margarita in Caine's hands, and she jabbed a finger at it. "Is that for me?"

"I brought it specially for you. My name is Caine." He took a seat across from her in the booth, and Rosalind followed, squeezing in next to him so she could anchor herself to his aura.

Sambethe snatched the drink from the table, extending a long, pointed tongue to lick the salt off the rim.

Caine leaned in close, peering at Sambethe from below his lashes. "Is it true that you are very discreet with your oracles?"

"Don't try to flirt with me, boy. I'm far too old for that." She lifted her drink. "You keep these coming, and I'll do whatever you want."

Smiling obsequiously, the red-haired waitress rushed over to the table, her tray laden with two Manhattans.

Caine leaned back in his seat, eyeing the redhead. "How did you get those so fast?"

She glanced away, blushing. "I took them off another waitress's tray. I thought you were more important."

"Well done," Caine said, snatching them from her tray. "Now, we'll need five margaritas."

Sambethe chuckled. "Now we're talking."

The waitress hurried away, and Rosalind turned back to the sybil. Was she still supposed to pretend to be mute? This was getting old.

Sambethe drained her cocktail. "We'll need a private space."

Caine closed his eyes, whispering an incantation. As his aura swirled through Rosalind's body, a black curtain closed around the booth's opening.

Sambethe's milky eyes swerved to Rosalind. "You can stop pretending to be a courtesan. I know what you are."

Rosalind's chest tightened. *Is that a warning?* "But you won't tell anyone?"

Golden light shimmered over the sybil's skin. "What do I care? I'm seven thousand years old. Ask your question."

Rosalind took a long breath. "I have another soul in my body. A mage's soul. If I take off this ring—" She lifted her hand. "—I plummet into a world of hell. It's like my mind is fracturing, and my body is on fire. I want to know how to fix it. How do I get the mage out of me?"

Sambethe held Rosalind's gaze for an uncomfortably long time. "Hold on to your cocktails. This could get messy." She slid her own empty glass out of the way and climbed onto the table.

After throwing back her head, the Sybil began to sway and jerk. Her arms twitched to the rhythmic pulsing of the club's music. Then, with a frantic snarl, she hunched down to a crouching position, her head weaving around in the air like a snake's, her muscles taut. Her eyes locked on Rosalind's before she reached out to grip Rosalind's head. A powerful aura coursed through Rosalind like a mountain wind, clean and ancient.

"Blodrial's child, split in two." Her deep voice howled like a gale. "The mage, tormented by fire. Nyxobas's servant made her burn." Her head lolled, eyelids fluttering. "On a full moon, find the hawthorn grove. The spell belongs to Blodrial. Coat yourself in iron, and the incubus will chant. He will take on the extra soul."

Relief flooded Rosalind. They had an answer—a solution at last.

Sambethe threw her head back, sighing. She wasn't done. "The incubus will take on the extra soul. Three souls in one body. Two that don't belong together, shattered by broken love. Someone must be sacrificed. The incubus's body will sicken and die."

Horror slid through Rosalind's bones. *The incubus's body will sicken and die.* If Caine took on the soul, he would die? That was supposed to be the solution?

Sambethe's muscles relaxed, and she slid back into her seat just as the black curtain disappeared.

Rosalind dropped her head into her hands as panic clenched around her lungs. This had been her one hope.

Caine took a gulp of his drink. "Just to clarify, I will die if I take on the other soul?"

The sybil lifted her empty margarita glass, shaking it. "Seems that way."

Devastated, Rosalind trembled. This was it—her life was over. She lifted her eyes to the sybil, fingers tightening around her drink. "Is there another possible solution? Couldn't the soul go into the afterworld, where it belongs?"

The waitress sashayed over to the table, lowering the tray of margaritas, and Sambethe grabbed another. "No. It's stuck in a body until someone dies with it. That's your parents' fault."

"What about another person?" Rosalind asked, desperation eating at her.

"Who would want to take that on? You could force someone, I guess." The sybil rose, licking the salt off her drink as she shuffled out of the booth. "You kids have a lot to talk about. I'm going to dance."

The news knocked the wind out of Rosalind, and she could hardly breathe. She was ruined. And, with a wave of dread, she realized Tammi's life was destroyed too. Unless Rosalind turned herself in, the Brotherhood would hunt them both to the ends of the earth.

Her fingers tightened around Caine's arm. *Corrupted. For good.*

He eyed her warily. "I can feel your panic. You need to calm down. The other demons will be able to smell your fear."

She shot him a dirty look, then gripped her Manhattan and chugged it down in one go. "Of course I'm freaking out. I'm cursed. And Tammi's life is ruined too."

He leaned in close, his breath warming her neck. "You can't make a scene here. You're supposed to be a courtesan."

Anger burned through her body. "What difference does it make? My life is over. I might as well let one of these monsters drain my blood now. Then maybe the Brotherhood will stop coming after Tammi."

Caine narrowed his eyes. "Your life is not over, but it will be if you don't get a hold of yourself."

The weight of the sybil's revelation crushed the air from her lungs. "Tammi and I have nowhere to go. We can't escape the Brotherhood." She scanned the room, her eyes landing on the flame-haired courtesan, eagerly massaging the feet of a horned demon. "We'll have to become courtesans for real. I'll have to rub demon feet."

"Don't be ridiculous," Caine said. "You'd make a terrible courtesan. You're going to become a mage."

"You don't understand." Her pulse raced, and she couldn't keep her voice from rising. She needed to get a grip, but her world had just completely crashed down on her, and she could no longer control herself. She waved a hand at the crowd. "All of this disgusts me. Demons use humans for their own pleasure, and I don't want any part of the magical world."

"For a smart girl, you have awfully simple analyses of complex situations."

He wanted to distract her with his moral equivalence again. "Using humans comes easily to you, doesn't it? I saw how you treated Josiah. It's just in your nature. You were born to feed from humans for sustenance."

"And you were apparently born to make my life hell by recklessly invoking the wrath of every demon you encounter. Including me." He took a slow, steadying breath, clearly trying to control himself. "You need to stop talking. I'm going to help you calm down, not because I want to control you, but because it's the only way you'll get out of here without one of these demons murdering you." He whispered, and his aura wound around her skin before pulsing through her chest, relaxing her muscles.

Some of the panic ebbed, leaving behind a gnawing emptiness. The world as she'd thought she understood it was gone—the divisions between good and evil, the order of things, her place in it all. None of it had meaning anymore, so what was the point of her life?

Trying to ignore the hollowness in her chest, she rose.

Caine stood, taking her by the hand to lead her from the club. The lights flashed garish shades of red and orange, pulsing over gyrating dancers. The thumping bass rattled her bones, and she tried to push out all thoughts of the evil lurking in her body.

She caught a glimpse of Tammi and Aurora dancing, losing themselves in the music. How was she going to break this news to her friend?

The question didn't linger in her thoughts long because, in the next moment, the valkyrie stepped into Rosalind's path, her cold eyes scanning Rosalind's body. "You're not a real courtesan. You don't behave like one."

Dread rushed up Rosalind's spine, mixed with an odd sense of relief. Maybe this encounter would end it all.

"I'm a novice courtesan," she said, her voice hollow.

In a blur of white and copper, the valkyrie lunged, long fingers clamping tighter on Rosalind's throat. Mists's aura, cold and furious as storm clouds, flooded Rosalind's body.

As the aura filled Rosalind, she surged with icy rage, and a deep desire to hurt anyone around her. *Kill.* She slammed her arms through the valkyrie's grasp. She ducked to avoid a punch, then brought her fist up hard into the demon's ribs, hoping to snap something. Caine pulled her back, wrapping his arms around her.

With Caine's arms around her, her body began to calm again, her pulse slowing. What the fuck had Mist just done to her? The demon wasn't lunging again, but her gray eyes locked firmly on Rosalind, glowing with a stormy fury. From the growing crowd, Aurora and Tammi looked on, eyes wide.

"Get Tammi out of here," Caine shouted to them.

The valkyrie's steely stare had Rosalind rooted to the spot. "I knew you were a fighter." Her eyes flicked to Caine. "You brought a human warrior in here?"

Caine began whispering a spell. His aura swirled through Rosalind's chest, stroking her skin. Heat shot through her core, and she could think of nothing but his warm, strong body pressed up against hers. She had a sudden desire to spin around and kiss him hard. *What the hell?*

The valkyrie seemed to be thinking the same thing. As she approached Caine, cheeks flushed, her finger trailed down her chest. She licked her lips.

That was when Rosalind understood: Caine was using his incubus magic, and she'd been caught in the crossfire. Right now, she wanted nothing more than to run her hands all over his bare skin.

Mist stepped closer, a low moan escaping her lips—until her gaze landed on Rosalind again. A look of confusion crossed the valkyrie's beautiful face, and she clamped her eyes shut, shaking her head. "Don't use your magic on me, incubus." Her voice was a low growl, and when she opened her eyes again, savage rage contorted her features.

She ripped Rosalind from Caine's embrace before raising her clawed hands, transfixing the pair in place.

A pale blue light flowed from her hands, freezing Rosalind's body.

"Let's see which of your lovers is stronger," the demoness said.

As the light hit Rosalind's body, the valkyrie's aura slammed into her like a hurricane wind. A cold, deadly battle fury coursed through Rosalind, so powerful that her limbs trembled. Anger blinded her like a white light, and she clenched her fists, fingernails piercing her palms. She wanted to break through bone and gristle, to slice through necks with a sword.

I need to kill.

Her vision cleared, and before her stood the one person that she'd been waiting for. Pale gray eyes, tousled brown hair—his whole existence was a lie, a grotesque monster wrapped in a veneer of beauty. A devil sent to test her faith.

His gaze bored a hole in her. "I should have known how you'd turn out. You've always believed you were born better than others."

"I am better than beasts like you." Underneath it all, he was just like the other demons—a beast of prey, waiting for the right moment to rip her to shreds.

Her eyes lingered over his perfect form, stoking her anger further. *All beautiful things must die.* She wanted to crush his stunning body like a rose in her fist. She pulled the dust from her cleavage, ready to burn him.

When his eyes darkened to a deep black, and a ghost of wings rose behind him, dread whispered through her—but her fear only ignited her rage. Dark shadows curled around his muscled body.

Rosalind stared into the face of wrath itself, ancient and venomous—the face of floods and storms, trembling earth and mountains of fire. Something in the primal part of her brain shrieked at her to run, but her body would no longer obey. She needed to kill.

She was no longer Rosalind. She was a great queen of war.

With a lightning-fast gesture, she uncorked the dust, flinging it at the incubus. Primordial ferocity coiled through her, ready to strike its prey. She belonged to Rage now.

Caine growled—a deep animal sound that rumbled through her gut, chilling her blood. But she wasn't running away until she'd stopped his heart.

She'd snuffed out his magic in the most painful way possible.

He snarled, "Good. Now you know that when I win, it will have been a fair fight."

"I'll remind you of that when I'm ripping your ribs from your back," she said in a deep voice, one not quite her own. "I'll give you real wings, and maybe you can fly to hell with Lilu."

She slipped the thin hawthorn stake from her hair, just as the incubus lunged. He gripped her hands, forcing them down to her sides so she couldn't stab him. Her body pulsed with fury, and she head-butted him, listening to the delicious *crack* as she broke his nose. He dropped her hands.

A smile curled her lips. As she lifted her stake again, his hands flew out a second time, clamping down on both her wrists in a crushing grip. He was going to break her bones, but the anger dulled her pain.

Caine leaned in close, whispering into her ear, "Give up, little girl. You're outmatched."

Asshole. Rage burned through her, and she tried to kick him in the groin, but he pinned her arms to her sides with impossible strength. She strained against him, kicking at his shins, desperate to crack his bones. But instead of doing any damage, she struggled helplessly as he lifted her body in the air, as easily as if she were weightless. Her breath caught in her throat as he hurled her across the room.

She slammed against the dance floor, toppling out of her ridiculous shoes. The fall knocked the wind out of her. She gasped for air, fighting to catch her breath as Caine closed in. As soon as he closed the distance between them, she swung her legs in a wide arc, taking him down.

With a shrill battle cry, she leapt on top of him, raising the stake. His hands flew out, clamping onto her wrists, and he flipped her over, pinning her arms over her head. He pressed himself on top of her, and a low growl escaped his throat.

His eyes trailed down her chest. Something else was overcoming him—not battle fury, but another type of need. His distraction was a vulnerability. He lowered his warm mouth to her neck.

She arched her back, marshaling her strength to fling him off her. He slammed against the ground, and then she hooked her leg around him, straddling him.

His hands still gripped her wrists, but a sense of victory bubbled through her. *I am in control.* She leaned closer, momentarily distracted by his earthy scent, then bit into his neck as hard as she could. Her prey instinctively released his grip on her wrists. She lifted her arms high, and plunged the stake into his heart.

20

The rush of fury flowed from Rosalind's body, like the wind over the ocean. She stared down at her blood-soaked hands gripping the hawthorn stake. Caine's shocked eyes had returned to gray, and he glanced down at his chest.

Panic clenched her heart, and she ripped the stake from his chest. Her mind spun with horror, and she pressed down on his heart, as if she could staunch the flow. *What have I done?* Blood seeped through her fingers. Caine took a shuddering breath.

Lilu fluttered overhead, squawking, before flying for an open window.

If Caine were fully human, he'd be dead by now. But even so— she'd staked him with iron and hawthorn. *Seven hells, what have I done?* Both could be lethal to a night demon. Pressing on his chest, her hands shook uncontrollably. "Caine. I'm so sorry."

Heels clacked over the floor, and she looked up to find Mist, standing over her arms folded. The valkyrie appraised Rosalind with a clinical stare. "I see you're the stronger fighter. I guess that answers my question. Now get out of here before I slaughter you, too. Take his body with you."

Rosalind heaved a sob, and tried to lift Caine from the ground, her body shaking. At the sound of his pained gasps, tears stung her eyes. As she wrapped his arm around her neck, Aurora burst through the door, Lilu trailing behind her. *Thank the gods, the raven went for help.* It only took an instant for Aurora to hurtle through the crowd and snatch up the incubus. Carrying Caine, Aurora rushed for the door in a blur, and slammed it open to the night air. Rosalind ran after, her breath ragged.

By the time Rosalind got outside, Aurora had laid Caine out below a maple. The vamp frantically cleared the dust off Caine's skin while Tammi looked on.

Caine rested against the trunk, blood pouring through his fingers, and grief pierced Rosalind.

Tammi's hand flew to her mouth as she took in her friend. "Rosalind, are you okay? You're covered in blood."

"It's not her blood." Aurora flashed her fangs. "It's Caine's. What the bloody hell happened in there? Why is he covered in your dust, and why isn't he healing?"

Rosalind's hands shook, and she couldn't seem to make her voice obey.

She glanced at Caine, whose eyes were fixed on hers. He was still conscious, at least, though his skin had paled.

He took a deep breath. "We had a fight. She won."

Aurora snarled, "You did this, human?"

"The valkyrie," Caine said. "She imbued us with battle rage. It wasn't Rosalind's fault."

"A hawthorn stake," Rosalind managed.

Aurora's eyes widened. "This human girl *won?* You must've been holding back."

"I got distracted," he said, his voice choked. "She looks pretty when she's twisted by bloodlust."

Aurora turned her furious gaze on Rosalind. "Fix it, then. He needs a human female."

"What do you mean?" Rosalind knelt by Caine's side, holding her hand over his heart, as if her fingers could heal a shredded artery. Her hands shook wildly. *She'd* done this to him. "I don't know how to fix this. I don't know how to stop—"

"He's an incubus," Aurora cut in. "He heals through sexual contact."

Rosalind's mind raced. "You want me to have sex with him?"

"It doesn't have to be the full thing, but at least kiss him. It's not that complicated. Just hurry up."

Tammi raised a hand. "I'll do it."

Rosalind met Caine's eyes, her chest flushing as she thought of his warm, protective arms around her in the club, and his aura pulsing through her body. "No, I'll do it."

"Good," Aurora said. "We'll look out for that valkyrie arsehole, or Bileth, or anyone else whose wrath you managed to incur in the past few hours." She pulled Tammi away, leaving Rosalind alone with Caine.

Rosalind glanced at the blood pouring from his wound. "Does it hurt?"

"What do you think?"

"Sorry."

"Do you want to heal me? Tammi seemed willing."

She glanced at the blood on her own hands, her heart fluttering. "Yes, of course. I'm so sorry."

"Not your fault. You do understand how this works, don't you?"

"Yes. And I understand it's purely practical. It's how you heal. It doesn't mean anything." She wasn't sure why she needed to say that, but it was a reminder to herself more than anything.

Moving closer to him, she slid into his lap. As she slipped her arms around his shoulders, he gazed into her eyes, pupils dilating.

Her heart hammered against her ribs. *Don't forget what he is, Rosalind. Deep down, he's a predator, and he can't be trusted.*

But even if he wasn't human, his proximity alone heated her body.

His breath quickened, and he slid a hand around the back of her neck, his touch sending a jolt of energy though her. At that moment, she almost forgot he was a demon. She only knew she wanted to run her hands over his smooth skin.

His eyes darkened to a deep abyss of midnight black. As his aura strengthened, it fluttered over her skin in a thrilling rush. He slipped his fingers into her hair, and in the next moment his warm, soft lips were against hers. His magic rolled through her body, making her tremble with need. When his tongue brushed hers, heat shot through her belly.

He kissed her hungrily. One hand gripped her hair, the other tightened around her waist. All panicked thoughts flew from her mind, and there was nothing left but Caine.

As she curved into him, his kiss grew more sensual. He lightly traced down her spine with his fingertips, and she gasped.

He folded his arms around her and lifted her from the ground. As he pushed her against the tree, she wrapped her legs around him. She threaded her fingers into his hair, pulling him in for another kiss. Instead, he teased her—nipping her lower lip before brushing kisses down her neck. Her body burned, and she wanted more. She wanted all of him.

"Rosalind!" Tammi shouted.

Caine's face turned away from her. She could have killed Tammi right then, but thank the gods it didn't go too far.

"We were just finishing the healing," Rosalind said, her legs still wrapped around Caine. His aura caressed her skin, and she needed to get the hell away from him before this got really embarrassing.

Something about the stricken look on Tammi's face pulled her attention from Caine, but it was the person standing behind Tammi who sent a jolt of panic through Rosalind.

Josiah stood with his hands at his weapon belt, his eyes blazing with pure loathing.

21

With her dress hitched up around her waist and Caine's body pressed against her, it took a few moments to register what was happening.

Josiah gripped a can of iron dust, and before anyone could stop him, he unleashed a spray.

With Rosalind wrapped around him, Caine's muscles tensed. The dust burned the aura off his skin. It must be excruciating pain. His heart beat against her, strong and rhythmic—at least she'd healed him.

Rage contorted Josiah's face. "You're not going to control my mind again, incubus. I look forward to watching you burn."

Rosalind unlocked her legs from Caine as he lowered her to the ground, and she tugged down the hem of her dress. "Josiah. You found us." She tried to steady her voice.

"Rosalind. I came back to tell you about my progress. I've been on the phone all night, begging General Loring to consider your case, and I think he was starting to listen." His voice cracked. "And then I track you again, and I find you with your legs wrapped around a demon, letting him use you as his plaything. There I was, like an idiot, telling General Loring that you were pure. That you were going to get an exorcism."

All at once, her encounter with the sybil came flooding back to her. Caine's kiss had been a distraction, but it didn't erase the fact that she'd just learned her life was over. There was no way to get the exorcism she so desperately needed.

"Josiah—" she began.

"I told you to stay away from him. I should've seen what the other Hunters told me. You're nothing but a whore."

The disgust in his voice sent a flash of anger through her. This wasn't just about Hunters and demons, about good and evil, about fighting for what was right. Caine, for all of his arrogance and obnoxiousness, had been on to something: Josiah wanted control over her body.

She crossed her arms. "The incubus needed healing."

"He's a predator, you idiot," Josiah said. "He's using you."

"He's helping me, and I stabbed him in the chest. Anyway, why do I need to explain myself to you? For one thing, you broke up with me, and for another, you were supposed to be acting as my Guardian—not my stalker."

"He's an animal." Josiah took a step closer, flecks of spittle flying from his lips. "You should never have been anywhere near him, but you couldn't resist throwing yourself at him."

"I've been stuck with the demons out of necessity." Fury ignited in her heart. "That's what happens when the Brotherhood wants to throw you in one of their interrogation rooms. You end up fighting for your life and joining forces with the demons." *Seven hells.* She'd just officially declared herself on the side of the demons, to a high-ranking representative of the Brotherhood. Was this really happening? She was still hoping to wake from the world's longest nightmare.

Josiah stepped closer. "I should have known your softness was something other than compassion. It was merely your repulsive, corrupted soul, drawn to the other abominations like a bitch in heat."

She wasn't scared of him. Right now, loathing overwhelmed her. "I should have never let you convince me to do what we did, Josiah. If my soul has been corrupted, it was because of your influence."

"What we did saved lives," he spat. "*Human* lives. Thousands of them—though I can see you don't actually care about those."

"I need you to tell me if it's true." She searched his face. "Are the Brotherhood burning people?"

Josiah's eyes bulged, and he enunciated each of his words like he was talking to a particularly dim child. "They're. Not. People. The animals deserve to burn, and so do their accomplices."

Horror burst through her mind, and her knees nearly gave way. The realization that she'd been fighting on the side of sadists hit her like a punch to the gut.

And now, they were coming for her and Tammi.

Caine stepped in front of her, blocking her with his arm. "She's heard everything she needed to hear. Get out of here before I relieve you of your heart."

Red tinged Josiah's face, and he jabbed a finger at Rosalind. "You think this freak is going to look after you? That he's not just using you like a disposable toy?"

She had no idea what Caine really thought, but that wasn't the point. She belonged to no one—not to the demons or the Brotherhood. As anger roiled in her chest, she pushed past Caine. "I don't need people looking after me. And just so you know, I'm stuck with this witch's soul. I'm corrupted, just like Mason always said, and I'm going to stay that way. So the Brotherhood will have to hunt me down, but when you run back to the General Loring like a loyal little dog, you tell him he better stay the hell away from Tammi."

Rosalind wished desperately that Caine hadn't been covered in dust, or he'd be able to use his magic to make this all go away. He could have hypnotized Josiah into forgetting all about Tammi.

What had Caine called her? *A staggering hypocrite*. She was beginning to see his point.

Josiah's hand twitched by his weapon belt. "You want me to deliver a message to Randolph Loring from the demon's whore."

She cocked a hip. "Call me whatever you want, but you can tell Randolph I have the power of a psychotic mage in my body, and I'm not afraid to use it." At least, part of that was true.

She was declaring war on Randolph Loring, and her mind buzzed with an intoxicating mixture of thrill and terror.

Josiah's mouth tightened with barely controlled rage. "You think your evil possession is enough? It didn't work out so well for Miranda."

Caine stepped forward again, and she tensed with irritation. She could fight her own battles. She knew how the Brotherhood worked better than he did, but Caine's body was suddenly alert.

"The Brotherhood found Miranda?" Caine asked, his voice a growl.

Rosalind shook her head, trying to keep up. "Wait. Who the hell is Miranda?"

Josiah's eyes bored into her. "Interesting. Apparently your new lover didn't want to mention her."

Caine's voice was glacial. "I suggest you get out of here before I tear your spine out through your throat."

Josiah's nostrils flared. "You can threaten me all you want, but none of you will last long. The Brotherhood have been slaughtering demons like you for millennia, and we're stronger than ever. The angels will glory in your demise when the smoke from your body reaches the heavens." He glared at Rosalind, and the vein throbbed in his forehead. "I look forward to getting my hands on you in the interrogation room, and when Miranda burns, I hope to light the match."

In a fraction of a second, Caine's hands clamped around her Guardian's neck, and Josiah's eyes bulged.

"You will stay away from Rosalind and Miranda, or I'll make you wish for death." The wrath in Caine's voice chilled Rosalind to the core. "Perhaps I should grant you that now."

With a hammering heart, she watched as Caine tightened his grip around Josiah's throat. Caine was going to murder him. For a moment, she almost wanted to watch the life seep out of her former Guardian. After all, Josiah was going to report all this information to the Brotherhood, feeding them her location, and Tammi's too. It would bring the Brotherhood down on them like a plague of locusts.

But she couldn't stand by and watch him die. She'd cared for him once, and he'd cared for her, too.

A horrible, garbled sound escaped his throat.

"Caine." She grabbed his arm. "Please stop."

Caine's eyes met hers, and he loosened his grip. Josiah gasped for breath, stumbling back—right into Aurora. The vampire lifted him by his collar, baring her teeth before she yanked his cell phone from his pocket. She crushed it in her fist. "Run along, and we'll let you live, for now. You're a soldier, aren't you? You should know when to retreat." Growling, she hurled him out of the park, and he landed on the pavement with a loud thud.

Josiah slowly pushed himself up from the ground, shuffling over the pavement without sparing a glance. Even he knew there was no way to take on an incubus, a vamp, and an angry-ex girlfriend at the same time. As he slunk away, his shoulders slumped. She almost felt bad for him. At least, until she remembered what he'd said about looking forward to interrogating her and burning people.

Tammi's face had gone pale. "So I guess a reconciliation with the Brotherhood is out of the question."

Rosalind's chest tightened. "Honestly, we're screwed. I'm so sorry I got you into this, Tammi."

"You're not screwed," Caine said. "As long as you're willing to work with Ambrose, you'll have his protection."

Tears pricked Rosalind's eyes. She'd just declared herself on the side of the demons. "I don't know that I can do... whatever it is that he wants me to do. And what about Tammi?"

"I'll tell Ambrose she's your assistant. She'll get a salary." Moonlight skimmed over Caine's skin. "We'll work out the details later, but right now we need to hide the both of you before Josiah alerts the Brotherhood. I would use magic to get us home faster, but that twat glitter-bombed me."

"Let me handle the teleportation." With a determined look on her face, Aurora stepped out of the park—and directly in front of a car. A blue Toyota screeched to a halt, and Aurora flashed her fangs, smacking a hand on the hood. "We need a ride." She glanced at Caine, jerking her head at the car. "Get in."

Caine rushed over to the car, with Rosalind and Tammi close behind. As Tammi hopped into the back seat, Caine pulled open the door, beckoning Rosalind inside. An empty car-seat took up the middle, and she had to squeeze in on his lap.

The woman in the driver's seat turned to them, her dark eyebrows furrowed. "Um, are you all vampires?"

Aurora slid into the front seat, slamming the door shut. "Just me. Take us to the end of Hardy Street."

"Please take us there, Ma'am," added Rosalind from the back seat. Her bare feet rested on a collection of discarded sippy cups.

The woman frowned. "Call me Marisa. Now, I don't mind working with vampires. In fact, I run a demon-human ally group to improve inter-species community relations. But I will not drive if you're not wearing a seatbelt."

Caine's arms folded around her. "She'll be fine. Trust me."

"Seatbelt," she repeated, her voice stern.

"Yes Ma'am." Caine reached around, pulling the seatbelt to strap the two of them in.

"Marisa," the woman corrected.

As the car took off, Rosalind leaned into Caine. She could feel his heartbeat through his clothes, and his warm breath against her neck. She resisted the urge to nuzzle his throat. She had no idea if that kiss had actually meant anything, but she was probably stupid to even consider the possibility. He *was* an incubus, after all, and he was obviously deeply untrustworthy.

Tammi let out a long breath. "I'm going to need to process everything that just happened. I don't suppose I can call my Thorndike counselor about this. I'm just a little confused about what the fuck is happening with my life."

"You and me both," Rosalind said. Her mind still reeled from that awful encounter with Josiah. While Caine's warm body was a welcome distraction, she couldn't stop her thoughts from running wild. For one thing, she'd just learned that the Brotherhood were as bad as the demons. And then there was the valkyrie fight, the kiss, the threats from Josiah...

Exhausted, she rested her head against Caine's shoulder. "Imagine if my parents had never done this to us. We'd been living happily in Maremount still."

"You would have been living happily. I would not."

"Why not?"

"That's a long story. Some time I will tell you all about Maremount."

"Now that I'm apparently on the side of the demons—" Her voice broke. "I should probably learn about my homeland."

Caine took a deep breath, and she sensed something was roiling through his mind. "If you're on the side of the demons, do you still think we're evil?"

She gazed into his pale eyes. Did he actually care what she thought? "I guess the idea of good and evil isn't as clear cut as I once thought it was. I'm sorry I called you an abomination. That's what Mason used to call me, and it just popped into my head. I don't know why. He's a complete asshole, and you're not an abomination."

He let out a sigh, his breath warm against her skin. "I wouldn't go that far," he said, his voice barely audible.

Whatever he meant by that, now wasn't the time to get into it. "Also I'm sorry about the stabbing thing."

"If it gets your legs wrapped around me again, I might risk another stake to the heart."

She almost smiled, but something else whispered through the back of her mind. *Miranda*. Both Josiah and Caine seemed to know who she was, and Caine actually seemed to care about her.

Unable stop herself, she touched his chest, feeling his body's heat through his shirt. "Caine. Who is Miranda, and why did Josiah say he wanted to watch her burn?"

His muscles tensed. "It's complicated. I don't want to get into that now."

His constant evasions irked her. "Will you at least tell me what Ambrose wants with me?"

"Yes. We're pulling up to my house."

"Hardy Street!" Marisa said. She pulled over by the empty green field.

After thanking Marisa, Rosalind stepped out of the car, her thoughts whirling. Whoever Miranda was, both Caine and Josiah seemed to find her important, and they weren't letting Rosalind in on their secret.

22

Still barefoot, Rosalind paced the warped wooden floor inside Caine's house.

It only took a few seconds for Tammi to find his whiskey decanter. She poured herself a glass. "I was an art history student. Less than three semesters till graduation."

"I know," Rosalind said. "Everything is a disaster."

Tammi took a sip, then wiped the back of her hand across her mouth. "Maybe we need to move to France or Vietnam or something."

Aurora leaned on a granite counter in the open-plan kitchen. "You both are starting to spin out. Do you need a snack or something?"

Rosalind *was* starving. But it wasn't just her hunger—her mind was a raging storm, and she could hardly concentrate on one thought at a time. "What I need is for the Brotherhood to drop my case and to leave Tammi alone."

Tammi knocked back her drink. "I don't blame you. I blame that stupid cult. Your ex-boyfriend is an *asshole*."

Aurora rifled around in the cabinets. "The two humans are losing it. I'm making them a snack of food."

Rosalind's fingernails pierced her palms. "We need a plan. Caine, what exactly is Ambrose's grand plan?"

He leaned back, stretching out his arms on the sofa's back. "Ambrose's plan is for us to take on the Brotherhood. With the combined auras of two powerful mages, we can find a way to get past their security systems."

Dread whispered through Rosalind. He wanted her to *take on* the Brotherhood?

Aurora sliced through the top of a tin can with a knife, spilling juice all over the counter. "Have some faith in Caine. He's a brilliant military strategist. Ambrose made him a Duke."

Tammi ran her fingers fretfully through her hair. "Is there another plan? Like, one that doesn't involve provoking the wrath of an ancient society of lunatics?"

Rosalind stared at Caine in disbelief. "Just the two of us are supposed to topple their security systems."

Aurora dumped a pile of mandarin slices onto a plate. "You're more powerful than you know."

Caine ran a finger over his lower lip, studying her. "We break into the building, and then we free the captives, so the sadists you once worked for don't burn them to death. Aurora can tell you all about their torture techniques."

Seven hells, the torture. She couldn't let this happen to more people, not after what she'd done with Josiah. Maybe this was her chance to atone. She knew what it felt like to burn now, and couldn't subject others to the same fate—not if there was something she could do about it. "I'll do it. I'll help you free them."

Caine let out a long breath. "Good. And now I have to teach you magic. We haven't got much time."

Rosalind stopped pacing, folding her arms. "Before what? Is there a specific deadline?"

"I have a good friend in there," Caine said. "Two, actually. And I don't want them to die."

"I don't really want Rosalind to die," Tammi said. "Do I get a vote in this?"

"No," Aurora said, spearing mandarin slices with toothpicks.

Two friends. At least one of them had to be Miranda, but she didn't need to ask about that now. And the other—she could only hope the other was not an incubus too. *Oh gods, what if the demon I interrogated was Caine's friend?*

All at once, a wave of guilt slammed into her. She'd been trying to keep the memories at bay, but she couldn't hold them back anymore. *I've done terrible things.* She slid her hands over her face, and her chest heaved with a sob. *Such a simple set-up for an interrogation. A chair, cinderblocks, cloth, and water.* She suppressed the urge to be sick. *It could have been Caine.*

Caine clenched his jaw. "There's no need to cry. You're supposed to be a warrior, and I'll make sure you don't die."

Josiah had looked her straight in the eye and told her she needed to hurt the incubus. He'd sworn the demons were planning a massacre to rival the Boston Slaughter, and that the only way to stop it was to break the monster's will. Josiah had said it was her duty to force the incubus to confess everything he knew until the Brotherhood could stop the carnage. It was the life of one monster sacrificed for the lives of thousands of innocent people. Simple math.

But half the stuff Josiah had told her was a lie. She wanted to smash his smug face in.

She lifted her eyes. "That's not why I'm upset. You don't understand. I'm not a good person."

Confusion flitted across his features. "What are you talking about?"

She was half tempted to confess everything. "I thought demons and mages were all evil. I never would have agreed to the things

I did if I'd known the truth. Maybe some demons deserve to die, but it's not like we took the time to find out." Every second they stood here was another moment wasted. "Why are we wasting time? We need to get in there now before anyone else gets hurt."

Tammi raised her hands in the air. "You've officially lost your mind."

Aurora handed Rosalind a plate of mandarin slices and raisins, each speared with a toothpick. "You can't just go in there now. You sound like a nutter. Have a sodding snack and a nap, or you'll be no good to anyone."

Caine caught her eye. "The whole building is rigged with iron dust. That means I can't use my magic until we disable the sensors. There are scanners to block our exit, and machines rigged with stakes."

He was right. With all the defense systems at the entrances and the ID scanners, no supernatural creature could gain access to the building.

At Aurora's insistence, Rosalind forced herself to eat a raisin. "And how do we disable all that?"

"We have a plan," Aurora said. "I learned about the building's design during my escape, and I'm guessing you can fill us in on what we don't know."

Caine shrugged. "Basically, I want to blow up half their building and disable their dust."

"Why do you need magic for that?" Tammi gripped her plate of speared fruit. "Why not just use explosives?"

"Too messy," Aurora said. "We might kill the people we're trying to free. We want to save all the captives we can."

Rosalind swallowed a mandarin. "How do we make sure no one from the Brotherhood gets killed?"

Caine furrowed his brow as though this question was absurd. "We don't."

Rosalind closed her eyes. "I don't want to kill people. That's the whole point."

Caine eyed her. "Am I wrong in thinking that just yesterday, you were trying to kill a vampire?"

"Yes, but not everyone in the Chambers deserves to die." She shot an uncertain glance at Aurora. "I know you were tortured, and you have every right to want to hurt the people who did that to you, but most of the novices don't know about that. Most of them just thought we were stopping demons from massacring humans."

The vamp glared at her. "Caine can hypnotize the novices to leave the building. Then the two of you need to blow up the front entrance, the great hall, and the offices. All of this means you need to take off your stupid ring and start learning Angelic, like you should have started yesterday."

Rosalind froze, the full implications rolling through her mind. On the side of the demons, she'd have to abandon the only thing keeping her remotely sane—though, given her whirling emotions, maybe it wasn't doing its job so well anymore.

She closed her eyes, trying to lock her terror into her mind's vault. Her atonement would depend on her ability to master her fear. No longer hungry, she set the plate on the table. "Let's get started now."

23

As they stood in Salem Woods, the wind rushed between birch and ash leaves, and Lilu circled overhead.

Caine stood across from her in the grove. Before they'd left, he'd created a new outfit for her—black jeans and a long-sleeved shirt. Of course, because he was Caine, they fit her like a second layer of skin. But at least if the spirit wanted to jump his bones again, Rosalind wouldn't end up with a skirt around her waist.

Caine looked down at her. "When you take off the ring, I want you to imagine the mage's aura inside your mind. Concentrate on trying to condense it smaller, so it no longer takes over your whole body. I want you to imagine it as a ball of light, right here." He touched her sternum, and her skin sparked at his touch.

"Is that how you stay sane?"

"Eventually I figured it out," he said. "Are you ready to start?"

"I thought we would learn some spells first."

He shook his head. "The mage already knows the spells. I'm going to prompt her to think of them, and then you need to draw on her knowledge."

"What if she tries to assault you again?"

"I don't mind."

"I don't want it to happen." Sure, Caine was beautiful, but it wouldn't be *Rosalind* kissing him. It would be the mage. On top of that, she knew better than to get involved with an incubus. "What happened outside Elysium was just strategic so you could heal. And anyway, we're here to learn magic so we can save the captives, not to get distracted by having fun."

"Fine. If you're worried about what the mage will do, I can tie your arms and legs."

Just like Mason used to do when he beat the crap out of me. "No way."

"It would help keep you safe. If she wants to do something against—"

"—I said no. The whole idea of it makes me want to stab you with another hawthorn stake."

He glanced at her shaking hands. "Gods below. What's wrong with you?"

Shit. Why was this coming up now? She didn't need to dredge up her screwed up childhood with Caine. "It doesn't matter. I'm just overtired. Let's get on with what we need to do."

"Fine. I'll keep control of the spirit. And when we get home, you need to eat and sleep, because you seem like a mess."

"It's been a rough night." *Understatement of the year, right there.*

"You're a warrior. Your enemy has made a move, and its time for you to fight back. Muster your mental strength and take off the ring." He closed his eyes, marshaling his patience. "Please take off the ring when you choose to."

She twisted the ring around her finger, trying to work up the nerve. "If I seem like I'm burning, will you touch my shoulder or something? It seemed like your aura helped stop the pain."

"Of course."

After closing her eyes, she yanked the ring from her finger, shivering at the tumultuous presence of the aura. It swirled through her body, skimming over her skin with a tingling and buzzing. Tendrils of green unfurled in her mind like spectral ferns.

Rosalind tried to curl them up again, forcing them together into a small sphere, but the aura wouldn't obey. In the heavy spring air, her body vibrated with exertion.

The spirit was winning, forcing her to move, making her open her eyes. She stared up at the stunning incubus. Pearly moonlight filtered through the oaks, dancing on his smooth skin, glinting in his pale eyes.

The spirit wanted Rosalind to run her hands over his strong, tattooed arms, his perfectly muscled chest. But it wasn't just how he looked. Something in his aura drew her closer, like a gravitational pull. The spirit *knew* his aura.

She took two steps, slipping her arms around his neck, reveling in the warmth coming off his body. She thrilled at his sharp intake of breath when the spirit pushed Rosalind's body against his.

She studied his face, and the ethereal silver aura spiraling skin. Another soul lay inside the incubus, one the spirit knew well. "Richard."

His muscles tensed, a hint of confusion in his beautiful eyes. "Cleo." He gripped her forearms. "Rosalind. You need to control the aura."

His touch sent thrills through her body, but the spirit looking out through her eyes didn't like the name *Rosalind*.

"That's not my name," she warned, her voice laced with venom, no longer her own.

His grip tightened. "Rosalind. I need you to gain control. Close up her aura."

The aura surged through her body, and her voice came out

low, strangely accented. Her arms tightened around the incubus. His body was rigid against hers, and she tried to pull his head down for a kiss, but his perfect lips were out of his reach.

He swallowed hard, closing his eyes, and took a steadying breath. "Rosalind. Crush the aura."

The spirit forced her to stand on her tiptoes, but she couldn't reach his mouth. "Richard. I missed your touch, but I like your new body better."

Caine pulled her arms from his neck, gently pushing her back. "Rosalind. Get control of the aura."

The green tendrils spiraled through her in whirlwinds, and she tried to get control of them, but the spirit was stronger. It began speaking in Angelic, and Rosalind's body hummed with the growing aura, a thrilling rush of power.

At her words, the incubus's eyes widened, and he spun her around, wrapping his strong arms around her. He clamped a hand over her mouth to silence her.

She didn't like being pinned. Rage burned through her nerves, and she bit into his fingers, drawing blood. He released her, and she broke into a run through the forest, the damp air whispering over her skin. This was Cleo's true home, her world before the evil ones snatched it away from her.. *How would you like the flames, Rosalind?*

The spirit forced her to stop and hold out her arms. Somewhere inside, Rosalind screamed, trying to regain control. The scent of burning flesh filled the air, and in the next instant, searing pain ripped her apart. Flames blazed from her limbs, and she loosed an agonized scream.

It must have been only a few moments before a pair of masculine arms surrounded her again, cooling the flames.

In the next instant, Caine slipped the iron ring on her finger, and Rosalind let out a long, shuddering breath. Her body trembled. She'd only been on fire for a few moments, but the ghost of her torment still whispered through her nerve-endings, reverberating in her skull.

"Fire," she whispered.

"I'm sorry." His voice was so quiet she hardly heard him.

Her breath rasped, and he held her from behind, his skin smooth over muscled arms.

Exhausted, she melted into him. "She called you Richard."

"I never knew my spirit's name before," said Caine. "But as soon as she said it, I recognized it."

"You said the name Cleo."

He took a deep breath. "Richard knew her. There was some connection between them. I'm guessing they were lovers."

"She was starting to chant a spell. What did it mean? Why did you stop her?"

His arms loosened. "An aphrodisiac," he said, his voice husky. "If she'd finished it, I wouldn't have been able to control what happened next."

"She has a one track mind."

"Can you blame her? It's probably been hundreds of years since she inhabited a human body. She obviously wants to make the most of it."

She stepped out of his arms, turning to look at him. "That was a total disaster. She *wanted* me to burn. She was vengeful, and I had no control over her. I don't think I've ever failed at anything so shockingly. I'd rather fight the Brotherhood with weapons."

"That won't work."

"*This* won't work." Her nerves were frayed, the memory of pain still whispering through her. "I can't control her. She's too powerful."

"It was only your second try. Aurora was right. You need to rest and eat. You won't be able to gain control of anything when your body is falling apart."

She dug her palms into her eyes, trying not to think of what might be happening to the captive incubus. "We need another plan."

24

By the time they reached Caine's house, the rising sun stained the sky a pale coral, streaked with steel. Caine opened his front door into a quiet house.

In his living room, someone had drawn the curtains closed, and only a faint glow filtered in through the edges, dimly lighting the living room and kitchen.

In the darkness, Rosalind could just make out that Aurora had fallen asleep on the sofa, while Tammi dozed in an armchair, wrapped up in a blanket.

Caine trod quietly into the kitchen, motioning to one of the chairs that stood by the marble island. "Have a seat. I'm going to make you some food."

He lit a candle, and it cast a wavering light over the countertop.

Her stomach grumbled, and she wasn't going to argue with that declaration. "You said you didn't know how to cook."

"I lied." He pulled a bowl of eggs and another of ricotta from the refrigerator.

At the sight of actual human food, her stomach rumbled. "What are you making?"

He cracked an egg into a bowl. "Something you may remember from Maremount. Or not, in all likelihood."

She straightened, suddenly alert. "I don't remember the food. The one thing I remember clearly is your eyes."

He paused for a moment, his hand hovering in the air, clutching an egg. "You remember me? Are you sure?"

"I remember a boy with eyes your color. They're quite memorable." Her gaze roamed over his muscular arms, and an uncomfortable thought twisted in her gut. "You promise you weren't my stepbrother?"

He worked the eggs and ricotta into a batter. "Would it bother you if I was your stepbrother?"

He loves making me uncomfortable. "You know it would be weird. I mean, after I healed you."

He opened a metal canister, scooping out a measure of corn flour into the batter. "You can calm your fluttering heart. I'm not your stepbrother. The few remaining incubi are enslaved in Maremount. All the succubi have been killed. In fact, the entire city is built around the Lilitu fountain, where the last remaining succubus was killed. Her petrified head spews the town's drinking water. A few incubi were kept around for the pleasure we provide. You and I were not of equal standing in the Atherton household."

"Atherton." It struck her suddenly that she hadn't ever known her own birth name. "Rosalind Atherton."

"*Lady* Rosalind Atherton. It has a nice, noble ring to it."

"And you were some kind of *slave?* I don't remember a boy in chains." That didn't suit his imperious nature at all, though neither did the fact he was cooking her breakfast. She watched as he pulled out a steel skillet, turning on the burner to melt a hefty dollop of butter. "How could they keep you enslaved?" He was far stronger than any human.

He shot her a perplexed look. "Magic. I wore an iron collar, charmed by a powerful sorcerer. Your father." He salted the batter before pouring a thin layer into the hot pan.

Her stomach turned. Every new tidbit she learned about her parents only made her dislike them more, but she was still desperate for more information. This was the first conversation with Caine where he was actually willing to divulge information. Still, she knew if she pushed too far, he'd shut down. "If you're half-incubus, does that mean your father was a full incubus? Did you know him?" she asked. *Shit.* That was probably too personal.

The look he shot her iced her veins. "Just because I'm making you food and teaching you magic doesn't make us friends. You need to keep up your strength so we can achieve our objectives. That's all."

"I didn't say we were friends," she shot back, too exhausted to come up with a better retort. His rebuke stung, though she had no idea why. He'd already warned her not to trust him, and he'd offered nothing more than an uneasy alliance. That was all. "I get it. You're very mysterious and you don't like personal questions. So tell me about my own parents. Why were they so eager to experiment on us?"

He flipped her cakes onto a plate and slid them across the table. "They wanted you to be the most powerful mage Maremount had ever known. It was a time of turmoil for the city, and they wanted to take advantage of it."

"Lovely people," she said drily. She picked up a fritter, biting into it, her mouth exploding with the rich, buttery tastes. "Mmmmm."

Thunder cracked outside, and the room darkened further. She glanced at Caine, his skin warmed to a deep gold by the candlelight. "Tell me, is Maremount still in turmoil?"

He leaned on the countertop, holding a fritter. "No. A war broke out a few years ago. Eventually, the monarchy was overthrown."

"Were you involved in the fighting?"

A muscle worked in his jaw. "Is there a reason you need to know that?"

She swallowed a mouthful of her breakfast. "Right. No personal questions. But do you know what happened to my parents?"

He paused for a long time, and she almost wondered if he hadn't heard her. "We didn't stay in touch."

Considering they'd ruined her life in the quest for power, she wasn't sure she even wanted to see them. Still, she felt an overwhelming urge to ask Caine what had gone so horribly wrong that her parents had shipped her off to the Brotherhood. But the last time she'd tried to pose that question, his eyes had turned black, and he'd nearly murdered her. She took a large bite of the corn cakes, and her mouth rejoiced. "This is the most delicious thing I've ever eaten. I think I could die happy after this."

His face changed, and he flashed a brilliant smile. She'd never seen him smile so genuinely before, and his beauty nearly took her breath away.

Rosalind swallowed. "Was I nice to you and the other servants?"

He quirked an eyebrow. "You used to dump things on the floor just to have the servants clean them, and you only referred to them as *Servant,* never by name. But you were only four, so it was hard to take you seriously. Especially since you couldn't pronounce anything properly, so it sounded like you were calling them *swabents.*"

She shielded her eyes with her hands. *Oh, gods. I was a nightmare.* "Please tell me you're joking."

Something struck her about the way he'd phrased that. He'd referred to the servants in the third person. Was he not among them?

He swallowed a bite of his fritter. "Truthfully, you were a horrible, spoiled brat."

"I'm so sorry."

"It doesn't matter to me. You were only four."

Imagining herself ordering around servants, even as a little girl, made her cringe. "Maybe it's a good thing my parents had me sent out of Maremount so I didn't turn into a full-blown asshole." She finished her breakfast in silence, and glanced down at her crumb-littered plate. "I'll clean up."

"No need," he said. He whispered a spell, and crumbs disappeared off the dishes.

Thunder cracked outside, and a hard rain battered the house's old wooden exterior.

Rosalind rose, stretching her arms over her head. "Where should I sleep?"

He beckoned her to a stairwell. "My room is upstairs. Since I'm feeling generous, I'll let you take my bed." As they climbed the stairs, he shot her a sly look. "Don't worry. I'll sleep in the study."

It was such a big house, she was surprised there was only one bedroom. "Are you sure?"

"You need proper rest if you're going to learn magic."

Right. It was all part of meeting their objectives.

At the top of the stairs, he led her into a hallway. Dark wood arched above, and sharply peaked windows overlooked sailboats bobbing in the stormy harbor. Lightning speared the water, followed by a loud crack of thunder. The sky was black as smoke.

She shivered. "There's only one bed in the house?"

"No one else has ever been here. There was never a need for more than one bed. I do all my entertaining in my other apartments."

"I guess with all those vampire women trying to kill you, you'd need a secret hideout." She almost felt a pang of jealousy, but that was stupid. He was an incubus, and there was nothing real between them—not even friendship.

"Precisely."

She followed him past several closed doors to the end of the hall. "What about human lovers? Isn't that where you draw your energy from?"

"They want to kill me too. Only, human women aren't much of a threat." He stopped to open a large oak door, glancing back at her. "Though you did put up a good effort with the hawthorn stake. I've never had a woman come that close before."

He held open the door, and she stepped into a tidy room. A four-poster mahogany bed took up most of the hardwood floor. The soft gray blankets and pillows looked inviting, and she wanted to sink into them. Black curtains framed tall windows. Rain hammered the glass panes.

Lanterns hung from the ceiling, carved with stars and moons. Bookshelves covered one wall, crammed with faded tomes. A painting of an imposing stone castle hung on the other.

Rosalind pointed to the picture. "That doesn't look like the castle in Lilinor. What is it?" She was stalling. For some strange reason, she didn't want him to leave. In fact, she really wanted to slide her arms around his neck again and find out exactly what he did to drive all those women so crazy.

"You don't recognize it? It's the Throcknell Fortress in Maremount. It dominates the city."

"Have you ever been inside?"

He stared at the painting. "No."

So much for that conversation. It obviously had some meaning to him, but—of course—he wasn't up for sharing.

"Okay," she said. "I don't suppose you have an extra toothbrush?"

He walked over to a small table by the window, set with a pewter cup and pitcher. "Another thing you don't remember from Maremount." He poured a pale green liquid into the cup, handing it to her. "Charmed sage water. All you need to do is drink it."

She took a sip, rolling the clean taste around on her tongue. He pulled the cup from her, sipping from it before setting it down. "Don't worry about our attack on the Brotherhood. I'm not going to let anything happen to you."

"What if you can't control it?"

"Don't say that. It's not a good idea to dwell on your worst fears right before you sleep."

"That's not my worst fear. I don't want to to die, but my worst fear—"

He stepped closer, touching a finger to her lips. "Not before you sleep. You'll have bad dreams. I'm a priest of the night god. I know these things." He lowered his hand, studying her. "And anyway—if you solidify your worst fears in your mind, they can be used against you. Some demons are just as awful as the Brotherhood have said."

She took in his smooth skin, and the lean, muscular physique molded by years of leading Ambrose's army. It was no wonder women lost their minds over him. Part of her wanted the release he could give her—the quieting of her raging thoughts, a short respite from her most disturbing memories. She wanted to feel his calming aura flood her body, and more than that, she wanted to feel his perfect mouth on her skin.

But getting involved with an incubus was a terrible idea, and he'd just said it himself: he wasn't her friend. He was only working with her because it was what Ambrose wanted, and because it served Nyxobas's goals. If she started to think of him in any other way, she'd only turn into another one of his jealous maniacs.

And more than that, she could never forget the darkness lurking inside him. Even if she'd changed her mind about the sharp divisions between good and evil, demons were fundamentally *different* from humans. A part of any demon's mind would always see humans as toys to manipulate and use.

"Get some sleep." As he walked to the door, he whispered a spell, and the curtains closed, shrouding the room in darkness. He gently closed the door behind him.

She crossed to the bed, pulling off her boots. She still wanted to know who Miranda was. *Caine's girlfriend, probably.*

She slipped out of her pants, leaving them in a crumpled pile on his floor. *No point mulling it over now.* She was a warrior, and had a job to do.

She slid into his bedsheets, pulling the duvet tight around her shoulders.

She closed her eyes, and the pounding rain lulled her into sleep. Her mind offered up an image of Bileth, stalking though Salem's winding streets on a pale, white horse, hooves clopping against the pavement. As he approached, a drumbeat sounded, slow and deep, rumbling through her gut.

Rosalind stood with Caine, holding his hand in the cool moonlight, while Bileth walked closer, his eyes burning red. When he grinned, Rosalind felt horns grow from her head, her teeth lengthen. A knife appeared in her hand. Bileth howled, and forced Rosalind to jam the knife into Caine's neck, plunging in and out until blood soaked her body.

Her eyes snapped open, and she gasped, her heart pounding. Caine had warned her about dwelling on her worst fears before sleep.

What if Caine knew the incubus she'd hurt? Her pulse raced. She'd have to tell him. A part of her wanted to tear through the hallway and confess everything, but she was terrified of what he'd say.

Taking a deep breath, she closed her eyes again. This time, she imagined Caine's strong arms around her, his aura caressing her skin, soothing her muscles. His bed smelled like him—the heady scent of fresh earth after a rainstorm. She shouldn't let herself think of him like that, but she was too exhausted to fight it. The sensation of his presence was so vivid that it almost seemed real, like his perfect body was pressing against hers in a warm embrace, and she melted into the illusion.

She drifted off to the sound of the rain battering the windows and steep-peaked roof. She dreamt of a hawthorn grove, with a ground blanketed by falling petals.

25

$\mathcal{A}$ hanging noise jolted her from her sleep, and she sat up.

"Rosalind." Caine shouted through the dark, his voice urgent.

She threw the covers off, suddenly alert, and jumped out of bed. "What's going on? What time is it?"

He sparked the candles, and for a moment, his eyes trailed over her bare legs. "Bileth is near, and you need to leave before he finds you."

Her pulse raced. "Where is he?"

"He's a few streets away. The house is invisible to him, but he's scented us somehow."

"What time is it?"

"Nearly ten at night. You slept for fourteen hours." He was dressed for battle—sleek, black clothes, dark armor over his chest, and a sword slung over his back. Smaller blades glinted from holsters strapped to his legs and arms.

She crossed to the window, pulling aside the curtain. Moonlight glinted off the harbor.

"Can he get in here?" she asked.

"No, but if he figures out where the house is, he can draw us out with fire. I'm going out to speak to him, but I want you to get out of here with the other girls."

Something about his phrasing irked her. *Get out of here with the girls.* "I'm a trained fighter, you know. I don't need to run away from demons."

He stared at her in disbelief. "You're the one he's hunting. If he gets anywhere near you, he'll torture you to death. I need to keep him as far away from you as possible. He'll forget about you eventually, but right now he wants to impale you. Repeatedly."

Even though her vision of stabbing Caine had only been a nightmare, guilt still weighed heavily on her, crushing her chest like a load of rocks. On top of that, she was starting to feel strangely protective of the incubus. "I'll hang in the shadows or in the house, but I'm not leaving you alone. You were too closely matched last time for me to feel good about it. I'll only step in if I think you're about to die."

He inhaled deeply before handing her a knife. "Fine, but you must promise to stay inside. I'm still hoping to fix this with diplomacy." He eyed her carefully. "What, exactly, do you know about high demons?"

Hardly anything. When encountering a high demon, novices were just supposed to run. "I know they're immortal. Speaking of which, can I have more blades? I don't feel like one is enough."

He pulled two more daggers from his holsters, and a thin stiletto. "There are ways of killing them, but the weapons need to be charmed. To deliver a death blow, you need to be a powerful mage. I fit the criteria, but let's hope it doesn't come down to that. If we killed Bileth, we'd have far worse problems than the Brotherhood."

"You mean we might have eighty legions of demons hunting us."

"Precisely." His eyes trailed up her legs again, lingering on her tiny black underwear. "As much as it pains me to say it, you should probably put on some clothes."

"Oh." She hurried over to her pile of clothes, slipping into her pants and boots. She slid two of the blades into her boots, and the stiletto into her belt. "Where are Tammi and Aurora going?"

"They're taking a boat to Great Misery Island. I know a sorceress there who is quite fond of me. She should be able to keep them hidden for now."

Footsteps pounded up the stairs, and within seconds, Tammi's flushed face was in the door. "Rosalind. Let's go. We're taking a sailboat from the dock."

She shook her head. "I'm staying here. Caine might need me."

Tammi's face blanched. "Are you high? I haven't heard such a terrible idea come out of your mouth since you decided to dress as a slutty sheep for Halloween."

Rosalind scowled. "You already know I hunt demons. Why is this surprising?"

Tammi stared, her voice incredulous. "You hunted pixies who screwed up the plumbing."

"Is that true?" Caine arched an eyebrow. "And the slutty sheep outfit, too?"

Rosalind looked between them, her resolve growing. She projected her voice, imbuing it with as much authority as she could. "I'm not going to argue with you two. I'm staying. I'm the one who caused this situation, and I'm not letting Caine take the fall for it by himself. And then I'm going to help tackle the Brotherhood. Got it?"

Caine glanced at Tammi. "We'll meet you on the island. Aurora knows the way."

Tammi pointed at him, scowling. "You make sure Little Ho Peep comes back in one piece." She turned and hurried down the hall.

Caine approached Rosalind, standing so close she could feel the heat coming off his skin. He brushed his knuckles against her cheek, studying her face. "You're brave for a noble-born girl, but please stay in the house. You have a tendency to screw everything up by making stupid decisions. I'm even firmer in that belief now that I've heard about the slutty sheep costume."

She tightened her fist around the knife hilt. "You need to stop talking or I'll stab you with one of your own weapons."

"Wouldn't be the first time. Would you heal me again?"

A deep, rumbling noise resonated through the house, shaking the walls and rattling the windowpanes.

"He's outside," Caine said. "I'm going. Please stay in here." He wrapped his fingers around her knife-holding hand. "If he gets past me somehow, use this."

He turned, stalking down the hall, moving silently as the wind through the trees.

She closed her eyes, taking a deep breath and trying not to think of her nightmares. *I can't dwell on my worst fears.*

She stepped into the hall and peered out the window, staring at the moonlit street outside Caine's house. Mounted on an ivory horse—just like in her dream—Bileth strode into a streetlight. Tendrils of his red aura curled off his skin like smoke. His steed's eyes blazed red, hooves clopping slowly over the pavement. He carried a scythe slung over his enormous, bare back. Curling tattoos covered his pale, muscular body, and horns swooped back from his forehead. She almost thought she heard the low rumble of a drum...

At the sight of him, fear stole her breath.

Caine pushed open the front door and strode toward the high demon. Bileth halted and dismounted, nostrils flaring. When the demon's feet landed on the pavement, the ground trembled, and shock waves shuddered though the earth.

Caine held up his hands, as if trying to placate Bileth, but the high demon pulled his scythe from his back before charging.

Bileth swung, but Caine lifted his forearm, blocking the attack. In a blur of movement— so fast Rosalind's eyes could barely track it—Caine maneuvered behind Bileth, pinning the demon's arm behind his back. As Caine pushed Bileth's neck down, forcing him lower, the high demon lost his grip on the scythe. Caine leaned into him, whispering in his ear, no doubt trying to placate him with promises of submissive courtesans.

But Rosalind knew what the high demon really wanted. He wanted *her*.

Bileth's body vibrated with fury, skin blazing bright red with his aura. When he flung out his arms, he threw Caine back in a blast of magic. The incubus landed hard on the pavement; in the next instant, he was on his feet again, his silvery aura whirling around him.

What the hell is he supposed to do? He was clearly the stronger fighter, but he couldn't kill Bileth, which meant he was at a severe disadvantage. Diplomacy clearly was not on the table, and neither was an all-out battle with Nyxobas's crony.

Bileth snatched his scythe from the ground, and Caine slid his sword from his scabbard, blocking another swing. The two demons whirled and parried in an intense blur of movement, their blows ringing out into the air. Metal sparked in the night air.

Bileth's aura burned hot around him, and he intoned a spell. His voice rang through the air like the knell of a hundred discordant church bells. As he spoke, Caine's spine arched, and his body lifted into the air, suspended in apparent agony. Caine dropped his sword, and a look of intense pain contorted his beautiful features. His eyes turned black as pitch while his primal instincts took over.

Bileth was torturing him. Caine's fingers curled, his body shaking.

Horror spread through her. This was her fault, and she needed to help him. Clutching the iron blade, she sprinted through the hallway, thundering down the stairs. She had no plan beyond ripping Bileth's attention away from Caine, and her seething fury leant her courage. She slammed through the front door, heart pounding.

Bileth whirled, locking his red eyes on her.

"Bileth," she said. "I think you were looking for me. What the fuck do you want?"

His lips curled in something like a smile, and he beckoned her closer with a long, taloned finger. She gritted her teeth, but his noxious red aura seeped into her body, infecting her limbs. She clamped her eyes shut, imagining a clear sphere that forced out the red tendrils. Her pulse raced with the effort. When she'd pushed his magic out, she threw the knife.

The blade pierced Bileth's shoulder. He roared, and the sound slid through her bones. In the next instant, his hands were around her throat, pressing hard on her airway. In about six seconds, her neck would be crushed. "You filthy, human animal. You were born to serve," he whispered.

Panicking, she strained her foot up until she could yank a knife from her boot. She slammed it hard into his arm, and he lurched back, roaring. She reached for the other knife, ripping it from her boot.

A burst of powerful magic from Bileth surged through her veins, overtaking her. It seeped into her limbs, claiming territory in her muscles too fast for her to block it out. Her stomach churned as Bileth compelled her to stalk over to Caine.

Caine's large eyes landed on her, black as smoke from a funeral pyre. Her heart squeezed in her chest. Bileth would force her stab Caine.

This is my nightmare come true. I'm going to murder him.

Her arm reared back, ready to plunge the knife into Caine's neck, and dread ripped her apart.

Caine's silver aura exploded from his body, and in the next second his hand darted out to grab her arm, lightning fast. He tightened his fingers around her wrist until she dropped the knife, and pulled her closer, slipping the iron ring from her finger.

Power bloomed in her body as her mage took over. Caine chanted an ancient spell, and something in her mind recognized the words: a spell for traveling. Instantly, she joined in, the familiar Angelic words tumbling from her lips. As they spoke, their bodies glowed with a protective light—a thick, vernal aura that rushed over her skin, whirling around the pair like a storm wind.

At the spell's completion, mist surrounded them, and Caine slipped the ring onto her finger again. His arms encircled her protectively, his heart pounding hard against her chest.

Where were they? She didn't want to utter a word in case Bileth still lurked nearby, but when the air thinned, she found herself looking at a thick grove of firs. This wasn't Salem.

Rosalind let out a long, slow breath as relief flooded her. "Where are we?" she whispered. Caine's body was a beacon of warmth in the cool forest, but she forced herself to step out of his embrace.

He smiled. "Great Misery Island. You do realize we just performed a powerful spell together? Our auras mingled beautifully."

Her head throbbed. "You mean, your aura mingled with Cleo's perfectly."

"Either way, I couldn't have done it without you," he said.

In the chilly sea air, she hugged herself. "I didn't feel the flames. The mage seemed more focused."

"I was with you the whole time. And Cleo must have known it was life or death. Maybe she hates you, but she doesn't want her host's body to die. Especially not before she got a chance to get her hands on me."

Rosalind studied him. "Were you pinioned by Bileth's magic the whole time? It seems awfully convenient that you only broke free at the last second when I was about to stab you."

"I let Bileth torture me," Caine said. "He wanted revenge, so I let him have some. And I wanted to see what you would do. I would have stepped in if it seemed like you were about to die."

"Seven hells, Caine. He practically murdered me."

"I did tell you to stay in the house. If you were a foot soldier in the army I commanded, I'd have to punish you."

She forced *that* image out of her mind. "You're not my commanding officer, and I don't foresee that happening. We've already established I can take you in a fight. But maybe you should find some courtesans for Bileth so he'll leave us alone. Perhaps you could glamour yourself to look like a beautiful, submissive woman and tend to his needs. I hear you're an expert in the seductive arts."

He grimaced. "Ugh. That sort of comment would get you a severe punishment if you were my foot soldier."

"Stop with the punishment thing. You like that idea a little too much."

"Right." He turned, trudging through the thick undergrowth. "We need to keep going. We must find Tammi and Aurora. Omerelle lives somewhere nearby, and they may arrive soon."

She followed him, snapping over twigs. "Omerelle? Who is this woman?"

"She's a mage. She's quite lonely out here. Her husband died a few years ago, and I keep her company sometimes. She'll probably be thrilled at the visit."

Rosalind didn't want to think about what sort of "company" he provided.

Lilu circled over their heads, fluttering through oak leaves. Streams of cold moonlight pierced the canopy, and a cool breeze kissed her skin. A heavy scent of brine, moss, and oak leaves hung in the damp air. She could envision herself living out here in the wilderness, lulled to sleep every night by the gentle sounds of the waves against the shore, and the wind rustling the trees.

"Rosalind," Caine said. "There's something I have to ask you."

His grave tone had her full attention. "Yes?"

"You said you remember my eyes from your childhood. Do you remember anyone else?"

"No. Just you, and glimmers of the sea and of flowers. And—weirdly—I remember seeing my own face a lot. When I told Tammi that, she thought I must be a narcissist."

Caine paused, lightly touching her arm. "That wasn't your face."

His words made her stomach swoop. "What do you mean?"

He inhaled sharply. "That was Miranda."

She gasped. "Who is she?"

"Your twin."

The ground seemed to tilt beneath her feet as this news hit her. "I have a *twin?*"

"Miranda, yes."

"And the Brotherhood have captured her?"

"According to Josiah."

"Why didn't you tell me about this before?"

"You've only just given up your allegiance to the Brotherhood, and I had no idea if you were trustworthy. And moreover, you're impulsive and overly emotional. I didn't think you'd approach it strategically. You've been very worked up this whole time."

Everything about what he was saying made her blood boil. "You can't trust me because I'm impulsive?"

"You followed me through a portal into another world, with no thought for your own safety. You decided to defy the orders of the Vampire Lord." He held up his fingers, counting out her offenses. "You threw a fit in Elysium that drew attention to us. Oh, and you stabbed an ancient high demon—three times—in a direct contradiction of my orders. You're not trustworthy."

"Well when you list it all out—" She stopped herself. She didn't want to get sidetracked by an argument. "Forget about all that. I need to know more details. Where has Miranda been this whole time? In Maremount?"

He started walking again, and she followed. "Miranda has been living in Maine. Your parents sent her to live with another member of the Brotherhood, but he didn't treat her well. She ran away at some point."

"Where did she go?"

"I have no idea. She must have been sleeping in the streets like a peasant."

A flood of guilt and anger rushed through Rosalind. "I wish I'd known."

"I wish I'd known too," Caine said. "I assumed you were both living safely in the pedestrian world, until Ambrose told me otherwise. I was supposed to bring you both to safety, but the Brotherhood came for you first."

"And she's possessed, like me?"

"Yes. And that's why Ambrose is interested in the both of you," Caine said. "He wants all three of us together for a triumvirate of power."

Stunned, Rosalind tried to picture her twin. "I think I remember her braiding my hair."

"She was the sweet one. She used to give the servants food when they were hungry."

The servants. There was that third person again. "And I used to torment them. Are you telling me that I'm the evil twin?"

"If you forced me to choose between good and evil, that would be my best guess."

"What else can you tell me about her?"

"I haven't seen her since she was four or five. But I know she completes our circle. Three mages, each aligned with one of the shadow gods. Together, our power would be unparalleled. He has a few old scores he'd like to settle, including one against the Brotherhood."

Rosalind's knees felt weak. "Three shadow gods."

"Right. The night god, the forest god, and—"

"The sea god." Her mouth went dry. She'd felt the sea mage on Thorndike's campus.

She'd sent the Brotherhood after her own sister.

She stumbled over a tree root, her mind a whirlwind of revulsion and guilt. "Caine. What if I've done something terrible?"

"What have you done?"

Her heart pounded in her rib cage. She had to tell him about Miranda, and the temptation to confess about the incubus was overwhelming.

She closed her eyes, an image flashing in her mind of Josiah, handing her the knife. "If you don't do this, humans will die," he'd said.

Rosalind's body shook like a leaf in the wind. "I did terrible things for the Brotherhood. And I think I'm responsible for—"

"Shhh," he lifted a finger to his lips. "Something's happening."

She listened to the wind whispering through the trees. Distant screams floated along the breeze, and her chest tightened.

"We need to go." Caine broke into a run.

She sprinted with him, snapping through twigs and branches. The screams grew louder as they ran. As orange flames came into view, Rosalind's heart constricted. Was this their destination—burning?

She pushed on faster, her breath ragged in her throat, until they reached the clearing. A young woman stumbled in front of a blazing gothic mansion. Blood streaked her beautiful face, and a tiara hung limply from wild, blonde tangles. A black cat stood before her, its back arched.

"I fought them," the woman said, her eyes frantic. "I fought them with magic, but they'll be back for me. They found me here."

Caine rushed to her, grabbing her hands. "What happened?"

"It was the mage Hunters. I used a protection spell, but it won't last. They wanted to burn me. They burned my house."

"How did they know you were here?" Caine's voice was urgent.

She wiped a shaking hand across her forehead, smearing the blood. "I never thought they'd come for me. I didn't have the shields up."

Caine gently wrapped his fingers around her arms, staring into her face. "Omerelle. Tell me what they said."

"They didn't say anything, but I read inside their minds." Her sorrowful, brown eyes glistened. "The witch-Hunters had been spying on two women—a vampire and a pedestrian. The Brotherhood heard them saying they were coming to Great Misery Island. The girls are friends of yours. The witch-Hunters are accusing me of aiding the fugitives."

At Omerelle's words, a crushing panic began to take root. "Do you know what happened to the two women?" Rosalind asked.

Omerelle stared at her, and the woman's willowy body trembled. "The witch-Hunters had already taken them by the time they got to me. They're in the Chambers."

Bile rose in Rosalind's throat, and she covered her face with her hands. Not only did the Brotherhood have her twin sister, but they had Tammi and Aurora, too.

Anger crackled through her body. She wanted to storm the Chambers and punch a hole through Josiah's face. As Caine tried to calm Omerelle, Rosalind took a deep, shuddering breath, trying to steady her nerves.

Omerelle picked up her cat. "I'm not staying here. Alu and I are going to hide from them." She closed her eyes and chanted a spell; her body shimmered away.

Caine's shot a worried look to Rosalind. "We need to get out of here now. Do you think you can do the teleportation spell again?"

She glanced down at the ring. "I think so. If you stay near—"

A hail of bullets cut through her thought, and pain speared her body. She crumpled to the ground, gripping her ribs. Caine rushed for Rosalind, his eyes black. He touched her chest, chanting the beginnings of a spell. Rosalind could feel the wound start to heal, until a spray of iron dust blasted Caine's skin, snuffing out his aura. Another hail of bullets blasted Caine onto the ground. She looked up, catching a glimpse of a tall, thin man walking closer. *Longshanks.*

She gasped for breath.

Before she could sit up, pain exploded through her skull, and her world went dark.

26

Icy water ran down Rosalind's face, and she gasped. Her eyes snapped open, but she could see only white light filtering through dark canvas. Panic coursed through her, nearly drowning out the screaming pain in her lungs. Something covered her head—a hood, probably, and a rough piece of fabric gagged her mouth, compressing her tongue. She coughed, nearly choking on the cloth. Its oily taste was suffocating.

She needed to get out of there, but she couldn't move. Coarse rope bound her wrists behind her back at an awkward angle. She tried to tear her wrists free, and her skin chafed against the rope. Terror exploded through her skull. Her arms had been fastened tightly to behind the back of a chair. When she tried to move her legs, she found they were trapped by rope, too. She was completely helpless, unable to do anything except exist.

She took a deep breath, the air burning her lungs. *Gasoline.* She was in one of the interrogation rooms.

By the deep ache in her chest and the sharp whistling sound, she could tell a bullet had collapsed one of her lungs, even if Caine had partially healed it.

Heels echoed on a concrete floor, and someone yanked the hood from her head. Her captor strode in front of her, peering into her bleary eyes.

Rosalind stared into the pale, freckled face of Randolph Loring. She glanced to the right and caught a glimpse of Caine, his body bound to a chair with thick, iron chains—chains that would leach all the power out of an incubus. Black duct-tape covered his mouth, and blood soaked his chest from gunshot wounds to his shoulders.

She gazed around at the iron-walled room. It was nearly bare. A bright light shone overhead, and a metal watering can stood on the floor by two cement blocks. There was a video camera mounted on a wall. She'd seen this setup before, and the sight turned her blood to ice.

Caine's blackened eyes burned into General Loring with an ancient, primal hatred.

Loring leaned down, examining Rosalind's eyes. His cold fingers slid over her cheeks, and she shuddered.

In desperation, she wanted to tell him how much she hated being tied up, but the cloth still gagged her. Raw panic gripped her lungs like a vise.

"Mmm. I can see you'd like to speak," he said tonelessly. He pulled a knife from his belt, cutting through the cloth.

She gasped, looking up at him. "Please untie me."

"I don't think so, Rosalind. You look so much like your sister." He shook his head. "Do you know, Rosalind, that I'd wanted to promote you? We were alike, or so I thought. Not everyone understands that we must take extraordinary measures to fight evil, or that there are strict lines separating the pure from the corrupted. Not everyone has a visceral revulsion to magic like I do. Not everyone understands that the demons won't respect us if we're weak and refuse to fight back. I thought you and I were the same."

"Magic still repulses me," she said. Apart from Caine's magic, but she wasn't going to bring that up now.

"It is a poison. A toxin that corrupts a human body. You seemed to understand that. I'd been watching you from afar. I'd hoped you'd work on our security team. I'd heard about you, and your clever skills. I thought perhaps you'd make a nice wife for one of my officers, or even me. I didn't know we had a traitor in our midst. We'll have to be more careful in the future."

They were in one of the cells deep below the ground in the Chambers. A thick metal door blocked their exit. There was no way in or out of this room without a retinal scan. Even if she could get out of this chair, her own retinas wouldn't make the "approved" list. She was thoroughly screwed. In a frenzy, she tugged at her wrists, the chair rattling on the floorboards. "General Loring. I didn't realize you knew so much about me. It is nice to finally meet you."

Randolph folded his hands behind his back, pacing. "I think Josiah was in love with you. It must have broken his heart to learn you're corrupted with filth. I've promised he could interrogate you. I think it will make him feel better. He asked if Caine could watch, and I granted him his wish."

Her mouth was dry, and she tried to focus on his words as she tugged at the ropes. "Watch what?"

Randolph tilted his head. "Watch what he does to you. It's an acceptable strategy. The demon may choose to confess everything to save you. But of course, demons have no compassion at all, nor do you, I suppose. You're not human anymore. It's fascinating, really. You do look human. Beautiful, even. Though when Josiah is finished with his interrogation that may not be the case."

Cold dread snaked up her spine. "I want a trial."

Randolph crinkled his brow. "What for? We know you're guilty. We're no longer required to waste time with paperwork and legal nonsense. We're at war. Moreover, the sixth amendment only applies to humans. Same for the eighth amendment."

"The prohibition against cruel and unusual punishment."

"Exactly. They don't apply to your species." He stared at the floor as he paced, his eyes never meeting hers.

"I'm human."

"We've changed our thinking about that. Once a person uses magic and creates an aura, they are no longer considered human. A person who provides protection for a witch is no longer human, either."

She struggled frantically against the ropes, sweat beading on her forehead. This was insane. "You can't just make up your own definitions."

"Of course we can. It is people like me who create reality. It is people like me who define our terms. This is the way it's always been. The Brotherhood is an empire, and Blodrial has called on me to lead it." His cheeks reddened, his pace increasing. "Weak-minded scholars might huddle in libraries, arguing over semantics and ethics. Fine. With their noses stuck in books, they're out of my way while I create reality. Meanwhile, I'm going to act, molding the world into the way it should be according to divine principles."

She gasped for breath, her lungs burning. "If you torture people, what makes you any better than the demons?"

"We don't call it torture, so it isn't." His heels clacked faster over the floorboards. "Anyway, that you would even question me in that way shows how far you've fallen."

She wanted to distract him—if only because she knew what was coming next. "Your lack of introspection is breathtaking."

He paused his pacing, cocking his head but refusing to meet her eyes. "I do often request that our interrogators refrain from leaving marks, because they can make for unfortunate pictures in the wrong hands, but I can't promise Josiah will heed that request." He turned with a tight smile. "Well, it was interesting to meet you in person. I'll let Josiah know you're ready for him. You already know how this works, Rosalind. You've been in here before."

Terror vibrated in her skull, and she tried to rip her arms from their ties as Loring strode from the room.

Tammi. Where was Tammi right now? Rosalind's pulse raced. She needed to get out of here and search the other interrogation rooms—but even if she could get out of here, there was no way to unlock the secure rooms without the retina scan.

As she tugged the ropes, her chair legs banged against the floor. Caine remained still, his black eyes cold as glaciers, devoid of humanity. He must have flipped some kind of switch.

"Caine," she said. "I need to find a way—"

The door opened, and Josiah stepped into the light, his brown eyes boring into Rosalind.

"Hello, my darling," he said, voice seething with anger.

"Josiah. You don't want to do this."

He crossed the room, reaching out to stroke her hair, eyes glistening. "That's where you're wrong. I've been so looking forward to this."

"Why? You know what happened to me. I was turned into a witch against my will."

His nostrils flared. "Fine, but then you opened your legs for the incubus and declared war on humanity."

"I haven't declared war on anyone."

"You're either with us or against us. You know that." He straightened, staring down at her. "When I was five, I hid in a closet and watched as demons ripped into my parents' necks, drank them dry. They did things to my mother that no child should have known about. Your lover here not only lives among them, but he acts as their leader." Josiah's eyes burned with fervid intensity. "To see you lusting after this beast set a fire blazing inside me that can never be extinguished. I want you to feel my pain. I want this monster to feel my pain when he watches me hurt you."

Caine's growl reverberated through the room, his demonic eyes dark as voids.

"Tammi didn't do anything wrong," Rosalind said, in desperation.

Instead of responding, Josiah shoved her shoulders so hard that the chair tipped back. As it slammed against the floor, she gasped in pain. The full weight of her body landed on her hands, bound behind her back. She struggled to catch her breath.

"Did that hurt? I see you're injured." He knelt down, pulling a knife from his pants, before cutting through the front of her shirt.

Revulsion spread through her. She couldn't believe she'd ever cared for this maniac. She should have let Caine kill him when they had the chance. "What are you doing?"

"Looking at the damage to your corrupted body." He studied her gunshot wound before pressing down on it with one of his thumbs.

Agony lanced her ribs. Caine had sealed up some of the wound, but fragments of her broken ribs still pierced her lungs.

"That must hurt a lot," Josiah said. "Your demon lover didn't get to finish healing it. He won't be able to heal your broken corpse when I'm done with it, either."

"You're a monster," she choked out. Her thoughts raced, and she tried to slow them, to think tactically.

What did the Brotherhood teach her? *Use the tools from your surroundings.* But what the hell was she supposed to use here? She was tied to a chair, and...

The stiletto knife. She still had the small blade in the back of her pants, she could feel the hilt jabbing into her spine. She pinched it between her fingers.

"You're going to torture me because you're mad about our breakup. Do you realize what kind of psychotic, bunny-boiling asshole that makes you?" Slowly, she inched the knife from her belt, but she couldn't get much leverage with her hands crushed beneath her.

"I'm not saying it won't hurt, but we don't call it torture, Rosalind. We've talked about this. It's an interrogation." He glanced at a small camera in the corner of the room. He crossed to it, covering the lens with a small cloth. "It may get a bit unconventional, so I don't want any of this recorded. But it will be an interrogation, nonetheless. I do hope you'll be as willing to share with me as you once were. Did you know that your information led to Miranda's capture?" He raised the legs of the chair on to a cinderblock, so they were now higher than her head. As much as she dreaded what was coming next, this position made it easier for her to move the knife, since her hands were no longer pinioned.

"The sea-witch I told you about," she said through labored breaths. Slowly, she inched the knife up and down against the knots.

Josiah picked up the watering can. "She looks so much like you. I enjoyed breaking her. Though, I'm not sure she was sane to begin with."

Rage flowed through Rosalind like molten lava. She wanted to crush him.

She cut a glance to Caine, who remained still as a statue, watching. In a room rigged with iron dust, his magic was useless here.

As she rubbed the knife's blade against the rope, Josiah pulled a dark hood over her face, and her heart rate sped up. She knew how this worked. It made it easier to torture people when you couldn't see their faces. Right now, the spotlight still penetrated the cloth, but that wouldn't last long. Next, Josiah would wrap her head with a towel, shrouding her vision in darkness.

She'd watched him do it to the incubus. She didn't want to think of the demon's name, but as Josiah blotted out the light with the second cloth, it came to her anyway: Malphas. Fair-haired, but with gray eyes just like Caine's. Josiah had staked him earlier that night. The hawthorn wood had still protruded from his shoulder when Josiah brought Rosalind into the cell. His pale eyes had looked so tormented, and she'd wanted to yank it out, but Josiah had stayed her hand.

I can't think about that now. She needed to focus on getting the hell out of there. Josiah was drawing this out, enjoying her panic. When she'd said humans didn't enjoy torture, that they only acted tactically, she'd been lying to herself completely.

Still, the longer Josiah drew this out, the better chance she had to get herself out of here.

Her heart galloped in her chest, and she slid the knife against the knots.

Maybe she deserved this, after what she'd done to Malphas. Josiah had told her that the incubus had brutally raped and murdered three women just days before. He'd said that the demon had left their naked, broken bodies in a Walden Woods. There were the pictures of three brutalized corpses, shown to Rosalind in the cell as she stood just inches from the incubus.

As she'd stared at them in horror, Malphas had eyed her evenly, his breath rasping. He hadn't said a word.

Josiah had done all the talking: "That's what an incubus will do if you ever get near one. This monster would tear you to pieces if we let him free."

The pictures of the broken corpses had twisted her gut with disgust.

After Josiah had wrapped the demon's head with the towel, he'd told Rosalind to pour the water over his face. All part of her training. She was too soft, apparently, since she made the fatal mistake of viewing demons as humans instead of as cold, sadistic predators. In a fight for survival, there was no room for gray areas.

She scraped the knife against the rope.

It was too late by the time she realized Josiah had a bad habit of passing on shitty information. There was every chance that Malphas had never been anywhere near those girls.

The watering can scraped across the floor as Josiah shifted it, and fear rushed through her body. She'd gotten nowhere with the ropes. You couldn't seriously cut through a thick rope by slowly rubbing a blade against it—

Her mind froze as the cloth dampened. It started with the slow flow of water trickling into her nostrils. She held her breath, still rubbing at the robe with the knife, trying to rip through the fibers. She held her breath for what seemed like an eternity, one agonizing second after another, and pain exploded through her lungs. When she couldn't hold it anymore, her body forced a breath out.

She knew not to breathe in, but her lungs burst with agony, and she couldn't control it anymore. Involuntarily, she breathed in, sucking the wet cloth against her face. *No air.* Panic burst through her mind. *There is no air. I'm going to die.* Her body shook, rebelling against the suffocation. Her vision burst with images of Malphas, his body convulsing as she poured the water on to the towel, the stake still protruding from his chest.

I'm going to die. All rational thought flew from her mind. She'd beg Josiah for mercy, do whatever he wanted to get out of this.

I poured the water. I'm the monster. Sheer terror and agony warped her mind.

After ten lifetimes, she felt the chair tilt up again. *Please.*

Josiah pulled the towels off her face before yanking off the hood. She gasped for breath, sucking in air. Her wet hair plastered to her face. Icy water soaked her shoulders.

Josiah looked into her eyes. "This is the part where I ask you questions."

What had her plan been? *The knife—gods help me.* She'd dropped the knife.

27

She glanced at Caine, but he wasn't moving. He just stared at her, his eyes empty.

"He can't save you, Rosalind."

Josiah touched her cheek, and she flinched. *He's going to drown me again. He's going to kill me. I'm going to die at the hands of a sadist.*

She clamped her eyes shut, trying to get a grip. She needed to master her fear, to keep her wits intact so she could figure out how to get the hell out of here.

"Tell me about the Vampire Lord," Josiah said.

Shit. She'd already divulged too much. "The Vampire Lord?" she repeated, stalling. Frigid water dripped down her chest. Her teeth chattered; her body shook.

Josiah gripped her sodden hair, yanking her head backward. "Start with his name."

"I don't know," she stammered. She wasn't telling this asshole anything until her mind broke completely. "I just heard everyone call him the Vampire Lord."

"Where does he live?"

She gasped for breath, and her throat burned. "No one told me."

Josiah slammed his fist into her face. Pain burst through her cheek, searing her skull.

She glanced at Caine, who watched her impassively. In fact, he seemed completely unperturbed by this whole thing. *What the fuck, Caine?*

The incubus obviously had no plan to help, and couldn't get out of the chains, anyway.

Use what's around you, Rosalind, her mind screamed. But she couldn't get her hands on a single weapon. The only thing she could manipulate in the room, was—

Josiah.

Whatever it was he wanted, she could use it against him.

He yanked her hair tighter, nearly ripping it out by the roots. "Does the Vampire Lord have an army?"

"He didn't tell me," she said, staring in to his blazing eyes. She wasn't about to tell him that the General of Ambrose's army sat just a few feet away, staring at the two of them.

Josiah's breath was hot on her cheeks. "I know he has an army. And I want to know everything about it. How many are there? What are their plans? You will tell me every single thing you know," he said through gritted teeth.

"It's hard to think when you're hurting me," she said—stalling, again.

He tightened his other hand around her waist. "I want you to know that I will never let you out of my sight again. You're mine, Rosalind."

Fuck this guy. What he wanted was glaringly obvious: he wanted complete control over her, and he wanted to hurt her in the most brutal ways possible.

But what else did she know about him? He had an intense curiosity for all things demonic. He tended to underestimate her strength and her ability to look after herself. On top of that, he had a serious rage problem. These were all things she could use against him.

"I don't know. Josiah, please," she let out a sob. "None of this is my fault. I don't want this spirit in me. When the ring comes off, I burn with excruciating pain. It's like my whole body is on fire."

"You've told me this already." He slipped a large hand up her body, tightening it around her throat. "Tell me about the Vampire Lord, or I'll put the hood on you again for more water."

"It's a curse, Josiah," she said. "I don't want that magic. I never want to feel that pain again. You can't imagine the agony."

He looked into her eyes, licking his lips. "Oh really?"

She'd laid the bait. It was working.

"I never wanted this curse, Josiah. It's the worst pain I've ever felt."

He yanked a knife from his weapons belt, and slipped behind her back, cutting through the knot that bound her hands. He gripped her wrists hard, pulling her hand in front of her face so she could stare at the iron ring. "You still wear Blodrial's ring. He is your saving grace, and you betray him."

If she acted as fragile as possible, he'd let down his guard even further. "Josiah. You're hurting me," she whimpered.

"Good." He tightened his grip on her wrists. "Tell me what you know about the Vampire Lord, or I'll take the ring off and let you burn until you beg for mercy."

Manipulating Josiah was easier than she'd thought. In fact, a kernel of an idea began to bloom in her mind—a way to free every captive in the building—if she could manage to get out of there alive.

She lifted her eyes to his, letting them glisten. "I don't know anything about an army. But please, Josiah—"

With a tight smile, he stared at her ring. "I've wanted to see what would happen when the spirit takes over you." He dropped her other hand to slip off the ring, but he didn't get that far. As soon as he let her hand out of his grip, her hand flew to his throat. Within moments, she had both hands around his neck. She dug her thumbs into his Adam's apple. His eyes bulged, but she wouldn't be strong enough to choke him out like this. She just needed more of his rage to break her out of this chair.

"The truth is, Josiah, you could never satisfy me like an incubus could."

His face contorted with rage, and his fingers dug into her wrists before he ripped her hands from his throat. Snarling, he kicked her hard in the chest with one of his boots. The chair flew, slamming against the wall. The blow knocked the wind out of her, but it also had the desired effect. The crash splintered the chair into dozens of pieces.

She was free.

With an exultant smile, she grabbed a fragmented chair leg. When Josiah rushed for her, she jammed the splintered end into his thigh. It wasn't enough to kill him, but he wouldn't put up much of a fight after that.

Stunned, Josiah stared at her and staggered back—right into Caine, whose muscular arm tightened around Josiah's neck.

Where the hell did Caine come from?

"Caine?" she shouted. Wood splinters pierced her back, and at this point, she was sure half her ribs were broken. "How did you get out of the chains?"

His black eyes were fixed on Josiah. Instead of answering, he tightened his grip. *Shit*. She was quickly formulating a plan, but it was one that required Josiah to be alive.

"Caine!" She shouted. "We need him to live."

Caine's midnight eyes, as dark and empty as the opening of a cave, met hers. She wasn't getting through to him.

"Caine!" Panicking, she rushed forward and slapped him across the face.

He dropped Josiah, whose body landed on the ground with a thud. Rosalind knelt next to the Hunter and felt for a pulse. Blood still pumped through his veins. He was alive, but unconscious. Assuming someone found him before he bled out from the stab wound, he'd pull through.

Caine looked down at her. "You'd better have a very good reason for asking me to leave him alive. If this is sentimentality again, I'm going to kill him."

Pain wracked her body as she rose. "I know how we can use him to save the others, but we need to get out of here first. We won't be able to free them from their cells until I can get to a computer."

"What are you talking about?"

"I need you to trust me."

"Fine. Josiah was an idiot to underestimate you, and I won't make the same mistake." He eyed her torn shirt. "Hang on."

He stripped off his blood-stained shirt, tossing it to her. She tried not to stare at his muscular chest. *Focus, Rosalind.* They needed to get the hell out of there.

A voice crackled over Josiah's walkie-talkie. "*Agent Endicott. Please tell us the captives' status.*"

Rosalind slipped into Caine's shirt, and it nearly hung to her knees. "Thanks."

"What's the best way out of here?" Caine asked.

She closed her eyes, trying to visualize the building. "Right now, we're underground. There are no secret tunnels, and there's no way to get out discretely. We're going to have to blend in. We'll need better outfits."

"Since you didn't let me kill Josiah, I'm feeling a bit unsatisfied. I'll be happy to divest some guards of their clothing."

Josiah moaned, and Caine kicked him in the head.

The walkie-talkie crackled. "*Agent Endicott. Please report immediately.*"

"Let's go," Caine said.

Rosalind eyed him. "I still don't understand. How did you get out of the iron chains? I didn't even hear you escaping. The iron should have sapped your power."

"No. That's succubi. We're different creatures. Like I said, the Brotherhood gave you a lot of misinformation. We don't have time to get into that now. Let's go assault some guards."

Her pulse raced. "The chains didn't weaken your strength?"

"No. They did nothing, really. Not that I want the Brotherhood to know that. The less they know, the better."

Her pulse raced. "So—that whole time I was being tortured, you could have stopped it?"

His eyes remained black as pitch, cold and bestial. "Yes, but it would have been a tactical error."

Whatever he meant by that, one fact burned through her mind: Caine had sat there and watched Josiah beat the shit out of her. He'd let her think she was about to die. He could have stopped it, but he'd sat there impassively, watching it like a spectator. The betrayal burned. She rushed at Caine, shoving him hard in the chest.

"You watched me get tortured when you could have stopped it?" she shouted. "What the fuck is wrong with you? Did you not see him drowning me? I thought I was going to die."

Caine's voice was low and controlled, and he grabbed her

wrists. "Stop shouting, if you want to get out of here alive. You're supposed to be a soldier. That's what you signed up for when you joined the Brotherhood, even if you joined the wrong side."

Seething, she ripped her wrists from his grasp, just barely restraining herself from snatching another wooden fragment from the ground and ramming it into Caine's neck. "Half my ribs are broken. Josiah ripped my shirt off like a sex offender. He punched me in the face, kicked me into a wall, prodded my bullet wound, and practically drowned me. You're just lucky I didn't give up any real information to him."

"I was planning on killing him, so that wouldn't have mattered."

"I see. But apparently the state of my broken bones wasn't enough to move you off your ass. How much would you have let me endure?"

"Did no one ever tell you that war could be a bit uncomfortable? General Loring seemed to think you were familiar with the interrogation room, so I can't imagine that its unpleasantness is news to you."

"*Agent Endicott. I'm ordering you to report your status immediately. Your video monitor has been disabled.*"

His words stung, and tears pricked her eyes. He'd *wanted* her to get hurt. "I get it. So that was revenge."

The black in Caine's eyes faded. "No, that's not it at all. The point was—"

An alarm sounded, and Caine's eyes flicked to the door. "We need to go."

She pointed to the circular scanner. "We can't get out without a retina scan."

"What about Josiah's eyes?" Caine asked. "I'd be perfectly happy to cut one out and aim it at the thing."

She shook her head, grabbing two shards of wood from the ground. "The scanners sense small movements. They won't work for an unconscious eye. We need to wait until the guards come in here. We'll kick the shit out of them and steal their clothes."

"Fine." Caine walked over the spotlight hanging from the ceiling. He reached up, crushing the light with his hand, and darkness fell on the room. "They're coming," he whispered. "Stand against the wall."

A buzzer sounded at the door, and a guard kicked it open. Four guards rushed in, guns ready. Rosalind threw one of the stakes for the door, jamming it open slightly. Pain screamed through her chest. She was in no condition to fight.

"Agent Endico—" A guard's words were cut off by the crunch of bone and the sound of a gun hitting the floor. Only a faint stream of light illuminated the room, and she struggled to see in the dark. Bodies whirled around her, and the room filled with the sound of fists slamming against flesh. Someone unleashed a hail of bullets, but a cracking sound cut the assault short. The sound of a bone snapping, maybe. After a few moments, silence descended.

"Rosalind?" Caine said. "I've disabled them." He handed her a bundle of fabric. "Put these on."

Her breathing came sharp and fast as she pulled off her boots to change her clothes. It was a small mercy she could get out of her piss-soaked pants. "Did you kill them?" she whispered.

"Of course."

She slipped out of her clothes. She was now an accessory to the murder of four humans—people who had once been her colleagues. "You couldn't have just knocked them unconscious?"

"They signed their death warrants when they volunteered to work in torture chambers," he said.

She'd worked in one of these rooms by Josiah's side, an instrument of misery.

The walkie-talkie crackled again. *"Agent Endicott, we sent reinforcements. Please let us know your status."*

She buttoned the new uniform as Caine began speaking into the walkie-talkie. "This is Agent Endicott." It was an exact replication of Josiah's voice. "The reinforcements have arrived, but you didn't need to send them. I have everything under control. The interrogation continues. *Lux in tenebris lucet.*" He dropped the walkie-talkie.

"Please report to the head offices, Agent Endicott."

"Are you ready, Rosalind?" Caine asked.

She pulled on the guard's hat before crouching down, groping around for a discarded gun. "I'm ready. Just keep your eyes down." A fragment of wood still propped the door open, and she pushed it.

The alarm continued to blare, and red lights flashed from the ceiling, pulsing over iron walls that stretched far into the distance. This corridor covered nearly half a mile beneath Cambridge's streets—a dizzyingly long line of cells, each filled with a monster—or, so she'd once thought. Now, she knew ordinary people like Tammi were locked in here, too.

"You're walking like you're injured," whispered Caine.

"I am injured, no thanks to you."

She had to mask her pain, or the guards would see it in her limping walk and rasping breath. Josiah had promised to break her body, and he wasn't far off. She felt as if she was breathing through a tiny straw, and pain ripped through her limbs.

She was out of the cell, but not ready to celebrate just yet. She was fairly certain several of her ribs were broken. She had a bruised tailbone, a wrist fracture, and she remained stuck in the bowels of an institution that wanted to torture her to death.

She swallowed hard, trying to block out the pain as they drew closer to the corridor's end. What hellish torments had the Brotherhood unleashed behind those doors in the name of humanity?

Miranda, Tammi, and Aurora were just a few feet away from them right now, but there was nothing she could do about it. It wasn't like she could break through six inches of metal door without getting caught; even Caine couldn't do that.

At last, they reached the end of the hall. Two guards flanked another set of metal doors, and Rosalind slowed, letting Caine take the lead. She couldn't let the guards see her face. Even if they didn't recognize her features, the raw pain written in her eyes would spook them.

A tall, dark-haired man nodded at Caine. "What's going on with the traitor?"

"Interrogation got messy." Caine kept his eyes down and mimicked Josiah's voice. "It's still going on, but the others are handling it. *Lux in tenebris lucet.*"

The blond guard pushed a button, opening the metal doors. "You get your hands on that bitch? I want a turn on her when they're—"

Fury rushed through Rosalind, and before she could stop herself, her leg swung up, and her boot connected with the man's face. His neck snapped back, hitting the wall, and a fraction of a second later Caine slammed his elbow into the other guard's skull. The two men slumped to the ground.

"Unconscious," Caine said. "At your request."

"Thanks." She gripped her ribs, suppressing a moan.

The door had swung open into the older part of the chambers—a brick hall that opened into a stairwell leading to the ground floor.

"We're almost out," she said through labored breaths, climbing the stairs. She tried to catch her breath, her lungs still burning. She held on to the rails, gasping for air. What she really needed was a goddamn hospital. Caine glanced at her before slipping an arm around her waist.

"Are you okay?" he asked quietly.

"I'm alive."

At the top of the stairs stood another set of doors. While these doors required scans to get in, there was nothing to stop them from leaving. Rosalind pushed open the door, trying to project an air of confidence as she strode past the guards into the central hall. A sigh slid from her. They were now clear of the maximum security part of the Chambers, and they just had to make it through the lobby and onto Oxford Street. She cast a quick glance around at the lobby's towering ivory columns, the busts of famous Hunters, and the crimson walls lined with portraits of the Brotherhood's most illustrious members: King James I, Cotton Mather, and England's witchfinder General. This had felt like her home once.

Was it only a week ago that she'd strode through here, certain that her future was secure in this building, that she'd one day lecture to a crowd of students in the Chambers' old Mather hall?

Her heels clacked over the marble floor as they crossed the lobby, striding past the wooden security desk to the glass doors, illuminated by streetlights outside. So close to freedom, her heart pounded harder.

Still, guilt tightened her throat. She was leaving Tammi and the others at the hands of the psychopaths.

With a final glance at Caine, she pushed on a glass door, but it didn't budge. *What the hell?*

Caine pushed another door, with the same result.

Locked.

The security guard's voice broke the silence. "You gotta use the scanner. When the alarms are going off, no one can leave without scanning."

28

"Of course." Caine kept his voice even when he spoke to the guard. "The scanners."

Any minute now, they'd be found out. She couldn't let herself imagine the torture they'd endure after an escape attempt that left a trail of bodies.

"Get ready to run," she whispered to Caine.

She took a few steps back before pulling the gun, aiming it at the glass doors. If she couldn't scan her way out, she'd have to shoot her way out. She squeezed the trigger and broke into a sprint. Glass shattered all around them. Shards blasted against her skin as she bolted to the pavement outside. They cleared the door's entrance just as the guard unleashed a round of bullets. Caine pulled her out of the crossfire, taking shelter behind the building's brick facade.

He folded her in an embrace and pulled off her ring. In the shadows, he began chanting in Angelic. The mage joined in as their mingling auras whirled through her body. Panicked shouts echoed from within the building, but the magic was already rippling over her skin, and a thick, protective mist enshrouded them.

Caine slipped the ring back on her finger, and the mist thinned. Rosalind let out a long, slow breath. They stood in Mount Auburn Cemetery, dwarfed by Abduxiel Mansion. Blood streaked Caine's neck.

Pain splintered her shoulder. She pressed her fingers to her collarbone, wincing. "I've been shot three times in two days. This is not how I imagined my life turning out."

Caine slipped his arm around her waist. "Let me get you inside. I'll heal you."

As they approached the tall oak door, it swung open, revealing a cavernous hall. Moonlight shone through a stained glass window—an image of an angel. Twinkling lights hung suspended in the air like stars, flickering over an empty marble floor. If she weren't half-dead, she might actually enjoy this place.

Orcus rushed from a darkened archway. "I tried to keep her here. She wouldn't listen," he hissed. "Are you injured, Master? And what is happening with Bileth?"

"I'm fine, but she's badly hurt."

Orcus pulled off his hood, revealing black eyes and a pale, bald head the color of bone. "Take her into the celestial room. Try not to get blood everywhere. I've just cleaned up. I'll draw a bath in the adjacent washing room."

She leaned into Caine, and agony burned through her shoulder. He led her through an archway, pushing open a door into a candlelit room. Midnight-blue wallpaper, marked with silver stars, surrounded them. A silky, blue bed stood in the center of the room, and a twinkling chandelier hung from the ceiling.

"Lie down," instructed Caine. "You're walking like you're in agony."

She pulled off her boots, wincing as she bent over. *Nice of him to notice.* She lay on the soft bed, barely able to restrain the tears welling in her eyes. "I *am* in agony. And what about you? You're covered in blood."

"I was shot in the neck, and the rest is from the glass."

Her stomach clenched. "Shot in the neck? Why aren't you dead?"

"I can't be killed that easily, not unless it's a hawthorn stake."

A hawthorn stake—so that was why Malphas had been weakened. Her sense of relief at their escape was crushed by the weight of guilt—not just because of Malphas, but the friends she'd left behind. "What about the others? What if Josiah and Randolph punish them for what we did? We need to get back there." Miranda probably looked exactly like her, and Josiah would be sadistic enough to act out his most depraved revenge fantasies on her.

Caine eyed her with concern. "You need to calm your breathing. You won't heal as well if you're panicking. We'll save them, but I need to heal you first. And then you can tell me about your plan. Open your shirt, please."

She unbuttoned the front of her shirt, grimacing at the pain when she moved her arms.

Caine brushed his hands over her sternum, chanting in Angelic. His aura seeped into her skin, soothing away the pain. He trailed his fingers lower, lingering lightly over her broken ribs and lung, before they moved to her neck and face, lanced with shards of glass. With each stroke of his fingers, the pain began to ebb, leaving behind only a dull ache in her muscles.

"Is there anything else?" he asked, his eyes roaming over her body.

"That's it. Just soreness."

His gaze met hers. "I didn't realize how bad it was. You had five broken ribs."

"You let him torture me." She sat up. "Why didn't you stop it?" She wasn't quite sure she wanted to know the answer.

"There were two reasons." He spoke quietly, gently picking up her hand. "One—the Brotherhood believed that iron chains were enough to bind an incubus. I didn't want to dispel that myth. If they believe iron alone can hold us, it works to our advantage. That meant I had to wait until it looked like you were the one to break us out—until you very ingeniously found a way out of that chair. And the other was simply that Josiah's interrogation gave me valuable information. I now know what's important to him and to the Brotherhood. I know what he knows about us, and what he doesn't."

"Sounds very practical." She pulled her hand from his grasp and drew her knees up to her chest, hugging them. "Is there anything he could have done that would have spurred you to action, or would you have sat there and watched him murder me as long as you got the information you wanted?" She wasn't sure why she felt so betrayed. He'd never promised her anything more than an uneasy alliance. Like he'd said. They weren't friends.

"Don't be absurd. I wouldn't have let it go that far." He looked down at his hands. "I didn't realize the damage he was doing. I forget sometimes how fragile human bodies are. But you need to get over it. You're alive. And if it makes you feel better, I plan to kill him in the most excruciating way possible."

"I'm not sure that makes me feel better. And that's another thing—how are we any better than the Brotherhood if we kill everyone just like they do?"

He shrugged. "We aren't any better."

She'd been expected some kind of argument, and had no idea what to do with that response. "But I hate them and what they do. I don't want to be the same as them, or I'd have to hate myself.

I used to think it was okay to kill people as long as they weren't human, but I've changed my mind. It's immoral to kill people unless it's pure self-defense. Like, if you're about to die."

"We're at war, Rosalind."

"Only because everyone keeps *saying* we're at war." Loring was right about that much—words had power.

"Mmm." He apparently couldn't stop his eyes from roaming over her bare skin now that it had been healed. "Well, let me know when your semantic argument convinces the Brotherhood to stop hunting demons, and I'll let things lie." Blood still poured from the bullet hole in his neck, and he winced.

"Can you heal yourself?" she asked. Even if he was a demon, a bullet to the neck had to hurt.

"No. It doesn't work that way."

"You can only be healed by human women."

"And Orcus. He's not quite as enjoyable, but I don't imagine you're going to volunteer."

"Orcus it is." She heaved a sigh of relief. It wasn't that she didn't want to kiss him again. She wanted it a little *too* much. His touch could distract her from what they needed to do. Maybe some moral quandaries were murky, but spending the night in the arms of an incubus while your best friend and sister were being tortured went into *full blown sociopath* territory.

The door creaked open, and Orcus poked his head in.

At the sight of his shining skull, Rosalind pulled her shirt closed. It was one thing for Caine to see her half-naked, but the grim reaper was another matter.

Orcus cleared his throat. "The bath is drawn for the lady. I left you both a change of clothes in the washing room. But could you please tell me what I'm supposed to do about Bileth? He has been here three times looking for you, and I'm fairly certain he intends to send you into the shadow hell in a most unpleasant fashion."

Caine rubbed the center of his forehead. "Arrange for ten courtesans to visit him. And find ones that look like Rosalind. Tell him they're a gift from me, and that I've already punished her severely."

"Of course, Master."

Caine glanced at her. "You should go soak your muscles. The bath he's drawn will heal the ache in your bones."

She clenched her fists. "We need to talk about breaking into the Brotherhood. I want to get in there now."

"I'll join you in a moment, and we'll talk." He eyed her thoughtfully. "I'll keep my gaze on the floor, if you want."

"Good."

Orcus's heels clacked over the flagstones. "Master, I must heal your neck."

Rosalind rose, holding her ripped shirt closed, and strode across the cold flagstones in her bare feet. She pushed open the door into a stone washroom. A silver, clawfoot bath stood in the center, filled with bubbles and herbs, and candles guttered in spidery sconces. A silver-framed mirror hung over a sink.

She draped the blanket over a chair before slipping out of her underwear and padding over to the tub. She climbed in, lowering herself into the warm water scented with rose petals and foxglove. She leaned back, resting her neck on the tub's edge. If she weren't battered by worry, this would be heaven.

As the water melted the ache from her body, she mentally ran through her plan. Magic was useless in the Brotherhood's chambers, and technology controlled the whole building: retina scanners, key cards to get in and out, auto-locking doors, sensors that detected magical auras, the sprinklers of iron dust... If she controlled the technology, she controlled the Chambers.

She dipped lower in the bath, inhaling the steam. It all started with a laptop. What were the chances that Orcus had a laptop lying around—that he spent his nights gaming or watching online porn?

Behind her, the door creaked open, and she turned her head to find Caine, his eyes downcast. "I'm going to be exercising a lot of restraint for this conversation."

"I need a laptop."

"A *what*?"

"A computer. You know—a digital device? Zeros and ones? Do you have any idea what I'm talking about?"

"I've heard the word before, but Maremount technology is about four hundred years behind yours."

She turned to look at him. "Well, magic is no use to us in the Chambers, so we've got to use what's available. I don't suppose you have a spell that creates a laptop?"

"No. Most of our spells are medieval. I could blight someone's cabbage crop without a problem." He pulled off his shirt, and she caught a glimpse of the red streaking his perfect chest. Facing the mirror, he grabbed a cloth, scrubbing at some of the blood. "What, exactly are the details of this plan?"

"If I can hack into the Brotherhood's computer systems, I can control the building. We can get in; the prisoners can get out." Suddenly excited, she sat up, and the suds dripped down her skin. "I can turn off the dust, shut down the scanners, unlock the doors. I can control it all."

His eyes met hers in the reflection, and he paused, his cloth hovering mid-air. He swallowed hard. "I forgot what we were talking about."

"We were talking about you looking in another direction."

"Right." He finished cleaning off the blood and pulled off his pants.

For a moment, his strong, athletic form distracted her. *Focus, Rosalind.* She was turning into that full blown sociopath she'd imagined before. "So how do we get a laptop?"

He stepped into a pair of freshly-laundered black pants. "I could just take one from someone."

"Half of Cambridge will have one," she said, pushing aside any moral quibbles about theft. "We're not far from Harvard. The students will be walking around with them."

He slid his shirt over his broad shoulders. "Give me ten minutes."

29

$\mathcal{A}$fter Caine left, Rosalind stepped out of the bath, drying herself off with a towel.

She slipped into the clothes that Orcus had laid out—a pair of black leggings, a T-shirt, and a leather jacket. He'd even included a pair of bright red underwear, exactly her size. Either one of Caine's conquests had left these items behind, or Orcus had created them through magic, perfectly gauging her size. She wasn't sure which possibility was weirder.

Either way, she had more pressing matters on her mind. She pulled on her boots, zipping them over her pants. She was desperate for a computer.

She racked her brain for everything she could remember about assembly languages from her class last semester. Right now, lives depended on her ability to recall Professor Carroll's murderously dull lectures about compiling.

She pushed through the door into the celestial room, sitting on the edge of the bed, her nails digging into the blanket. An image burned in her mind—Miranda tied to a chair, her limbs beaten bloody by Josiah. Rosalind shook her head, trying to force the picture from her mind. This wasn't the time to lose it. *Think of something calming: the water running over my toes at the beach, a hawthorn grove.*

It was strange. Lingering around the edges of her most cherished childhood memories were Miranda and Caine, ephemeral figures in the hollows of her mind. Caine's eyes were her only solid memory. Gray irises and sun kissed skin— such a beautiful combination of warm and cool, like when sunlight pierced the storm clouds. It was so much like Malphus...

She shuddered. She couldn't think of Malphus now.

She couldn't let herself picture the pained look in his eyes as Josiah had twisted the stake in his heart. Did the other incubus live still in those dungeons, or had she unknowingly participated in his brutal murder?

She stood, pacing the room. She'd have to tell Caine—maybe she should have told him already. An ache welled in her chest. She tried to force out the images flitting through her mind: Josiah beating Miranda, Tammi trembling in the corner of an empty cell room, Rosalind's own face as she poured the water over Malphus...

She forced back tears, gripping her hair by the roots. She had to keep it together. Tammi and the others *needed* her to stay sane, and if Malphus was still in the Chambers, this was her chance to make up for what she'd done, by saving him.

The door creaked open, and she glanced up to see Caine holding a laptop bag. He slid the bag onto the desk. "I got the thing you wanted. I hope this works." He eyed her. "Are you okay? You look a little... upset." He approached her, gently touching her shoulder.

"That's what happens when you get tied to a chair and tortured."

He folded her in an embrace, his strong arms encircling her, and she melted into him, listening to his heart beat. He ran a hand down her hair. "You're okay now."

"Maybe I deserved it."

"What are you talking about?"

Her heart thudded in her chest. "You said that you knew someone else in the Chambers."

He pulled away, studying her. "Yes."

"Was he an incubus like you?"

His eyes narrowed. "Yes. Did you see him?"

She nodded, hugging herself. "I saw him. Malphus. But he couldn't get out of the chains. He'd been staked in the heart."

Caine backed away, his eyes darkening. "Is he dead?"

She shook her head. "I don't know. I never saw him after that day. Josiah told me he was a murderer and a rapist. He even showed me the pictures."

"Josiah lies." His eyes flashed like storm clouds.

She tried to force back the tears. "Josiah said if we didn't interrogate Malphus, it would lead to hundreds or thousands of human deaths. We hurt one to save many. A demon for many humans. It was simple math."

"Math," he repeated, his voice glacial. "That's an interesting way of putting it."

"You know him." A hollow opened up in the pit of her stomach. "Who is he?"

"It's none of your concern."

Caine glared at her, his eyes cold, black pools.

The judgment on his face stoked her ire. "What are you on your high horse about? You seemed perfectly fine with torture a half hour ago when it was *me* in the chair."

"When Josiah was interrogating you, you didn't have a hawthorn stake jutting from your ribs."

"Humans don't need a hawthorn stake to feel the blows," she shot back.

"And I would have stopped it before he did any serious damage. I would have got you out of there. Can you tell me the same for Malphus?" His voice sent a chill through her. "Is he even alive?"

"I have no idea, but I guess you could say when I interrogated Malphus, I was acting tactically. It is a war, after all. Isn't that what you said?"

"Well, then." Venom laced his voice. "If you plan to be strategic, you'd best get to work on your brilliant plan. And I really do hope it's brilliant."

30

*O*ver an hour later, and after three cups of coffee, she'd managed to piece together what she could remember of assembly languages. She was fairly certain her plan *was* brilliant.

Now, she needed to shove all the panic into her mental vault so she could focus—just like she was attempting to block out the open hostility radiating from Caine, who'd been pacing back and forth across the room like a caged animal for the entire hour.

She sat at the edge of the bed, laptop open. Before emailing Josiah, she glanced at the clock: 3:14 a.m. She'd set up the email to come from a burner account, *Cleo.X@sanguinebrotherhood. ca.* In the subject heading, she typed "Info about Rosalind." She clicked the paperclip, attaching a document called "Rosalind_ location.docx."

Only a lunatic would open a random file from a suspicious account, but Josiah probably fit that description. Her entire plan hinged on his fanatical need for control outstripping his judgment. The man was so desperate for revenge that he might not be able to restrain himself.

Once he opened the attachment, the worm she'd created would infect the system, allowing her to explore the network.

Her body buzzed with excitement—or possibly caffeine

overload. If she'd gauged this right, she had the potential to gain control over the entire security system. Finally, all the time she'd spent listening to Professor Carroll's monologues would actually pay off with a stunning takeover of the Chambers.

Caine paced over the floor, clearly riled by the inaction. "You realize that we can only rescue Aurora before the sun comes up, right? I think we should revisit Tammi's suggestion to use explosives."

"Explosions would risk killing the people we're trying to save."

"I want to kill people. And you want me to wait while you tap away with your fingers."

"There's a point to this. I've created a computer worm." She took another sip of Orcus's weird, herbal coffee. Ignoring Caine's fierce glare, she opened Terminal and typed *tail -F access.log*.

"You've created a *worm*," he repeated in a tone that said she'd lost her mind.

"The US government used something like this to hack into Iran's nuclear centrifuges. The worm will install itself, giving me access beyond the firewall. Though the server, I'll be able to command the system. I can survey the network to see what's there. I'll be able to figure out how to control the building."

Caine rested his palms on the table, staring down at her. "You're not talking about a literal wall of fire, are you? That was the only thing I could picture from what you just said."

She let out a sigh. "Let me put it this way: If this works, we can shut down the Chamber's retina and ID scanners. Anyone will be able to get in the building. All the prisoners will be free to escape their rooms. And I can disable the sprinklers that spray iron dust, so anyone with magic can fight back."

He straightened, suddenly interested. "If we went in, I could use my magic in the Chambers?"

"Assuming you can do it without destroying the place."

"Destroying the place would be the whole point."

She kept her eyes locked on the dark screen, waiting for an update. Everything—her chance to redeem herself, her friends lives—it all depended on one line of code. *Come on, Josiah, you psychotic asshole. Open the email.*

Her heart skipped a beat as a line of code updated in terminal—the Brotherhood's server had made a request. She loosed a long breath. "It's working. Josiah opened the attachment. Dumb fuck."

"What's happening?" Caine asked, leaning over her.

Her pulse raced, and she typed a command telling the Chamber's server to download mapping software. It would allow her to scan the network. "I'm looking for vulnerabilities."

"Exploit vulnerabilities," he said, a hint of admiration seeping into his tone. "Like you so cleverly did with Josiah."

"Same idea."

"Good. I look forward to finding out if your colleagues murdered Malphus."

She flinched, trying to scan through computer names in Nmap. "You're not helping me focus, Caine."

retinascan.brotherhood.agency.gov. And those would be the retina scanners. They weren't exactly very well hidden. The computers controlling the badge scanners had a similarly obvious name.

Probing further, she picked out the name *dust.brotherhood. agency.gov*—the iron dust.

If they'd promoted her to Guardian and put her in charge of their security systems, she would have renamed their computers, but they'd screwed that right up.

She inhaled deeply, picking up the gun she'd stolen earlier. "Are you ready to transport us? Once I make these changes, all hell will break loose in the Chambers. I want to make sure Tammi doesn't get lost. Or eaten by a starving demon."

"I've been ready for over an hour."

One by one, she picked through the computers—the ones that simulated sunlight to burn the vamps, those that blasted hawthorn stakes at incubi. She rewrote the code until *none* of them were functioning, and in a final masterstroke, she shut out the lights.

Chaos would rule the Chambers tonight.

After she disabled the last computer, she stood, facing Caine. Her body trembled with anticipation. "Let's go."

He wrapped his arms around her, anchoring her with his aura. This time, she pulled off her own ring.

31

$\mathcal{A}$ s the mist cleared, Caine slid her ring back on her finger—
only to yank her forcefully behind a tree. They stood a
hundred feet from the Chambers, shielded by an oak. On the
other side of grassy courtyard, a line of armed guards stood
before the old brick Chambers.

Red lights flashed from the roof, glinting off the shattered
glass that littered the ground from their earlier escape. In the
quiet night, the guards' feet crunched over the shards.

From inside the building, gunshots rang out, and her stomach
turned. She hadn't even *thought* about the guns. She'd been so
focused on fighting with magic, that she hadn't thought about
ordinary firepower—which, incidentally, could kill ordinary
humans.

From the streets of Harvard Square, sirens blared.
Reinforcements were already on their way.

Caine whispered in her ear, "I'm going to build a shield around
the building. We'll be able to get out, but no one can enter. And
I'll get rid of the guards. Stay a few paces behind me, and you'll
be protected."

He stepped out from the oak, holding out his arms to either
side. Rosalind followed behind, walking through the shadows

over the soft grass. Caine chanted in Angelic, and as he spoke, his silvery aura whirled around his body, curling through the air across the courtyard. The guards stood frozen. After a few moments, they dropped their guns, stumbling away.

Something didn't seem right, and dread whispered over her skin. Why weren't the prisoners fleeing the building? She clutched the gun tightly. She wasn't trained to use it, but she'd managed to shoot through the glass earlier.

Her breath came faster as they approached the shattered doors, footsteps crunching over the glass. The flashing red lights cast a garish hue over the abandoned security desk. Behind Caine, Rosalind tentatively stepped through the lobby, her gun raised.

A rhythmic sound, metal against wood, grew louder in the stairwell, and the door swung open, releasing noxious black smoke.

A bearded man stood in the doorway, his chest bare. Copper boots encased his feet, and he wore a red hat, dripping with gore. Blood ran down his chin. Fear coursed through her mind. *A redcap.*

The man's pale eyes landed on Rosalind. "I'm still hungry, and you look delicious," he growled.

When Caine stepped closer to the demon, his body crackled with magic. "Get out of here while you still can, redcap."

Behind the demon, two large, black dogs bounded through the doors, their eyes glowing yellow. *Hellhounds.* At least some prisoners were making it out.

The redcap glowered, baring his long, yellowed teeth. "I'll eat elsewhere." A moment later, he sprinted from the building, metal boots clanking over the ground.

From the prisons below, screams pierced the walls, and the sound curdled Rosalind's stomach. *Gods, what is happening down there?*

The building smelled of burning wood and fumes, and Rosalind covered her mouth with her shirt. *Tammi must be terrified right now.*

Caine pulled open the door to the stairwell, glancing at her as smoke billowed past. "Please be careful down there."

She stepped into the stairwell, her heart squeezing in her chest as she glimpsed two guards' bodies lying crumpled at the bottom of the stairs, their throats ripped out. Blood pooled around them—no doubt the red cap's most recent meal.

As he descended the stairs, Caine chanted a spell, and tendrils of magic curled around him. Through the security doors, the prison corridor glowed orange, but as Caine chanted, the air grew damp. Thunder rumbled through the walls.

At the bottom of the stairs, he pushed open the doors, just as heavy rain began falling from the ceiling. Red lights flashed over the halls, and the acrid smoke burned Rosalind's eyes. Something felt *wrong*. Where was Josiah?

Rosalind followed after Caine, and the deluge he'd created soaked through her clothes. The air hissed with dampened fires, and she rushed to the first open cell.

A thin, ginger woman stood shivering in the center of the room, her green eyes large. Her feet were bare, and she wore a ragged white dress, the fabric now singed. Around her, the rain doused a circle of fire, and tiny licks of flames still lingered over the scorched floorboards.

A sharp ache pierced Rosalind's chest. Apparently, this was the Brotherhood's primitive back up system in case technology failed. This explained the gasoline stench that always pervaded these rooms. It only required a simple mechanism—something to drop a lit flame from the ceiling when the electricity cut out, trapping the prisoners with fire.

"Go!" Rosalind yelled to the woman. "Get out of here."

The woman flinched.

"The doors are open!" Caine's voice boomed through the corridor. "You're free to go!"

The woman scuttled past Rosalind.

When Rosalind turned back to the corridor, she gasped at the slew of prisoners pouring from their cells. Some sobbed, others growled. By their auras, she could see that some were witches and demons, but many were simply pedestrians.

Rosalind lowered her gun, tucking it into the back of her belt. *We've won.* She just needed to find Tammi. And why couldn't she shake the feeling that something was *wrong?*

Ignoring the pit in her stomach, she followed Caine against the stream of fleeing prisoners.

Through the crowd, Aurora hurried toward them, her dress torn and bloodied. "Caine!" She threw her arms around him. "I knew you'd come for me."

In the next moment, Tammi's voice cut through the crowd. "Rosalind! Those fuckers tried to light me on fire!"

Rosalind's throat tightened as she caught a glimpse of Tammi, her lips swollen and cheeks bruised. One of her eyes had swelled shut.

Rosalind gently ran her fingers over her friend's face. "Oh my gods, Tammi. What did they do to you?"

"Your fuckstick of an ex-boyfriend paid me a visit."

Hot rage burned through Rosalind's blood, and she had an overwhelming desire to hunt Josiah down and stake him again. "Do you know where he is now?"

Tammi shook her head. "I'd like to think one of the demons ate him, but I have no idea."

In the corridor, the crowd was thinning out, and Caine turned to them. "I have to find Miranda and Malphus. I can handle this on my own. The three of you should get out of the building. Wait for Miranda out there if I need to send her to you."

Rosalind shook her head, marshaling her resolve. She was the whole reason Miranda was in here, and she was going to find her. "I'm staying with you."

"Who the hell is Miranda?" Tammi asked.

"My twin—" Rosalind stopped herself. There wasn't any time to get into this now. "Just go outside, and if you see someone who looks like me, that's Miranda."

"I'm taking Tammi to safety," Aurora said, grabbing Tammi by the arm. "With a bit of my blood, she'll be right as rain."

Apart from a few other stragglers, who limped on injured legs, the corridor was nearly empty. At least Tammi and Aurora were safe, but Miranda's absence was a bad sign.

Rosalind raised her gun as they walked quickly through the hall, checking one empty cell after another. If Miranda was a high security risk, maybe she wasn't even in here anymore.

As she looked into a dimly lit cell, she heard Caine's footsteps pause.

"Rosalind."

His tone made her stomach drop, and she turned, tentatively approaching across the corridor. Inside a cell, a man lay chained to a post. A hawthorn stake protruded from his shoulder, and his blond hair hung in his face. Deep bruises and gashes covered his body. *Malphas.*

At the sight of him, Rosalind's body began to shake. Josiah had completely brutalized him.

Caine ripped an iron chain from Malphus.

"Is he alive?" her voice cracked.

"Barely."

"Can you use your magic to heal him?"

"No. It only works on humans."

"What can I do?" she asked in desperation. "Can I heal him?"

"Not as long as he's unconscious. I think you should get out of here and leave me to sort this out on my own. Go find Miranda if you can, bring her to safety, and get out of the building."

Tears stung her eyes, and she turned to walk out of the room, crossing her arms. She'd been a part of that, and the guilt ate at her.

She walked further down the corridor, peering in each room for signs of Miranda. An eerie silence had descended—the only sound filling the hall was the distant rattle of Malphus's chains as Caine pulled them off, and the steady dripping of water. All of a sudden, her own breath sounded deafening.

She was about to meet Miranda, her own twin. The fact that Miranda hadn't run from her cell like everyone else was already making her stomach lurch. In the best case scenario, Miranda was unhurt, but in all likelihood she hated Rosalind. Why wouldn't she? Rosalind had sent her here.

Rosalind peered into a cell, expecting another empty room, but what she saw stopped her heart. Miranda—her mirror image— sat bound to a chair with an iron chain. She wore a ragged green dress, and faint bruises covered her skin. She looked exactly like Rosalind, except a network of ridged scars ran over her arms. This wasn't how a reunion of long-lost sisters was supposed to be. Still, at least she was alive.

Miranda blinked, staring at Rosalind. "You came for me." Her voice sounded small.

Rosalind rushed over to her, bending over to give her sister a hug. "I'm so sorry, Miranda. I didn't know it was you."

"Didn't know *what* was me?"

"I told the Brotherhood about the sea witch. I didn't know it was you. I was an idiot. I didn't know anything. I get it now. I'm not with the Brotherhood anymore." Her words tumbled out in a panicked rush, like she was some kind of maniac.

"Oh. I was looking for you." Miranda shifted in her chains. "Can you get the key, please? They left it on the floor where I could see it. But I can't reach it."

"Of course." Like an asshole, Rosalind had been blubbering to her sister instead of freeing her. She snatched a metal key from the ground, rushing around to slide it into the lock. She turned it, and it clicked open, releasing the chains. They fell to the floor in a heap.

Miranda sighed with relief, rubbing her arms.

"Do you need help walking?" Rosalind offered her arm.

Miranda took it, groaning slightly as she stood, and Rosalind led her into the corridor.

Rosalind eyed her sister's scars, and the collarbone that protruded from her chest. It looked like it had broken and healed over not long before. "Did Josiah do this to you?"

"Do what?" Miranda asked distractedly, wincing at the flashing lights.

"The scars and the beatings. Someone hurt you. I'm guessing it was Josiah."

Miranda glanced at her arms, as if seeing the damage for the first time. "Oh. That. Mostly Josiah, and Randolph. They were in my room a lot."

Rosalind felt sick. Where the fuck was Josiah anyway? She wanted to punch his face through the back of his head. "I didn't know what Josiah was like." She had a sudden desire to confess everything to Miranda, to try to explain herself. "I didn't know that he was a psycho."

Miranda squeezed her arm. "People aren't always what they seem."

They drew closer to Malphus's cell, and Rosalind peered into the room. Cain kneeled over the other incubus, and at her approach he glanced up.

His face brightened when he caught sight of Miranda. "Thank the gods. You're okay."

"Rosalind came for me." She pointed to Malphus. "Is he dead?" she asked sweetly.

Rosalind was starting to get the impression that Josiah had beaten some of the "normal human behavior" out of her sister, but Miranda would get better with time. She just needed to get out of this hellhole to recuperate.

"He's alive," Caine said. "I'm setting some of his broken bones before I move him. Go outside and wait for me. I'll bring him upstairs in a few minutes."

Rosalind gently pulled Miranda's arm, and they continued down the corridor, passing one empty cell after another.

"One thing confuses me," Rosalind said. "I still don't understand how the Brotherhood got to me so fast. I told them where you were, but they were already waiting for me by the time I got back to my room. How did they know about us?"

Miranda shrugged, her large eyes gleaming. "Malphus told them, of course. After Randolph Loring hurt him."

Rosalind's blood roared in her ears. "You know him? Who is he?"

They reached the stairwell, and began climbing the stairs.

"It's funny you don't remember him from Maremount. He was Caine's brother. I remember everything. I remember you. I braided your hair. And Malphus was the one who gave us bluebells and dandelions when our parents forgot our birthday. Malphus was the one who patched up your skinned knee with tree moss and barbery root. He was always good to us. I never knew he was a demon."

Rosalind's mouth went dry. The yellow and blue flowers, the person tending to her knee—it had been *Malphus*. She could hardly find her voice. "You remember much more than I do."

At the top of the stairs, Miranda pushed open the door. "I remember too much. Sometimes I can't quiet the voices in my mind."

None of this would have happened if Rosalind had never followed Josiah into the interrogation room. Revulsion climbed up Rosalind's throat. She'd been an instrument in her own downfall, and of the very people she should have protected. She'd told the Brotherhood where to find Miranda, and she was the reason they'd arrested Tammi and Aurora. On top of that, she'd tortured Malphus. When his spirit broke, her name must have rolled right off his tongue.

"I didn't know who he was. I didn't recognize him," Rosalind mumbled.

In the lobby, Miranda tugged on her arm. "It's okay. Come with me. There's something you need to see."

Rosalind shook her head, distracted. Flashing lights blared outside the protective shield that Caine had created around the building, and someone with a booming voice barked orders into a loudspeaker.

Rosalind glanced at Miranda. "What are you talking about? What do you need to show me?"

"It's in the Great Hall."

"What do you mean? How do you even know about the Great Hall?" Her skin prickled with apprehension.

Miranda tugged her hand, pulling Rosalind toward the great oak door. "My magic helps me see things. And I want you to see, too. You wear the iron ring. You're wedded to Blodrial. But I can show you something you've never seen before." She pushed through the door.

Rosalind didn't know what was happening, but she wasn't about to argue with the sister she'd sent to a torture chamber. Hugging her sodden clothes, she stepped into the Great Hall, and the door slammed behind her.

"Why are we in here, Miranda?"

Miranda walked to the circular stage. Through the darkness, Rosalind could now see an iron stake that stood in the center of the room, its base surrounded by a pile of wood. High above, moonlight streamed through the oculus, which someone had opened to the air, almost as if someone had prepared the room for... Her stomach hollowed out. "Miranda. Let's go. We shouldn't be in here."

Miranda backed away. Light sparked off metal on her finger—an iron ring. "I didn't have a choice. He makes me do things. He says he'll protect me from the pain."

"*Who* says he'll protect you?"

Miranda slipped into the shadows. "Josiah."

32

A fist slammed into the side of Rosalind's head, and her world spun. She tottered. Through her blurred vision, she caught a glimpse of Josiah's enormous form. *What the fuck, Miranda?*

She hadn't even begun the fight, and was already at a disadvantage. Stumbling, she reached for the gun in the back of her pants, but Josiah gripped her arm hard. He grabbed the gun and pointed it at Rosalind's head.

"You betrayed me." His voice cracked.

Rosalind's head throbbed, and she stared into the barrel. She choked down a thousand angry retorts. This wasn't the time to argue.

"I was supposed to protect you. I was going to find a way to marry you. You were mine." The gun shook in his hands. "And then I saw you wrapping your legs around that monster."

Rosalind seethed with rage. She'd just risked her life trying to save people from Josiah's torture, and he was going on about a kiss that hurt his feelings. "It was tactical," she ventured, trying on one of Caine's lines. "I was doing what I thought I had to do to get back to you. You've always been the one I wanted." The words tasted like poison in her mouth.

"I can't have a woman who lusts after demons. What about the other incubus? Did you screw him, too?" He favored his left leg—the one she hadn't stabbed with wood.

"No. I had no idea who Malphus was." She still needed answers. "How did you find him in the first place?"

"It was my job to watch over you. I followed you some nights after we broke up. I waited outside your window, looking inside. And one night, I saw someone else following you. It made me so angry. I started hitting him, but he was stronger than a human. That's when I knew. I had to stake him. That's why I had to make you interrogate him. I needed to see what you'd do. You were willing to hurt him. So I let you go. I had faith in you." His voice broke. "I was wrong."

A cold sweat beaded on her forehead. Malphus had been searching for her—just like Miranda had. And Josiah had attacked him not as a noble soldier in the fight against evil, but as a psychotically jealous ex-boyfriend.

As the truth of the situation dawned on her, the rage in her chest burned hotter, flooding her body like a hot magma. Josiah hadn't been her Guardian. He'd been her stalker.

Her foot flew to his gun, and she kicked it hard out of his hand. It spun over the marble floor.

Josiah glared at her, rolling his shoulders. "I don't need a gun."

He uncorked a right hook to Rosalind's head, but she ducked, and his swing failed to connect. He threw another punch, and his fist grazed her head. *Gods damn it*. His arms were much longer than hers. This was not a fair fight. What had Aurora told her? That she was awfully preoccupied with fairness, and sometimes bad things happen to good people.

She just needed to keep her distance until the right moment. She backed away, weaving away from his blows until he started to overextend his reach. When he pitched his body forward too far, she slammed her foot into his gut with a front kick, and he doubled over. She used that moment to ram an elbow into his lower back, bringing down the full force of the blow right into his kidney. Josiah grunted, trying to right himself. She threw a right cross, connecting hard with his temple, and he staggered.

Adrenaline coursed through her veins. "Screw you, Josiah."

As Josiah stumbled back, she scanned the floor for the gun. This was the moment she needed to end this, or get out of there fast. She heard the sound of a gun cocking, and turned to find Miranda pointing the barrel in her face.

Tears streamed down Miranda's face. "I don't want to do this. But I know it's what Josiah wants. And he's the only one who can keep me safe."

Horror coiled through Rosalind. "Miranda. You don't have to do this anymore. You're free. You can use your magic now."

Josiah straightened, pulling the gun from Miranda's hands. "She knows what's good for her. She's going to chain you to the stake." Josiah pulled out a small metal spray can and soaked Rosalind with liquid. The sharp smell of gasoline burned her nostrils. "You broke one of my teeth," he said evenly. "And you stabbed me."

A pale, pink light glowed through the oculus. The sun was beginning to rise, and for the first time Rosalind realized there was someone else in the room. A stream of rosy light fell on Randolph Loring, who sat on one of the benches, watching.

"Are you here to watch the show?" Rosalind asked him, her legs trembling.

Randolph leaned forward, resting his elbows on his knees. "The flames will purify you. They illuminate the truth." He lifted a hand to the sunlight. "*Lux in tenebris lucet*: light shines in the darkness."

"Stand in front of the stake," Josiah said, still pointing the gun. "Miranda will bind you."

She glared at him. Maybe she could get close enough to kick him right in that injured leg. "No fucking way."

Josiah pulled the trigger, and pain exploded through her thigh. She moaned, and he unleashed another shot. Agony ripped through her stomach, and she clutched the bleeding wound. She was going to die here. She staggered back, stumbling over the wood that surrounded the stake.

Josiah drew closer over the marble floor, and her mind blazed with pure panic. *Run, Rosalind.*

"Stand by the stake," he said through gritted teeth. "That's how it's supposed to happen."

Another gunshot ripped through her ankle, and she whimpered, nearly collapsing. *Stand up, Rosalind. Show him you won't bow to him.* Blood seeped from her stomach.

Randolph rose. "This is your chance to atone, Rosalind. This is the only way you will keep your soul. Better that you burn now than suffer an eternal torment in one of the shadow hells."

The door slammed open. Caine stood in the entrance. His black eyes glinted with ancient, primordial rage.

His sterling aura radiated around him, filling the large space. His magic enveloped Josiah's body, making him tremble. Josiah still held the gun, but his body stood immobilized. Clutching her stomach, Rosalind shuffled over the floor. She threw a punch to his temple, as hard as she could, though pain screamed through her gut.

Wrath burned through her blood. "You're a monster, Josiah." A part of her wanted to bash his skull into the floor, but she didn't have the strength, plus she'd lose the moral high ground. Still, she could get in one more punch. With a grunt, she slammed her fist into his throat, and he emitted a choking sound.

"Stop it!" Miranda screamed, pulling at her hair. "He promised to protect me!"

Rosalind stumbled back, and the pain she'd been ignoring flooded her body. She clutched her bleeding stomach, ready to collapse.

She watched with awestruck fascination as Caine's magic forced Josiah's arm to bend. Grunting, Josiah pressed the barrel against his own head.

"Stop!" Miranda shrieked.

Josiah's face reddened, sweat streaking his temples. He cocked the gun and pulled the trigger. The gunshot echoed off the high stone ceiling, followed by Miranda's anguished screams—almost as if she *cared* about her torturer. Sobbing, Miranda ran from the room, slamming through the oak door.

Rosalind glanced away, unwilling to look at the carnage. When she forced herself to glance back, she shuddered at the sight of Josiah's crumpled body and the gore pooling across the floor in a crimson puddle.

Caine glanced at her, and concern glinted in his eyes as she struggled to stand. He stepped over Josiah's corpse. Something moved in the shadows behind him, and her gaze darted to Randolph. She'd forgotten about him. There was something in his hand—

"Caine!" She shouted.

Randolph hurled a stake right for Caine's chest. Rosalind's hand flew to her mouth, and her world stopped as she watched Caine's tall frame crash to the floor by Josiah's. Caine's silver aura snapped into his body.

"Caine!" With pain fragmenting her leg, she tried to hobble to him, but Randolph blocked her path.

Stepping over Josiah's corpse, the Brotherhood's leader aimed a flamethrower right at Rosalind's gasoline-soaked clothes. "Your demon lover murdered one of my finest Guardians. It's okay. Josiah wasn't a true believer. He didn't belong with us. But I did want to watch you burn—not for my own pleasure, of course. But because it is Blodrial's will."

Fear tightened around Rosalind's heart like a honeysuckle vine, crushing the life out of her. With the flamethrower pointed right at her chest, Randolph was about to set her ablaze. She'd felt the flames before—when Cleo had taken over her body—but this time, her skin would blister for real.

Cleo. The mage was her one hope.

Rosalind pulled off her ring and hurled it at Randolph. The moment it was off her finger, Cleo's aura exploded from her body, and Rosalind's mouth began to form ancient, Angelic words.

Randolph's eyes bulged, and his flamethrower clanked against the marble floor.

He held up his hands, screaming in Latin, *"Exorcizamus te, omnis immunde spiritus, omnis incursio infernalis adversarii."* His words seemed to shield him from the tendrils of Cleo's vernal magic that curled around him. His body glowed with a golden light, and he backed over Josiah's body, chanting. *"In nomini et virtute Domini nostri Blodrial!"*

Cleo's temper flared. She would protect this body from the evil ones. Cleo chanted in Angelic, and her magic lashed out at him. She wanted to hurt him, to force his guts out of his throat, but those words he spoke shielded him.

They made Rosalind's body shake, as though he was forcing the aura out of her. Hot agony coursed through her. Still, he continued to retreat, his face reddening with the effort, and Cleo felt a thrill of raw power as he scuttled from the room like a bug.

When the door slammed shut with finality, Cleo turned her attention to the beautiful incubus on the ground, his breathing labored. Richard was in there somewhere, but the incubus's body was dying.

Trapped somewhere within Cleo's powerful vernal magic, Rosalind's mind screamed *save him*.

She walked closer. Ignoring the pain that wracked her body, she knelt down, her blood pooling on the floor and mingling with Josiah's.

Cleo pulled the stake from his chest. Caine gasped, his back arching with the pain. *Still conscious.* She lay next to him, stroking her hand over his chest, and pressed her mouth to his. His perfect lips parted, warm and soft, and he kissed her deeply. Hungrily, he drank in her energy, and his arm tightened around her back. At his intensifying touch, heat shot through her body.

The incubus's aura strengthened deliciously, swirling through her belly, caressing her skin. He pulled her on top of him, the kiss energizing him.

She had no idea who she was, or where she was, only that she wanted more of him.

She nearly gasped when he pulled away, looking into her eyes, searching.

"You're Cleo, aren't you?"

Cleo needed his mouth on hers, and moved closer to kiss him again, but he held her at bay, staring at the blood streaming from her shoulder. "You're hurt. I need to get you out of here. Say the spell with me, Cleo. Rosalind will die if I don't heal her."

He reached out, snatching the iron ring from the floor before he returned to her. Wrapping his arms around her, he chanted a spell for teleportation, and she joined in, their auras mingling together with an intense, euphoric power.

33

*I*n the celestial room, Caine carried Rosalind across the room. Thick, starry curtains blocked out all the sunlight, and candlelight danced over the room.

Caine gently lowered Rosalind to the bed, propping her up on the pillows. With the iron ring back on her finger, she gripped her shoulder, no longer able to block out the agony.

Excruciating pain blazed through her stomach and collarbone, and blood poured from her wounds.

She heaved a sigh of relief as she heard Aurora and Tammi's conversation pierce the walls from the next room. *Thank the gods—they're safe.*

Caine pulled off her jacket, and the pain took her breath away as she moved. "I need to heal you—now. You're losing a lot of blood." He ripped the front of her shirt open, unable to hide the fear flickering across his features when he saw her stomach.

"Miranda ran off," Rosalind said, her mind twisting with confusion. The blood loss made her dizzy, almost as if she could feel her heart rate growing fainter. "She thought Josiah was her protection."

"Don't worry about that now." Caine traced his fingertips around the wound, then closed his eyes, chanting in Angelic. His aura whispered over her skin. It pulsed through her body, slowly drawing the pain out of the wound.

She took a slow, shuddering breath. "What happened to Malphus?"

"I handed him over to Aurora before I went looking for you. I was nearly too late." He scanned her body. "You need to take off your pants."

She leaned back on the bed, unbuttoning the top of her pants as he pulled off her boots. Grimacing, she slid her pants down past her thighs, and Caine tugged them off the rest of the way. Blood streaked her legs, and Caine winced as he looked at her ankle. It was obviously in rough shape.

"You killed Josiah," she said.

"I can't imagine you'd object at this point." He ran his fingers over her ankle, and his aura assuaged the pain. She watched with fascination as the skin healed over, the wound shrinking.

"Not even a little."

His fingers traced higher up her leg, his touch tingling over her thigh, and the pain from the last gunshot drifted away at his warm, soothing touch. As he finished healing her, she took a deep breath, her body still throbbing with a faint ache.

"That should do it," he said, his gaze trailing over her body.

"I just want to clean the blood off before I find Tammi. She tends to freak out about blood."

"Give me a moment." His fingers still lingered on her leg, and as he chanted, his aura whispered over her skin, sweeping away the blood and gasoline. Her body thrilled at his touch. When he finished, she was suddenly very aware that she wore nothing but the red underwear, and that Caine's hand rested on her thigh. Her heart pounded harder, and her breath sped up as she looked into his perfect face. His soft, smooth lips had just been on hers, and—

The door slammed open, and Aurora stood in the entrance. "Seven hells. I heard someone's heart pumping hard, and I thought you might be injured, but no. We just barely got away from an evil cult with our lives intact and you two are stripping off to get it on with each other."

Caine turned, pulling his hand away from Rosalind's leg.

"I was healing her."

Aurora narrowed her eyes. "Is it just me, or are you two awfully fond of 'healing' each other? You know, you could just shag like normal people and not subject yourself to broken bones first."

Rosalind pulled her ripped shirt closed. "Josiah shot me."

"Josiah's a twat." Aurora cocked her head. "You know Caine doesn't actually need to touch you to perform magic, right?"

Caine rose, frowning. "It works better that way, actually."

With her body now healed and clean of blood, Rosalind slipped back into her pants. She tied the remnants of her shirt in a knot in front of her bra. "Is everyone okay?"

"Fine, yes," Aurora said. "Though I nearly burned to death in the sunlight on the way home. Next time you're planning on rescuing me from the death cult, please do it closer to midnight. And Tammi's not quite ready for this level of excitement. I had to give her two cocktails to stop her from babbling."

Tammi strolled in, her face now fully healed and slightly flushed. "There you are! What the hell happened to you? You were supposed to meet us outside the Chambers."

"Josiah," Rosalind managed. It was all she could get out right then. If she divulged the full details, she'd break into hysterical sobs—and she wanted to do that when she was alone.

Tammi frowned, approaching across the stone floor. "Caine said you found your twin. Where is she?"

Rosalind shook her head. "I found her, but she wasn't right. Mentally. I think Josiah warped her mind. The Brotherhood has a way of doing that to people."

"So what happened to her?" Aurora asked. "Ambrose will want to know."

Rosalind blinked, fatigue overtaking her. "She ran off. She seemed to think Josiah was her savior. My guess is that she's wandering around Cambridge, ranting about her protector."

"That's some serious Stockholm Syndrome shit," Aurora said.

Right now, Rosalind couldn't handle the guilt—the crushing weight of having sent her sister to the torture chambers.

Then again, maybe Rosalind was just as much a victim of the Brotherhood as Miranda had been—after all, the Brotherhood had a way of warping a person's mind.

"Is Malphus all right?" Caine asked.

"Orcus is tending to him," Aurora said. "What's our plan now? How long are we staying?"

Caine rubbed his sternum where he'd been stabbed. "Rosalind and Tammi should stay here for now. You and I will return to Lilinor with Malphus when night falls. We've just provoked an all-out war with the Brotherhood, and we need to report to Ambrose."

Aurora put her hands on her hips. "He won't be happy that we lost Miranda."

Caine glanced at Rosalind. "We'll find Miranda again. I promise. But right now I'm going to check on my brother. You should all get some rest."

Without a backward glance, he stepped out of the celestial room, and the girls followed behind him. Tammi closed the door, leaving Rosalind on her own.

Alone at last, she threw herself on the bed, her body burning with exhaustion. Caine was an amazing healer, but even he couldn't fix everything.

She pulled down the covers, climbing into the bed before blowing out the candles.

She closed her eyes, and the dreams that flickered through her sleep were of a girl whose face looked just like her own, of dandelions and bluebell flowers, and sea foam running over her toes.

When she woke in the darkness hours later, she was almost certain someone had brushed a soft kiss across her cheek.

34

*R*osalind heated the silver kettle in the cavernous stone fireplace, breathing in the strong, herbal aroma of Orcus's coffee. Since she'd met the night demons, her schedule had become completely screwed up. Strong coffee at seven p.m.—in a vast, stony living room—seemed a perfectly reasonable idea.

Tammi sat cross-legged in a mahogany chair, stretching her arms over her head. "I've never in my life slept as well as I have here. I don't know if Orcus is lacing our tea with opiates or if I'm just suited to sleeping during the day, but I feel amazing. What did Orcus say this place was called, again? I want to take up residence."

Rosalind sat across from her. "Abduxiel mansion. And, apparently, we're welcome here as long as we're in good standing with the night demons. It's kind of like a sanctuary for Nyxobas's allies."

Tammi sipped her coffee. "I wouldn't mind if a gorgeous vamp or two came in. I've read through half the library by now, and it's full of epic poems about hellhounds and angels of death. Not really my thing."

"I'll ask Orcus if he can find us some billionaire romances."

Tammi crossed her legs. "Speaking of romances—what's the deal with you and Caine?"

"The deal is that he's an incubus who flirts with everyone. Oh, and I nearly tortured his brother to death. We're not really well-suited."

"After Josiah, I'm not sure you can be trusted to choose your own boyfriends."

Rosalind flinched. "You have a point."

Josiah, for all his idiocy, had managed to lure her into trusting him. And what he'd done to Miranda had been even worse.

Though Orcus had forbidden it, Rosalind had been sneaking out during the day to search Cambridge's streets for her sister. She'd been desperate to feel that briny aura tingling over her skin, but she hadn't sensed the slightest glimmer. Then again, if Miranda was still wearing the iron ring, Rosalind wouldn't be able to sense her at all.

Footsteps echoed through the room, and Rosalind turned to see Orcus, his head covered by a hood. "Rosalind. There is someone here to see you."

Her pulse began to race, and she stood. *Miranda?*

Rosalind rushed through the door into the main hall, hurried over the marble floor, and pulled open the oak entrance. A tall figure lingered in the doorway, and the rosy sunset cast him in silhouette. *Caine.* Her breathing quickened.

"Rosalind. I just wanted to make sure you're okay."

"I'm fine."

He took her hand, his touch sending shivers over her skin, and led her out into the fresh spring air. The sunset hung hot in the sky like a ripe peach, bathing his skin in a tawny light. Around the gravestones, violet bluebells and broken acorns blanketed the grass.

Caine stopped by a towering oak, turning to look at her. "Ambrose has sent his men out to search for Miranda. Nothing to report so far."

"I've been looking for her too," Rosalind said.

"You're supposed to stay here. The Brotherhood want to murder you."

"You can't stop me from looking for her, just like I could never stop you from going after Malphus."

"Except that I *could* stop you." A muscle worked in his jaw. "Fine. I see your point."

"Why didn't you tell me you had a brother in there?"

He peered down at her, and the ruddy light stained his gray eyes a coral color. "If Josiah had known Malphus was my brother, Malphus wouldn't be alive right now. I'm not going to give up my secrets without a very good reason."

The lack of trust stung, but she couldn't blame him. After all, she had helped Josiah break him. "Miranda told me Malphus used to give me flowers. Is that true?"

"He did. I wasn't as nice."

"I want to meet him. If he doesn't hate me now."

"You'll meet him. Ambrose still has big plans for us."

"Plans that involve finding Miranda?"

"That's the first step. The Brotherhood will no longer be stupid enough to rely on technology the way they did. They'll be amassing an army of their own, and Ambrose wants to crush them with magic."

A shiver ran up her spine. "When Cleo was hammering Randolph with a spell, he protected himself with... magic. It was a different sort of magic. He was speaking in Latin, and his body glowed a golden color."

Caine nodded. "They don't use Angelic. But they have their own sort of magic. They give it another name. That's all."

Rosalind let her eyes trail over Caine's muscled frame, clad in a form-fitting black shirt. "Do Ambrose's plans involve me reporting to you as my commanding officer?"

A smile flickered over his lips. "Mmm. Yes. You'll be required to follow all of my orders."

"Good luck with that."

"Fair warning. There are a lot of female vamps in the army who will be competing for my attention. Can you blame them, honestly?"

She cocked a hip. "It must be quite a hardship for you to live in a vampire city. No mirrors."

"Nyxobas gives me the strength to endure. Speaking of Lilinor, I need to return before sundown, but I'll come back as soon as I hear anything." He nodded at the mansion. "You're safe here, but stay in Abduxiel Mansion."

Giving orders again. She crossed her arms, shooting him an irritated glare as he turned to leave.

He walked a few steps before pausing to turn back to her. "Stay here if you want, I mean. Your choice."

As he walked off to the crypt portal, a small smile curled her lips. For the first time in a while, something unclenched in her chest.

She now lived with a grim reaper in a cemetery, and her twin sister was missing. Yet after all the tumult of the past few days, she felt a strange sense of normalcy.

If nothing else, they were all alive—and somewhere deep within Rosalind, a sense of belonging was budding.

Stay in Touch

Readers who join our Newsletter get a **free ebook** of *Shadow Mage* a short story that gives Caine's perspective when he first meets Rosalind.

You can sign up to our Newsletter at *www.cncrawford.com*

And, if you have a moment, we'd really appreciate it if you would leave an honest review on Amazon and Goodreads. Word of mouth is the number-one way for new readers to learn of Rosalind and Caine.

Yours,
Christine & Nick

About

C.N. Crawford is not one person but two. We write our novels collaboratively, passing our laptops back and forth to edit each other's words.

Christine (C) has a lifelong interest in New England folklore - with a particular fondness for creepy old cemeteries. Nick (N) spent his childhood reading fantasy and science fiction which may partly explain why he is also a scientist.

Questions, comments, just want to say Hi? Don't hesitate to shoot us an email at *CNCrawfordAuthor@gmail.com* we try our very best to respond all messages.

Acknowledgments

We thank our wonderful editor Tammi Labreque; our cover designer Rebecca Frank; and our proofreader Sara Pinnell. Thanks also to Cady Vance for her input and advice. We also thank our ARC team and Author's Corner for their inspiration and moral support.

And a huge thanks to Michael Omer who has given amazing feedback on all of our books..

Made in the USA
Middletown, DE
16 December 2016